Second Sight

Second Sight

Mary Tannen

ALFRED A. KNOPF
NEW YORK 1988

F1C

THIS IS A BORZOI BOOK
PUBLISHED BY ALFRED A. KNOPF, INC.

Copyright © 1987 by Mary Tannen
All rights reserved under International and Pan-American
Copyright Conventions. Published in the United States
by Alfred A. Knopf, Inc., New York, and simultaneously
in Canada by Random House of Canada Limited, Toronto.
Distributed by Random House, Inc., New York.

Library of Congress Cataloging-in-Publication Data
Tannen, Mary.
Second sight.
I. Title.
PS3570.A54S4   1987   813'.54   87-45119
ISBN 0-394-56204-6

Manufactured in the United States of America
First Edition

For my parents

ACKNOWLEDGMENTS

Many thanks to Robert Gottlieb for his help and encouragement over the years, and to my editors, Alice Quinn and Victoria Wilson.

I also want to thank the following people who generously shared their expertise and experiences with me: Marilyn Lipsius, Jeffrey Spielberger, Cynthia Hildebrand, Curtis Velsor, Dorothy Nassar, Lorenzo Vega, Michael Feldman, and David C. Parris, Curator of Science for the New Jersey State Museum.

Second Sight

1

And you want to know—"

"If I should take it."

"Yes."

"Then you think it will be good—"

"Good for you?"

"In general."

"I can't tell that."

"I thought you were a psychic."

"I have second sight. I can see things as they are, in ways you might not."

"OK, go ahead. What do you see?"

"Queen of Pentacles. Is it a question of business? Something about your career . . . ?"

"This is where we began. I told you that—"

"Oh yes. I'm just laying out some cards. I'm turning up a lot of air signs. Are you an Aquarius, possibly? Gemini?"

"Capricorn."

"Oh. Earth sign. That's funny, because I'm coming up with a lot of air. Wheel of Fortune reversed—"

"Is that bad?"

"Arrested motion. Becalmed. Do you feel you're not getting anywhere, that your career has come to a standstill?"

"As I said, the only reason I'm thinking of taking it is that I haven't worked in a year."

"Uh-huh. Ace of Rods reversed . . ."

"Well? What does it mean?"

"Decadence. Fall from grace. Skill turned to cunning."

"From what? Why?"

"Negative forces in the environment, it looks like. All your cards are coming up reversed. . . . This might be the cause of it, here, the Emperor, especially in the layout, where it's in opposition to the Queen of Pentacles. Is there a very powerful friend, male or female, or relative, male or female, or institution that is having a heavy influence on you at this time?"

"I already told you that I'm living with Gareth Watts."

"Is that someone I should know?"

"Gareth Watts, the director?"

"Is he influential?"

"Are you kidding? Gareth Watts?"

"I'm sorry, I don't see movies very much."

"Believe me, he has a lot of influence."

"That's it then. What it is."

"What?"

"The negative force."

"What negative force?"

"That explains why you're drawing all these air signs. The Emperor, this influence, has cut you off from the roots of your talent. You are withering because you don't have access to the earth. Where did you say this movie was being done?"

"Arizona."

"Good. Go there. And try to walk on the actual earth, the dirt. Touch earth as much as you can."

"I don't understand. Why can't the Emperor—Gareth—do me good? Why can't his power be useful to me?"

"He's reversed."

"What?"

"In the cards I laid out, he's upside down."

"But what if I love him? I mean, I do love him. If I leave to make this film—you don't understand. It's like breaking faith. He'll be hurt, maybe find someone else. There are all these women around him. He attracts them without even meaning to. There are those kind of men, you know. It's not good to leave them. You're asking me to take a dinky part in a low-budget movie for—for nothing, for the chance to walk on dirt in Arizona. Plus I might lose Gareth—"

"I'm not asking you. You asked me. You wanted to know what I see. I see a powerful man who is—and it might not be intentional, it probably isn't—but he's doing something to stop your wheel of fortune. He's taken you too high, so your feet can't touch the ground, and it's important for people born under the earth sign to keep close to the ground. You are stranded in a hostile medium. I'm not saying you should take this part even though you may lose the Emperor, I'm saying take it because it will free you from him."

"What about love? Don't your cards say anything about love?"

"I thought you wanted to know about work."

"Well, yes, but there's love too, isn't there? I mean, I paid for a half an hour—"

"OK, let me see. . . . Here's something, someone who is attracted to you, no—more—is moving into your orbit. Someone young, fair-haired. Do you know anyone like that?"

"No."

"Of course, the problem is your receptivity—all these upside down cards—"

"Maybe you're holding the pack the wrong way. What do you

know about directors and films anyway? Nothing. You already told me that. I've wasted twenty dollars and the price of a phone call to New Jersey to hear—I could have gotten better advice from my Colombian cleaning lady. Tell me something useful for God's sake. Tell me something that makes sense."

"Fix the bannister."

"What?"

"The bannister isn't attached right. It's easy to fix, but right now it's dangerous. Someone could fall."

"Is there a Tarot card for that too?"

"It's just something I flashed on."

"That's real good. That's great."

"When they're good I can feel it. It's like a shiver up my spine. The rest I'm not too sure about. You'll have to use your own judgment, but the bannister—"

Clients sometimes hang up on her, which is why she has them pay in advance. It's too bad. The woman still had ten minutes left, and Destiny could have told her something about the Colombian maid and the silverware.

Delia crosses the name off the list. Two more calls tonight. She gathers up the cards, shuffles them, and lays them on the bedside table. November is a busy season, due to heightened anxiety caused by loss of light in the northern hemisphere. Primitive fears rise to the surface. Halloween, the night the dead walk. There's something to it.

Lazaro is not in his room. Delia doesn't call for him because the only other place he could be is the front parlor, where he never goes. He must have slipped out while she was working, although Delia told him not to.

She folds her arms across her chest and stands among the dresses hanging from the molding over her bedroom door. She keeps them there because she doesn't have a closet. They are old dresses she doesn't wear much anymore. It comforts her sometimes to stand where she can feel them around her.

Because of the dresses, Lazaro doesn't see her when he comes in, furtively tiptoeing across the dining room, his face arranged for going out on the street, baby cheeks sucked in, eyebrows gathered across an unlined forehead. Small for twelve, a late-bloomer. He's trying to leap the gap of puberty by sheer force of will.

"I thought I asked you not to go out."

He jumps, then scowls. "I had some business to do."

"What about homework?"

"That's what I came in to do. I could be working on it now if you'd leave me alone, for Chrissakes." He heads for his room.

"Knock, knock." Delia follows him.

He stops. She can see his shoulders soften. "Who's there?"

"Butcher."

"Butcher who?"

"Butcher arms around me. Knock, knock."

He grins. "Who's there?"

"Jimmie."

"Jimmie who?"

"Butcher arms around me and Jimmie a little kiss."

His body still melts against hers the way it did when he was small, but his arms are getting harder and leaner, like his face. And he's taller. Her nose is even with the top of his head. She smells gasoline and cigarettes.

He smokes when he's out of the house; she saw him once on Main Street. She recognized the jacket first, Jaime's from high school, still too large for Lazaro, although Jaime was small. Delia was going to call him when she noticed the fingers that just cleared the cuff of the jacket were holding a cigarette. Lazaro puffed, then flicked it into the gutter with such deliberate casualness that she knew he had smoked the whole thing so he could practice that one gesture. She hid in the bakery because she didn't want him to know she had seen. She bought him a chocolate chip cookie.

He never remembers to lock the door. Delia has to do it. She doesn't like to at night because she has to pass her hand through

Jaime's ghost, not a true ghost because it doesn't move. It's the afterimage of the way he was the last time going out the door, turning his head to look at her. Delia read in one of Lazaro's science fiction comic books about black holes in space and what would happen to someone entering one. The gravity at the edge would be so strong that it would prevent the light waves coming off that person from ever traveling. The voyager would be sucked into the vortex of the black hole, but his image would remain on the edge of what they call the "event horizon." Delia supposes this ghost of Jaime is something like that because it never changes, never moves.

She said, "Where are you going?" and he turned and looked at her, and that's what she sees, exactly how he was at that moment, dressed in his jacket, not the high school jacket Lazaro uses but the leather one he wore with the motorcycle, black jeans, and boots, his brown hair long to his shoulders, and his beard—like Jesus Christ, a Latin Christ with deep eyes, strong dark brows.

He knew. He must have and she did too, although if she did, why didn't she stop him, or at least try to? Because the part of her which knew was helpless, had no access to her tongue, her arms, her feet. It could only speak through her eyes, and Jaime's eyes understood but he couldn't say anything or move in any way to change. It was too late. That's what his eyes tell her in the ghost image that lingers by the door, taking on substance in the dark.

Delia reaches through Jaime's ghost and fixes the latches. She has invested a fortune in locks, more than the combined value of everything in the apartment. The only thing she wants to protect is their lives.

Lazaro is at his desk, shoulders pulled up against an invisible wind. Fingers covered to the second knuckle by Jaime's jacket sleeve are moving a pencil over a math book. Grand Land Development isn't very good with heat. Hugo found them some electric heaters for their bedrooms.

"Why don't you turn on the heater?"

"I'm not cold."

"You have your jacket on."

"I just don't want to take it off."

Delia pulls her robe more tightly around her and goes to check the kitchen latch, although they never open that door except in summer to let in a breeze. There's a small yard out back with a lilac bush, but no steps to get to it. She used to jump down and Jaime would hand the baby to her and a blanket they could lie on. Someone, a disciple of Jaime's, was going to build a little porch for them, and steps, but after the accident none of the followers came by anymore. Sometimes Hugo says he'll build one but he works in metal not wood. Delia asked Edgar Snow to build her a porch when Grand Land took over the property. He said it was a good idea but he never did anything about it, although he was a nice man, a charming man, a friend of Nestor's.

Edgar Snow came to visit when Grand Land bought the place and asked her to take down her sign. She explained that it was her only livelihood, her husband having died, and he said she could keep it there until renovation was complete.

He had white hair, which pleased Delia because of his name, a strong chest and shoulders, an expensive scent with tropical allusions, and a reptilian iridescent aura that changed colors as she talked to him. Delia had never seen one like it before and would have liked a chance to study it another time, but he hasn't been back since.

"What did your husband do?" he asked, looking around the parlor, wondering why Nestor Bird's daughter lived with painted plaster saints. They used to be Jaime's. Delia keeps them in the parlor for clients, the Spanish ones, who find them reassuring.

"He was a saint."

"I don't doubt that he was," Edgar Snow smoothly returned, "but what did he do for a living?"

"He was a saint, in the community. People came to him for healing and things. They brought us everything, food, clothes, blankets, money, whatever they wanted to give."

She showed him the framed photograph of Jaime on his float in the Puerto Rican Day parade. He was wearing a white robe, his arms raised in a blessing. The name of his botanica was spelled out in red carnations on the side. There are many pictures of him on his float. His mother has them, framed, in her living room.

Edgar Snow took her sign out of the parlor window to examine it. *Destiny Ortega. Palms Read. Tarot.*

"Did you make it yourself?"

"My son did, for Mother's Day, a year ago or maybe two. The old one was all faded and curled up."

The first one Delia made herself. Lazaro was a baby.

After Jamie died, Delia went into New York City to an employment agency where she learned she had no marketable skills —no shorthand, typing, switchboard, key punch, NCR, word processor—only a high school diploma. Walking back to the bus terminal, Delia passed a club featuring topless dancers whose names were painted on a panel by the door. "Jill, Lauren, Tiffany, Mercedes, Destiny."

Delia Bird couldn't do it, or even Delia Ortega, but she knew she could if she had that name. Destiny. Destiny Ortega. She went to the Señora, Jaime's mother, to ask for Jaime's place in the botanica. Delia had helped out in the store while Jaime was occupied behind the screen giving advice in his musical, light voice, almost as high as a woman's, soothing, sweet. Then he would come out and mix special ointments for them, recommend incense to burn, candles. She loved watching the clients, women mostly, making their purchases at the end. They looked peaceful, their hope restored.

She couldn't do it like Jaime. She knew that, and explained it to the Señora. She didn't have his connection to the saints. She wasn't even Catholic, probably not even Christian, but she could, under the name of Destiny Ortega, see certain things.

But the Señora was coming out of retirement to take over the job. When Delia explained, almost in tears, that she needed work in order to live, to feed the baby, the Señora suggested she give Lazaro to her. She and Carmen would raise him, and Delia could go back home to her mother.

Delia made a sign for her window. Then she applied for welfare. Some young Spanish women came out of curiosity. The social worker let her read her cards and sent some friends, young women who worked in the county courthouse. Delia charged them ten dollars, five for the Spanish clients.

If Grand Land ever renovates, she'll be willing to take down the sign. Not many come in off the street anyway. The competition is too strong. There are storefronts on Main Street with neon signs that read, *Tarot. Palms Read.* There are other botanicas besides the Señora's which sell room spray to bring love, money, ward off misfortune, ointments to smooth into your hair to confound your enemies. In the back of the botanicas, behind a screen, someone sits with a well-worn rosary, ready to read your fortune. Everyone in Wallingford is looking for miracles.

Most of Destiny's business is over the phone: New York, Los Angeles, and lately, Dallas. Delia charges twenty dollars but she thinks she could charge more. Destiny senses money on the other end of the line.

The questions are always about love or money, the callers mainly women. Whatever the questions, whatever they say, Destiny hears in the background the low buzz of turmoil, the sound of lives swirling out of control. It is very important that Destiny give the clients clear answers, specific tasks to perform, to make them feel they are part of a plan, that they have roles and functions. Destiny reestablishes the grid for them so they know how to move, what to do next.

Delia is often amazed at what Destiny says. No wonder clients hang up on her. This last one, for instance. Are there bannisters in New York City? She doesn't think so. In New York people live in apartments. But she never censors Destiny's words. It would ruin her flow to have Delia step in here and there.

Most of what Destiny sees is abstract: lines of force, sometimes blocking energy, sometimes releasing it. She questions her clients to bring the picture into focus, to guide them to the beneficial path. Most are forthcoming but some are closemouthed. They think it's cheating to help her, as if she's performing a magic trick. The most skeptical also expect the most—all or nothing, miracle or fraud.

Sometimes there is a flash—second sight, the real thing—but it is only a bright, fleeting fragment, some detail lifted out of context. Often even the client can't make sense of it. This is the case with the bannister.

Destiny is above personal concerns, for love or money. She is selfless and pure, a shuttlecock on the loom of life, existing only to move people along.

Delia worries about money. Rent isn't much, but electricity is, now that winter is coming on and they will be using the heaters. Lazaro is growing. He needs clothes and particular kinds of clothes with proper labels, the right look. He earns some money helping Hugo out at the station, but Delia doesn't like what it's doing to his aura. She sees a hard glint coming off him sometimes that worries her.

Firetrucks one block over are heading toward the river. Delia stands barefoot in the kitchen, thinking it's another one of the old mills burning, or a warehouse. "Wallingford urban renewal," Cass calls it. Cass is coming home for Christmas. Delia has a sudden need to speak to her, to tell her anything, that firetrucks are screaming through town again, that she suspects Lavinia is living on cookies, anything, something, but Destiny has clients tonight, calling any minute now, the next one from Oakland, California, a regular, someone whose life won't improve for ten years but who calls anyway with a broken, raging voice.

"Light candles," Destiny advises, "many sizes but all white, and arrange them on the window sill." She also tells her to stop drinking coffee.

2

Will Appleyard doesn't need road markers to tell him he's coming to Wallingford. Tall red cliffs announce it better than any green and white highway sign, red cliffs of basalt from Mesozoic times. A grinding of the plates on which the continents ride twisted the earth's crust until it cracked, releasing rivers of rock which crested and froze in a red wave above sleepy Triassic streams, red and brown mud patterned with three-toed dinosaur tracks, fernlike skeletons of fishes.

Perhaps begin the history with the volcano. It will annoy the department heads, who train their doctoral candidates to keep their history within boundaries, to turn out small, neat, detailed studies. They think he's doing his dissertation on the evolution of the silk industry in Wallingford from 1880 to 1920. They expect him to show the familiar arc of growth and decline. They teach the students to look at history this way, as a series of smooth arcs.

But Will has a different model in his head, in which curves break suddenly and begin again on other axes entirely, in which catastrophes occur in clusters, in which civilizations atomize overnight. He cannot visualize, as the history department would have him do, time moving evenly from past through present to future. He sees present leaping into future and past percolating in, so that all three are muddled and intermingled. He has difficulty cutting time into categories, which may be why he has yet to complete his doctoral dissertation. An historian who cannot differentiate past from future is like a deaf man who tries to be a musician, or a blind man who wants to be a painter.

From the elevated highway, Will looks down on a brick Victorian box factory, a squat fifties candy plant, a futuristic polymers company, and a warehouse of no recognizable era hunkering grimly over railroad tracks. Somewhere on the other side of town, near the river, are the old Appleyard mills.

Will does not look for his ancestral home because all the fine mansions in town burned in the fire of 1902. They were replaced by working-class two-family houses. Will can see them now, crowded together, with identical bay windows and exterior stairs. They are aging badly. Around them are red-brick housing projects built in the fifties, and interspersed like gray warts, concrete parking garages, underused and already crumbling at the edges.

The highway turns and church spires swing into view, along with a shining white and slender dome, the county courthouse, built in 1830 out of the finest Vermont marble. The graceful arrangement of spires and dome redeems the city, giving it a center both visual and spiritual, but only for a moment, before a brutal gray rectangle eclipses the dome and hides it from the highway. It's a prison—what else, with those narrow, slit windows? It's been recently built, conveniently if unesthetically, directly across the street from the courthouse. Cities generally like to put their palaces of justice in the center of town and hide their houses of detention on the outskirts. Is Wallingford to be condemned for its cynicism or applauded for its frankness?

The town was originally built on the banks of the Walling

River, but Will sees no evidence of river from the overpass. He takes the exit which promises *Historic Area and Falls.*

Narrow, dramatic, the falls were a spectacular sight to come upon out in the claustrophobic forests of New Jersey. They were considered one of the scenic wonders of the new world and were immortalized by European artists, in watercolors, oils, engravings. In these pictures there is often an underclothed savage posed on the cliff, an historical inaccuracy because the local tribe only went to the falls in groups and then only on special occasions. They believed the falls were protected by powerful spirits and that to approach the falls alone was to take the first step toward madness.

Alexander Hamilton, not of a mystical nature, or maybe accustomed since his West Indian childhood to overlooking the minor deities who lurk beside natural wonders, chose to see the physical, not the spiritual, properties of the falls. He organized a group of investors and commissioned L'Enfant to lay out canals, strings of mills, workers' housing. He took the dark unnamed force at the center of savage life and called it water power.

The sign promised falls, but the exit ramp dumps Will off in the middle of a barrio, with store signs in Spanish, and graffiti crawling up the walls.

At the gas station, men stand around in a knot, ignoring him, hoping he'll come to his senses and go away, but his gauge is on empty. Eventually one breaks off from the group.

"Yeah?"

"Fill it with regular, unleaded." Will gets out of the car and stretches.

"Something else you want?" as if he has encroached on private property, but he only got out of his car. At a service station. Surely that's permitted. The attendant is inches shorter than Will, can't be more than five-seven, and younger—looks in his late twenties. He wears his new leather bomber jacket open, displaying two heavy gold chains, one of them with a medallion. He's well built. His hands are clean, his loafers black and polished.

"Yes, I was wondering if you'd know a place I could stay, maybe a room or an apartment to rent in town for a couple of months—"

The attendant looks Will over, notes his topsiders, corduroy pants, down jacket. "Go down this road, turn left. Get back on the highway. Five minutes and you'll see three big hotels: Sheraton, Holiday Inn, and something else, I forget. You can get a room there. You can get meals. Around here you can't get neither one. You just get in trouble." He stands wide-legged and a little too close, rocking slightly in his pelvis.

The pump clicks off. He goes to pump some more into the tank. Will hates it when they do this. It just burns off anyway, and it makes the car smell of gasoline. "Don't top the tank," he usually instructs, but this time he stands as the attendant forces in an extra half-dollar, working the meter up to an even ten.

"I'm an historian," Will explains, taking out his wallet. "I wanted to live in town for a while because I'm writing a history of Wallingford."

"This place. You mean a history of this place?"

"Yes."

"I never think of it having a history. I don't think of it as a place."

Taking in Wallingford from the vantage point of the garage, Will can see what he means.

"Well, OK. Maybe I'll just drive around for a while," Will says, as if he owes this man an explanation.

"Hey, yo!" Before Will can get away, the attendant motions for him to roll down the window so he can lean in. His medallion swings free from his leather jacket. There's a leopard engraved on it, pouncing.

"You want some history, why don't you try the place across the street? You can get your fortune told too. It's expensive, but it's worth it. She's got some kind of sixth sense, you know what I mean? If you want my advice, that's the place to go. You can start there."

It's a *fin de siècle* mansion: three stories, mansard roof, cupola, the whole bit. The road has eaten up the front yard so that the porch steps come right down to the pavement. The reason he didn't see it before is that it is camouflaged by asbestos tile, patches of it in different colors and patterns, giving the house a leprous look. The upper floors are boarded shut. Through the clouded glass of the street-floor window, Will can see a sign: *Destiny Ortega. Palms Read. Tarot.*

Across the street, the attendant is still standing by his pumps, watching Will. Maybe Destiny Ortega is his girlfriend, or his mother. Will locks his doors and drives north on Market Street.

When the town was originally laid out around the canals, water was the dominant motif. Now, with the canals filled in and the river hidden by taller buildings, the chain-link fence seems to be the unifying element in the design of Wallingford. It snakes along the sides of buildings, marking boundaries. Sometimes it is cut and raveled, rusting, beaten to the ground. In other places it is shiny and new—around the prison, for instance, where it rises to triple height, crowned by silver spirals of razor wire.

The fence surrounding the old Appleyard mills is covered in vines and would be almost invisible in the summer. The buildings themselves are long and low, built of a mellowed brick, stark in outline but pleasing in proportions. They are reflected in the original canal which runs in front, surprisingly clean and clear. The river must be somewhere behind.

A sign in tasteful shades of gray and maroon announces that Grand Land Development Corporation is converting the mills into apartments and artists' studios, shops and restaurants. Will jots down the telephone number.

At last, Will finds the falls, under a bridge, hemmed in by an aging power plant. Will can't tell if it's the water he hears or the traffic on the six-lane highway above.

Nearby is what could have been the old lockkeeper's cottage, restored and converted into a gift shop. It isn't likely that a gift shop in a deserted part of town will be open at ten in the morning, but there's a light inside and a buzzer answers Will's ring.

A woman with a sagging jawline and expensively restored blond hair pokes her head up from behind a display of homespun yarns.

"May I help you?"

Is it all right if he looks around?

Of course, feel free. She thought he might be lost, needing directions or something. She doesn't usually get customers this early in the morning. She is having tea and a little chat with one of the talented craftspeople whom the shop is fortunate to represent.

Another head appears behind the yarn, this one younger, with strong golden hair parted in the middle and pulled back in a low braid. The older one, who insists that Will call her Bubbles because everyone does, offers a small plump hand across the yarn display. The younger one is Bridget Farthingsworth. Her handshake is hearty and callused.

Bridget is a blacksmith, creator of the andirons and trivets displayed on the back wall and also the elegant wrought iron gate which Bubbles is presently using to block off her little kitchen from the rest of the shop but which is for sale, if Will is interested—? The shop features the work of local craftsmen: woven wall hangings, hand-built porcelain teapots, sweaters that are works of art, really. It's a shame to wear them.

Is he any relationship to the Appleyards of the Appleyard mills? . . . Isn't that fascinating! What brings him back here? . . . He'll have to meet a dear friend, Edgar Snow, the man who is doing the old mills over into studios and shops. He's the one who convinced her to open this store, a marvelous person, who adores history. A man of vision. Is Will absolutely certain he doesn't want a cup of tea? Bubbles has all kinds.

"Actually, I was looking for a place to stay. They told me at the gas station that there weren't any good hotels in town, but maybe

you know where I could look for an apartment, something for a
few months while I do my research—"

"Oh of course! Of course! It's you!" Bubbles' eyes, which are an
extraordinary shade of green and match her sweater, go wide. "I
have your place, your new home. It's with my friend, not right in
town but overlooking it, about five minutes away. You do have a
car, don't you? Good, because you really need it. My friend takes
buses everywhere, but they are unreliable. I wonder if I should
phone? No, just go around and surprise her. Tell her Bubbles sent
you. She was in the shop yesterday saying she was going to look
for a boarder. She'll be thrilled. You are perfect, just the one."

> Your mama wears army boots,
> I saw when she took them off.
> She put them on the floor,
> Cock-a-roaches moved next door.
> Uh-huh. Uh-huh.

Lavinia, in old workboots Nestor left behind, sings as she shuffles
between pots of orchids. The boots are much too big, but she leaves
them in the conservatory to wear over her house-slippers. The
boots keep the cold from creeping up, and she enjoys seeing herself
reflected in the glass panels, in her nightgown and wool flannel
robe with the satin piping (worn but still good, purchased at Lord
& Taylor eighteen years ago), her gray hair back in a braid, tramping around in Nestor's big boots.

Lavinia works with energy, even though she hardly slept the
night before. Yesterday was unsettling, and then the fire last night.
She heard it on the radio this morning, another warehouse downtown burned and they suspect arson. She worries about Delia and
Lazaro living down there, although as Delia reminded her when
she phoned this morning to see if they were all right, they are a
good half-mile from the fire.

Lavinia restrained herself from speaking about the fire of 1902, when her grandfather's house and Nestor's grandfather's and nearly everyone's was destroyed in one horrible conflagration.

Lavinia also did not mention that Señora Ortega had warned her about the fire yesterday. Some saint, not a regular saint but one of their mixed-up voodoo saints, had had his day yesterday, and this saint or god was supposed to be very fond of fire. Lavinia doesn't like to mention the Señora to Delia because the Señora hates Delia. So odd, because nobody dislikes Delia, and the Señora is devoted to Lazaro. And then there's her friendship with Lavinia, which she separates completely from Delia. Of course, Lavinia and the Señora go back to before Delia and Jaime.

Delia had been—what? Fourteen? Delia and Cass had been just old enough so that Lavinia was feeling a little underused. She was looking for something to take her out of the house, take her mind off—things at home. The read-to-the-blind program at the library seemed easy enough. Nestor had his reservations; the library wasn't in a very nice section of town. He would have had a fit if he had ever found out where she was really going. He was very protective of her and the girls, right up to the day he left.

Most of the volunteers did their reading in the library, in one of the little rooms off the main one, but not all the blind were able or willing to come to the library. Miss Fox, the woman who ran the program, explained this to Lavinia. She assumed Lavinia would be more daring than the other volunteers because she spoke Spanish, spoke it fluently, since she had been raised in Madrid until she was a teenager and had majored in Spanish at Vassar. This skill set Lavinia apart, made Miss Fox treasure her above the run-of-the-mill volunteer, usually a bookish woman in late middle life, feeling lonely with time on her hands. Because Lavinia spoke Spanish, Miss Fox assumed she would also be unusually courageous and would be willing to make a house call. Lavinia found herself agreeing to go to the home of Señora Ortega, in the heart of Dublin.

It's called Dublin after the Irish mill-workers who settled there. When Lavinia's mother brought her to Wallingford from Spain, Dublin was Italian. Now it is mostly black and Hispanic—blacks from the South, Hispanics from Puerto Rico, the Dominican Republic, Honduras, Nicaragua, Guatemala.

For a moment, climbing the dark, narrow stairs to Señora Ortega's apartment above her botanica, Lavinia wished she had told Nestor, who would have forbidden her absolutely. But the minute Carmen opened the door, so pretty and slim, just Delia's age, Lavinia felt reassured, although Carmen did not smile. She never does.

Señora Ortega's front parlor was small, stuffy, dark, and cluttered, but clean, no dust on the religious statues or on the numerous tables, with their colorful hand-crocheted doilies under glass. Lavinia had to thread her way into the room to the plastic-covered maroon velvet armchair pointed out to her from the doorway. The lampshades were covered in plastic as well. Plastic runners lay in front of the sofa and chairs. It was as if the room had been prepared for a large group of careless people who came regularly to eat pizza and drink Coca-Colas, but Lavinia didn't think this was possible. More likely, the Señora used the plastic as a charm, a preventative against corruption and decay, the rotting, the organic breakdown that was so pervasive in her native Caribbean.

Lavinia took out her copy of *Don Quixote*, the one she kept from Vassar with her handwritten notes in the margin, and looked up to see Señora Ortega in the doorway.

All the blind people Lavinia had ever seen had been slightly sad and dim, with wisps of hair escaping in unfortunate places, amorphous bodies, dreary clothes put on with indifference. She was not prepared for the Señora, with her dark hair slicked back into a chignon, her rouge-burnished cheeks, her eyes outlined and highlighted with gold shadow, her brown skin shining. She couldn't have been taller than four-ten, although she was wearing three-inch heels. Her feet, hands, and head were small, but her body was ample, so she almost appeared to be floating in layers above her tiny feet—one layer of hips, one layer of bosom, with a small, round head like a bead on the top.

Lavinia rose quickly to lead her into the room, as Miss Fox had instructed, but the Señora, quicker still, made her way around the spindly tables, took Lavinia's hand between her own, and stood pressing it for what couldn't have been more than sixty seconds but which felt longer because it was such an odd thing to do. Someone flushed a toilet in the apartment above. A truck passed in the street. Lavinia felt her hand grow warm and slightly moist between the Señora's fleshy palms, but she dared not pull away or break the silence.

Finally, apparently satisfied, the Señora released Lavinia and retired to the plastic-covered sofa. Lavinia resumed her seat. She cleared her throat and picked up *Don Quixote*, trying not to be disconcerted by the way the Señora's blind eyes were traveling over her body, stopping at her breasts, her crotch. Before Lavinia could say anything, the Señora was off on a long, rapid, slurry monologue that Lavinia had trouble following because she wasn't used to Puerto Rican Spanish. As far as she could understand, the Señora was telling her that they would be friends for life because they shared the same protecting spirits. "We have many protectors, many protectors." Her short arms stretched out to include an unseen gathering of spirits. "We will be friends for life." She repeated that phrase. There was something else. Lavinia thought she said they would cause each other pain, or trouble, or they would bear the same sorrow; it wasn't clear.

Señora Ortega did not want to listen to *Don Quixote*. Instead she had some newspapers: *El Mundo* and *El Vocero de Puerto Rico*, which she asked Lavinia to read to her, everything—news, ads, comics. She corrected Lavinia's Castilian Spanish, making her say words over again until she learned to swallow the vowels,

Puerto Rican style. When Carmen came in with meringue cookies and coffee sweetened with condensed milk already stirred in, Lavinia was amazed to see that an hour had gone by. It had seemed only a minute, but when she was driving home, thinking of all that had happened, she felt as if she had spent a week in a foreign country instead of an afternoon in an apartment on Main Street.

"You have a daughter," Señora Ortega said, the first time she announced she would tell Lavinia's fortune. She held Lavinia's hand, which looked bony and translucently pale in the Señora's plump brown one. A cigar was clenched in the Señora's teeth. The Señora didn't ordinarily smoke cigars. This was for the sake of the spirit she was consulting. The smoke made Lavinia feel ill. She hadn't asked to have her fortune told.

"I have two daughters," Lavinia said pleasantly, trying to keep the exchange on a polite and superficial level.

"I am concerned with only one. Tell her not to come here. For all of our sakes."

"You mean here, to your house?"

"Yes."

"I don't see how she possibly would. She doesn't even know that I see you. Her father is very protective. I think it best not to tell the girls, that way they don't have to lie to their father. . . ."

Smoke exploded from the Señora's mouth. "Warn her never to come," she insisted.

To her regret, Lavinia didn't take the Señora's words seriously. Lavinia never told Delia any of this, even after Jaime's death.

Did the Señora see that the two children would fall in love, have a child? Did she see that Jaime would be killed? She must have thought it was all connected, that if Jaime met Delia, he would live with her, and if he lived with her, he would be killed. It's nonsense, but the thought always chills Lavinia. She tries not to think about it.

Lavinia sponges off the leaves of the Venerable One, her large paphiopedilum. She wants to have it blooming for Christmas when Cass comes home, although Cass isn't interested in orchids. Actually she hates seeing Lavinia puttering in Nestor's greenhouse, keeping Nestor's orchids alive. Cass always preaches that Lavinia should move out of the castle and get a little apartment somewhere, away from Wallingford. "What's the sense of living up there like a hermit, waiting for Dad to come back? After fifteen years, it's time to give up. He isn't coming."

> She put them in the sky—
> Superman refused to fly.
> Uh-huh. Uh-huh.

Cass doesn't like the idea of taking in a boarder. She called last night and Lavinia had to tell her, although she knew Cass wouldn't approve. "An old lady living alone, how do you know what someone might do. . . ." Wasn't it better to have someone else in the house then? And Lavinia could use the rent money. She could give Delia a little more each month if she had some rent coming in. She wouldn't even have to make renovations. The boarder could have the dungeon, Nestor's basement: wet bar (she would put in a hot plate); bathroom, full bath; sitting room with folding bed, TV.

"If you are determined to do it, I'm sure there's a safe, efficient way to go about it," Cass said. "Don't go sticking ads in the *Wallingford Gazette*. Let me think about this."

"Someone is coming to stay," Señora Ortega had said yesterday. Lavinia hadn't asked for a session. She never did. Señora Ortega lit up a cigar and coughed. Lavinia wishes Carmen would tell her to give them up; they can't be good for her health.

"My daughter," Lavinia said, trying to keep up a conversational tone. "Cass is coming in from San Francisco for Christmas." Señora Ortega never acknowledges that Lavinia has two daughters.

"This is a man."

Nestor! Lavinia's heart jumped. "Do I know him?"

"Someone with ties to the past."

Nestor! "Do I know him?"

"He will pay two hundred dollars a month to live in your house."

Not Nestor. "I was thinking of putting an ad in the paper for a boarder," Lavinia said helpfully.

"A friend will send him."

Lavinia doesn't really like it when Señora Ortega gives her one of these rare séances. She doesn't like the feeling that her life is being decided without her. She doesn't subscribe to all those saints and spirits Señora Ortega is forever calling on. Lavinia prefers the idea of free will. Of course, she has the option of turning away the boarder, as Lavinia has come to think of him, but wasn't she planning on taking in a boarder anyway? What if even her plan has been preordained, her own thoughts in the control of some outside force? Lavinia shivers and digs both hands deep into the bag of peat moss to steady herself.

She had hurried straight from Señora Ortega's up to Bubbles' shop by the falls. As usual, there were no customers, and fortunately, none of Bubbles' craftspeople, the knitters and potters who flock around her with their problems, who want to talk about their work. Bubbles' patience is boundless.

"You look as if you could use some Constant Comment," Bubbles greeted her. In addition to crafts, Bubbles sells wool for weaving and knitting, Caswell-Massey soap, and all different kinds of tea.

They sat out in the shop, behind the yarn display, most unprofessional-looking if anyone were to walk in, but people rarely do during the week. On the weekends, sometimes a bus of tourists will pull up and look at the falls. That's when Bubbles makes her sales—mostly the soaps.

"I can't wait to hear all about it," Bubbles called from the little kitchen in the back of the shop.

"About what?"

"The session. You were with the Señora, weren't you?"

"How could you tell?"

"You smell like cigars."

"Do I? How awful."

"Not strong. Just a little." Bubbles came out with the tea in two handmade porcelain mugs. She would never dare go to the Señora. Even if she did she wouldn't get anything out of it. French is Bubbles' language, not Spanish.

"A boarder! With ties to the past. How intriguing. Lavinia, wouldn't it be fabulous if it turned out to be a lover from your past—"

"I never had lovers, only Nestor. Besides, the Señora told me he will seek my daughter's hand. Those were her exact words."

"That's even better, isn't it, if Delia remarries and gets Lazaro out of that slum—" Bubbles also forgets that Lavinia has two daughters. But Delia needs a husband more than Cass.

"I'm just hoping he has a car so he can take me into town once in a while," Lavinia said, "although I imagine he works. If he works, he won't be around during the day. Of course, I don't believe a word of this. It's just that the Señora puts ideas in my head and then it's hard to get rid of them."

"I'm repotting the pleiones so they'll bloom again in the spring," Lavinia tells the boarder who in her imagination has taken on a hazy form lounging in the conservatory doorway, watching her in an amused but respectful way, like a grown son. He is, naturally, curious about the castle. Everyone is. Sometimes on a Sunday Lavinia has to turn people away who come in cars, attracted by the turrets, thinking the house is some kind of amusement. The castle, Lavinia tells the boarder, was built as a movie set, then outfitted as a home for the director. Nestor bought it from the director some years later.

Nestor calls the door that opens out from the basement the "sally port" and the paved parking area is Nestor's "bailey." The moat, to Nestor's disappointment, never did manage to hold water. The old castles with moats were built in rivers, not at the tops of hills.

They always use the sally port (she hopes this won't prove a problem for the boarder), never the two sets of eighteen-foot double doors that open from the great hall onto real drawbridges. The doors are difficult to open and close. They are warping. Lavinia stuffs blankets in them in the winter and when it rains.

The boarder's discreet but enthusiastic response encourages Lavinia to go on and describe the medieval banquets they used to hold in the great hall: Nestor at the head of the table in his absurd velvet robe (but he did look striking in it—a big man, he can carry off anything with authority); Lavinia in Elizabethan dress, which suited her figure; the girls, one fair, one dark, dressed as princess and page.

Lavinia, happily occupied with her potting and imaginary conversation, fails to see the red Saab until it is pulled to a stop directly outside the sally port.

She is hoping for a Jehovah's Witness or a meter reader or even a realtor out looking for property to sell. They sometimes come by. But even before he gets out of the car, Lavinia knows it is he. Wasn't she just chatting with him? Well, he's here. His hair is a little thinner on top than she thought, but now she's seeing him from above. Men always look balder from a bird's-eye view. He catches her glance before she has the presence of mind to duck behind the pots.

"Oh dear, oh dear," Lavinia tells the orchids, and then thinks, what an old womanish thing to say, and how cowardly to be huddled on the gravel floor while he rings at the sally port. Did he see her? Of course he did. He saw her silly gray head peeking out from the pleiones. There is no getting out of it. She is going to have to open the door in her housecoat and slippers, leaving Nestor's boots in the conservatory, hurrying downstairs, smoothing back her hair, and trying not to think about the Señora.

He is definitely flesh and blood, nothing apparitional about him; a tiny bit plump, as if he likes good food; smooth-faced, eyes somewhat obscured by wire-rimmed glasses; stoop-shouldered, a history professor on sabbatical, writing a history of Wallingford. He's looking for a place to stay in town. He went into Bubbles' shop and asked if there was an apartment to rent in Wallingford, and she sent him here. Lavinia can relax a little when she hears this, is able to take her hand away from where it's been, clutching her lapels—as if this moon-faced professor were going to snatch off her robe. For a moment Lavinia was terrified that some Caribbean voodoo was at work here but now that she knows it was Bubbles who sent him, she can see that he's a perfectly nice man, not metaphysical in any way. The Señora only predicted someone would come. She didn't send him by magic. He's not a zombie out of some horror movie on late-night TV, where the dead walk around in the jungles of Haiti. He's a perfectly nice man.

"Appleyard? Like Appleyard Road and Appleyard Lane and Appleyard Memorial Library?" Cass, on the other end of the line, sounds calm but a little stern.

"Am I calling you at a bad time, Cass darling?"

"No, it's all right. Tell me. He's one of *the* Appleyards?"

"The same. He's writing a history of Wallingford."

"It doesn't make sense. Why is he staying with you? Has he been disinherited or something?"

Cass always brings up questions Lavinia never considers. Why is he staying with her instead of renting a nice apartment or house of his own? "It's their method, these young historians—like method actors; they *live* it, you know, experience it as nearly as possible," Lavinia invents.

"He's delighted to be here. He loves the castle. You know, he considers it history, part of the history of Wallingford. And he's going to go through all the papers in your old room, sorting through and working out what should go to the historical society, what should just be thrown away. You can't imagine how happy he was to see all those boxes up there. Do you know, his mother didn't save anything, not even the last postcard he got from his father before he died? I think people who throw things out are sad."

"How much is he paying?"

"Two hundred a month. Do you think that's too much?"

"I think that's not enough."

"That doesn't include food. He's going to help me with the grocery money."

"You're cooking for him?"

"Well, yes. I thought it would be nicer for both of us."

Maybe it won't be so bad. She'll get some food in the house at least, instead of living on tea and cookies. Of course, most of the two hundred will go to Delia. Lavinia wouldn't think of repairing the roof or having the gutters cleaned. She worries about orchids while the house falls down around her ears. She thinks Nestor will come back and take care of it all, that he's just off on one of his peccadillos, as she calls them, only instead of lasting a weekend or a week, this one has gone on for fifteen years.

Cass wishes for once that there were someone she could tell this to, explain why she is always forced to be negative with Lavinia. It's because of Lavinia's maniacal optimism. It leaves Cass no choice but to adopt the cold voice of reason, a lawyer's voice, her father's.

A voice in the other room wants to know what the hell she's doing in there. Does she want to fuck or not?

Yes, of course she wants to. That's why she brought him up here, only now she would rather talk. He's lying on top of the blue and white quilt, displaying an erection. It's amazing how some men still think women care about the size of it. What kind of man would move in with an old woman? A homosexual. William Appleyard is probably gay.

3

---

avinia is a little eccentric. She talks about her husband as if he's living in the castle and yet when Will casually asked if he was away on a trip, she stammered and blushed, couldn't tell him. She went to cook dinner last night and all she had in the cupboard was a package of cheap, cream-filled cookies. Will ended up taking her out to a family-run Italian place in town. She was thrilled, a little shy, ate everything hungrily, said she didn't usually go to restaurants. Obviously.

Now she is sitting back in the passenger seat of the Saab, with the air of someone being driven in a limousine, humming a little song to herself. Will decided to drive to town to start his research, and Lavinia asked if she could ride along and do some grocery shopping. She called his three-year-old Saab a "marvelous little car," praised the interior, the way it rode.

It's Lavinia's enthusiasm, as much as her boxes of family records, photos, and letters, that is going to make this history live. Will told her as much last night over dinner. The combined effect of

Lavinia's almost superhuman cheerfulness, the discovery of the treasures in the tower room, and the good Chianti he had ordered with dinner had made him expansive—he could hardly believe it when he heard himself telling Lavinia that the history of Wallingford was the one he was destined to write. What did he mean by that?

It is true, however, that all his other attempts at writing a dissertation have been laborious, abortive efforts. Facts, dates, numbers, and names were hard to come by, and once he had them, they were as dry and meaningless as stones. But this time, the material is practically falling into his hands and every piece he uncovers glows with the promise of being part of a rich mosaic.

"You're like the prince in Sleeping Beauty," said Lavinia, her eyes shining from her share of the Chianti. "You know, nobody could get through for a hundred years, but when the time was right, and the person was right, the thorns simply parted in his path."

"Yes, yes, it's like that," Will agreed, although this morning it seems an odd image for an historian.

What if Lavinia is expecting something from him? Didn't Bubbles say he was "the one"? A prickle of warning creeps up his neck. But then seeing Lavinia supremely happy simply to be riding in his car, he decides that whatever Lavinia wants from him, it will be small, something he can easily give.

The town seems more alive today, or maybe it's the wind that gives the illusion of things happening. Lavinia wants to be dropped off at an Italian bakery on Main Street. Will goes back to Market Street, to the house across from the gas station. He checked his notes last night. A mansion like this, in this section of town, could only have been one thing, what they used to call a house of entertainment.

Pieces of newspapers go end over end past the gas pumps at the station, like tumbleweed through a Western ghost town. It looks so thoroughly uninhabited that Will wonders if he made a mistake and it was another place where he stopped yesterday. The house is the same, however, with the same sign in the window.

His Spanish is rudimentary, but he hopes he can make this Destiny Ortega understand. He has no idea what the Spanish word for historian is. She may speak English. The sign is in English. He'll start by having her read his palm or something and then persuade her to let him see the house.

"I never noticed wind before I came here." Faye hears her own voice echo inside her skull. It's the effect of the wind creating shifting vacuums, throwing her voice back to her. She is shocked to hear how artful she sounds, jejune, falsely innocent. *"Skill turned to cunning . . ."* The psychic's words keep coming back to her. Although she reasons them away, they have somehow lodged down deep where she can't get at them.

Her talent always lay in her ease, the unforced way she came to her craft—not actressy, not self-conscious in any way. Earthy. Yes. A woman with her feet on the ground. This is something she has always known, or does it seem that way after talking to the psychic? Which are Faye's thoughts, which the psychic's?

A year ago she moved in, arriving like a schoolgirl on vacation —as Gareth loves to describe it to his friends—with a carton of books, a few dresses, blue jeans, and a sweater, virtually homeless, although there's no virtue in it. There is no virtue in poverty. Try being a young actress in New York! How do you eat? Where do you sleep? You share a tiny apartment in a dangerous neighborhood with three or four other actors, and you wait tables or teach aerobics and go to auditions. If Gareth Watts offers to take you in—why, then you go.

Your closet begins to fill up, because you can't appear on the arm of Gareth Watts in places where you will be photographed by the press in the same little Betsey Johnson you used to dress up

or dress down for all occasions. Neither do you run around to
every little pissant audition, because with Gareth Watts behind
you, you can afford to wait for the right property.

They are waiting. Did she explain that to the psychic, or did she
merely say she hadn't worked in a year? If she told anyone, any
stranger, that she hadn't worked since coming to live with Gareth
Watts a year ago, whoever it was would have to answer that he
was inhibiting her career. That's the off-the-cuff response anyone
would give who didn't know the situation, no less a two-bit,
bargain-basement, phone-in psychic from New Jersey.

The windows shudder. The whole place sways slightly in the
wind. "Like a blade of grass," Gareth said, trying to explain to her
why it was necessary for the building to give in the wind, but it
makes her bilious, twenty-three stories up, cantilevered out over
East 70th Street.

It doesn't bother Gareth. He's up in his aerie, two floors above
at the very top of the building, playing his Bach, writing notes,
reading the properties people send him. He hasn't worked in a
year either. They are waiting for something they can do together.
She should have told the psychic that. If Gareth has turned down
work for her sake, it isn't unreasonable of him to ask her to do
the same.

Faye has been standing all this time in her underwear in front
of her closet, trying to decide what to wear. She is meeting Tina,
someone she doesn't see very often anymore. They are going for
a walk in Central Park. Faye feels the need to put her feet on land,
real dirt for once, instead of floors that hang out twenty-three
stories over 70th Street, for God's sake. The problem is that none
of these clothes seem right for walking with Tina in Central Park,
until a pair of old blue jeans appears in the back of the closet,
along with a sweater she forgot she had.

Bach fills the stairwell. She makes it to the living room, where
she tries not to look out. The walls are glass on three sides. "I like

to feel I'm on a ledge that I could leap from and soar over the city," Gareth tells people.

She stands at the bottom of the stairs to his study, his crow's nest. "I'm going out."

"What did you say?"

She sees his bare feet on the top stair, but it makes her dizzy to look up.

"I'm going out for a walk."

"Why don't you wait a half hour and I'll go with you."

"I'm meeting Tina."

"Come up and give me a kiss goodbye."

"No, you come down here. It makes me seasick to go up there." That fake little-girl voice again.

His foot comes down one step. He enjoys giving in to her small requests.

The stairs are steep and open on one side. Faye sees his hand grip the bannister, then wobble as a gust of wind hits the windows, and Faye thinks it is the wind, but it is the bannister coming away from the wall, making Gareth lose his balance.

Destiny is laying out the Tarot on the dining room table for her client. She sensed that the religious statues in the parlor, which put the Spanish people at ease, would only distance him, although he was interested in the room and said the interior was in remarkably good shape, considering the outside.

He is more comfortable here in the dining room. He fits in better. The cards are going to be especially talkative this morning. Their colors are rich as stained glass. They shimmer on the surface of the table. The configuration, the combination, is highly unusual.

It is important, however, to begin slowly. He is not sure why he is here. He's never had a reading before. His attention is not focused

on the cards but wanders around the house. Destiny brings him
back with a few questions.

"This card"—Destiny Ortega places a small, rounded index
finger on the picture of a knight laid out on a tomb, three swords
over him, one under—"would seem to indicate a loss in your life
early on, the death, perhaps, of a parent?" She looks at him with
round blue eyes, full of sympathy.

"Yes"—to Will's dismay, his voice cracks—"my father, when
I was ten, he died." He had pictured an old crone with whiskers
on her chin, muttering over his palm while he studied the house,
not this fluffy blond with tiny rings all over her fingers and two
sets of gold hoops in her ears, a child playing gypsy. He can't tell
how old she is, but he can see now that she isn't playing. She
really believes she's seeing something in the cards.

"This one"—she taps another—"is interesting. It could indicate
a chain of people or events impinging on your life right now."

They are masters at this, of the vague statement, which the
credulous can then apply to their lives. Will shouldn't have accepted the coffee. It's making him alert to the point of pain. He
hears the wind slapping up against the sides of the house, rolling
a garbage can in the street. The wind even manages to penetrate
the walls, making some dresses hanging in the doorway sway
slightly, like women waiting, teasing in a line. The phone rings,
but the fortuneteller doesn't seem to notice.

"Your phone," Will offers.

Destiny Ortega looks up from her cards. The blue of her irises
has receded, making her pupils unnaturally wide, as if she's had
eyedrops. Can she even see like that? She takes his hand in her
small, warm one. "Please, the cards are most interesting, the time
unusually propitious. Please give me your attention so we can
begin this journey together."

"Queen of Swords." Destiny has known clients to turn pale at
the sight of this card, but this one is unmoved. He is in a period

of retrogression. His aura lies like a dull purplish-brown smudge around him.

"I'm sorry," he says. "I'm not familiar with these cards. What is the significance of the Queen of Swords?"

"Well, a lot depends on her placement in your configuration. She usually represents a woman who is exerting a negative influence, a woman thwarted, in love perhaps or in pursuit of power."

"I was supposed to get married, but it fell apart. I wouldn't say Dagne, my fiancée, was thwarted, though."

"Hmm. The broken engagement seems right, but this would be closer and yet farther away. For instance, very near, near this place, but removed in time."

She is turning cards over rapidly now, as if looking for something, until she has five in a line. Out of the corner of his eye, Will sees a woman dressed in eighteen-nineties costume standing in the doorway. He turns, but it is only those dresses moving slightly in the ghostly wind. Absurdly, his forehead goes clammy. He should give up coffee entirely.

"There was a crisis recently. A brush with disaster when the Queen of Swords nearly had her way."

"I fell off a horse." Will's voice reverberates in the room. Did he actually say that?

"What?"

"A horse. Don't you want to get that phone? It might be important."

"Go ahead about the horse."

"My mother never let me ride, not even little ponies in a ring, because my father died in a riding accident, and my grandfather too, so she was kind of superstitious about it. I didn't mind. I'm not very athletic. But where I live, where I teach, it's horse country, a lot of riding, and not surprisingly, as it happened, I became romantically involved with a woman who was, is, a superb equestrian and she seemed to think she could teach me to ride."

She looks at him with round, black eyes, while her dresses gesture from the doorway.

"And she did?"

"I was doing pretty well. She's an excellent teacher—a bit of a perfectionist, a fanatic in ways, but she was pleased with me eventually and we were going to get married—that phone. Answer it. I don't mind."

"No. The horse. Go on."

"I was riding with Dagne, my fiancée, and some of her friends. We were on top of a hill. One minute things were fine, calm. Then suddenly I'm galloping down the hill, faster than I've ever gone. We were flying! Through a meadow and then into a bog, with trees. It only lasted a minute. The horse stumbled and I fell off, but Dagne was furious with me."

"Why was she angry?"

"Because I could have ruined the horse."

"But if it was an accident—"

"She said I did it, that I kicked the horse into a gallop. I don't remember that at all."

"Take my hands." He does so, feeling foolish. "Now close your eyes." She closes hers and sits up straight, attentive. Will lets his eyes fall shut.

He's aware of the wind snuffling around the window and of the blood going through their hands. Musty house-smells slowly give way to something sweeter, sun on grass and horse, maybe, leather and sweat, insects humming low, swish of tails, the invisible build-up, the tension of a day about to explode. Ringing. The telephone ringing. Will seizes it like a lifeline to pull himself back into the present, away from whatever memories she was conjuring up.

Destiny Ortega releases his hands. She sighs, then goes to answer the phone.

The wind is extraordinary, the way it whines and whistles and shakes the window panes. In the next room, the fortuneteller's voice, low and calm, seems to be trying to placate the wind's hysterical cry.

The elaborate moldings in this room and the parlor, crusted as they are with a hundred years of paint, confirm his suspicions about the mansion's original purpose. There must be records somewhere, maybe even in Lavinia's hoard in the tower room.

He means to examine the room, but the cards, worn, dog-eared, keep pulling him back. They are bright, as if constant use has not faded but deepened their color. What did she say about this one: three swords hanging over a dead knight. No, he isn't actually dead. He's alive but he doesn't dare move because of the blades hanging over him. Even with his eyes closed, he can feel the hard, sharp metallic threat suspended over his imperceptibly expanding and contracting, but still breathing, chest.

"It was a client." She steps out from her dresses in the doorway, making his heart jump. Coffee nerves. "Something I told her came true and she was upset. I don't know why they call me if they're not going to believe what I say."

"What had you told her?"

"To check the bannister, that it was loose, and it was. She was calling from the emergency room."

"She was hurt?"

"Someone she lives with. He leaned on the bannister and it came away from the wall. He broke his wrist."

"That's pretty impressive, that you knew."

She places both hands on the table and looks over the cards. "I have second sight," she says matter-of-factly. It occurs to Will that she is pretty, and that she reminds him of someone.

She bends over the cards, lifting her hair from her face with her fingertips. What was it she saw in the cards? Something significant in the way they came together. She could see lines of force between them. Now the cards lie flat and mute.

"I don't really care," he says, "about my fortune and the cards."

He doesn't want to look at swords and corpses anymore, malevolent queens, despairing youths. "I came for something else."

"All these swords," she muses, "like a curse—"

"Please," he hears himself almost begging, "I'd rather not."

"Maybe you're right. Maybe your way is better, going through the old papers. Maybe you'll find the connections that way. It's more your medium, history. Tarot cards, signs and portents, it's not everyone's thing."

"Good God, how did you know that?"

"Well, I'm not sure, but the Queen of Swords, the way she is with the nine of swords—"

"Told you I was writing a history?"

She looks at him with concern. "My mother told me that. Lavinia's my mother."

"What did that dude want?"

"I made some coffee. Want some?"

"Yeah, OK." Hugo follows Delia to the kitchen. "The character in the Saab. I know his car from the other day. He says he's doing a history of this place. That's what he claims, anyway."

Delia sets a fresh mug of coffee with condensed milk and sugar already in it beside the two cold, half-finished coffees from before. "He's searching for something."

"What do you mean?" He looks up fast, quick, alert. All the Spanish Delia knows are like that, even Lazaro.

"I don't know—"

"You don't think he's an agent, do you?"

"Agent?"

"An investigator. You know, a cop or something."

Delia laughs. Hugo watches her a moment, then laughs too. He leans back and stirs his coffee with a spoon he finds on the table. A heavy gold bracelet shows beneath the sleeve of his leather jacket, which he leaves on in the house to conceal the beginnings of a pot belly. His shirt is open and his gold medallion rests on bare skin, just a few chest hairs. His eyes are warm. Unlike Will Appleyard's, they are not afraid to travel over her.

"Lazaro's been hanging out at the station a lot."

"I hope he isn't in your way."

"No. He's a help. A boy his age, you know, needs a father figure. I'm like kind of a mentor for him." Hugo went to the community college in Wallingford for a year. His major was psychology.

"I'm afraid he isn't doing his homework. He's over there too much. Maybe if you sent him home a little earlier—"

He smiles sideways. "Yeah, I'll tell him. Kids that age, you know, they like to stay out. They think they're hot shit."

"I worry about him—"

"Of course you do. You're a mother. That's your role." His spoon clinks against the side of the mug. A wire sings in the wind. He sits up, looks around him quickly. "You don't, uh, have anyone coming—"

"No, mostly it's telephone now, and they usually call at night."

"What do you do all day?"

"I don't know. Something always happens. Today, for instance, he came over, and now you—"

"Yeah, but that's unusual. Usually, nobody comes. I know because I can see your house from the station. No one comes, no boyfriends, but you're still young. You're pretty. Don't you get lonely?"

"I don't think about it." She takes the two mugs, hers and Will Appleyard's, into the kitchen. He intercepts her at the door, smelling of sweet after-shave and gasoline.

"I could fix this place up. I could help you out."

"You have a wife. You have a baby," she reminds him.

Hugo shrugs. "She's my girlfriend."

"You live with her."

"I only stay there sometimes."

Delia turns away to put the mugs in the sink. "I have to think of Lazaro."

"What are we talking about? I'm thinking about Lazaro too. He's like a son to me."

"He needs someone to take him away—" Delia's hand flutters off toward the window.

"You mean not spic. Yeah, now I know what you mean. You let a spic get you into the slum, but now you want one of your own to get you out. Look, you know, I've got enough—you think I couldn't move you and your kid out to—I don't know, Larchmore or something? I could live there. We could live there. I got friends, Cubans, who live there. Some of my friends are Cubans. You want to do that?"

"It's not in my destiny, Hugo."

"Who is? This guy in the Saab? The professor?"

"I never thought of that." The sun, suddenly blown free of clouds, comes through the window and lights her hair from behind. "Maybe he is."

"You didn't tell me your daughter is a fortuneteller."

"You met Delia!"

"I was interested in her house," Will says, not wanting Lavinia to think he was having his cards read. "No tea, no thank you, Bubbles," but Bubbles is heading for her kitchen, wobbling a bit on slingback shoes, insisting that Earl Grey is what he needs on this windy day.

"Yes, it is an old thing, isn't it," says Lavinia, meaning the house.

"It's unusual for the area, being so elaborate—"

"It used to be a whorehouse. Have a cookie. They're my favorite kind, my secret vice. Whenever I feel flush I rush out and buy a bag from the Italian bakery."

"I wondered." Will takes a cookie and accepts his tea from Bubbles.

"Oh yes, notorious. I'm amazed you haven't come across it in your research. Delia's house, Bubbles, was a house of ill repute, loose women."

"Edgar owns it, I think." Bubbles brushes cookie crumbs off her lavender sweater, which matches her eyes exactly. "Wouldn't it be fun if he restored it? Now that would be a draw. What other town in New Jersey has a bordello museum?"

"Where is Edgar, Bubbles? I bought extra, thinking he'd be here."

"Maybe a meeting ran late." Bubbles cranes her neck to look over the yarn display, as if he could have come in without her knowing. "Edgar Snow is an Earl Grey man too," she confides in Will.

He's the developer, the one who is doing the mills, a man of vision. He loves history. Bubbles is certain there will be no problem for Will in getting into the mills. Maybe Edgar will give him a job, as a resident historian or something. Is Will aware that at one point they were going to tear down those beautiful historic mills to make way for a gigantic garbage disposal plant? Can he imagine a hundred trucks a day rumbling past, spilling garbage, not to mention the smoke, the pollution! Bubbles was on a committee to stop it but they weren't making much headway, when in rode Edgar Snow, like a white knight—

"Delia's not really a fortuneteller," Lavinia interrupts. "She's more of an advisor. People call her when they don't know where else to turn. She has all the hotline numbers by her phone: teen suicide, drugs, pregnancy, AA. She's sort of a clearing house for troubled people."

Bubbles reaches for something hanging on the wall. "Edgar

Snow presented me with the keys to this shop on this Tiffany key ring. Isn't it darling? It's a snake swallowing its tail."

Will admires the key ring, then hands it back to Bubbles. It feels cold and slightly slimy.

"In Delia's upbringing," Lavinia continues, "there was nothing magical. We certainly didn't plan this as a career," she tells Will, "but Delia wasn't a scholar. Even though she graduated from St. Agnes, which is quite a good school, college was out of the question. Nestor thought secretarial school, Katherine Gibbs, but I never could see Delia in an office, so I suppose this is the best, although not very lucrative."

"I should have Delia do me sometime," Bubbles' lavender eyes turn toward the door, "but I'm always afraid of what I'll find out."

"Delia's very careful not to scare her customers," Lavinia assures her. "She always looks for the good to temper the bad. For instance, someone came to her last spring about her mother, who was very ill with cancer. Delia said that by autumn the mother would be free from pain." Lavinia nibbles a cookie.

"And was she?" Bubbles asks.

"She died in August. But wasn't that a nice way of putting it? The woman called Delia and thanked her. It made her feel much better about the whole thing."

Delia believes that certain people, men and women, are destined for each other. She and Jaime were meant to be. Now that he is gone, she believes there is another in her future. She told Cass this when Cass came in for the funeral—she had dropped her studies and borrowed money to fly in from San Francisco.

"Yes, of course you'll find someone else," Cass reassured her, watching Delia carefully because there were none of the usual signs of grief. Delia was pale but calm, an island of stoicism in the flood tide of Hispanic sorrow, grieving, keening; banks of gladioluses; heavy, waxy wreaths; crosses made from carnations. Jaime, in a white tuxedo, was propped in his coffin, so that it looked as if he were attending to the proceedings and just resting for a moment on his white satin pillows. At the end, the followers, dressed in white, sobbing and wailing, women mostly, with a handful of young men, filed past to kiss their leader good-bye.

If an Episcopal minister had died under the same dubious circumstances, he would have been buried in secrecy and shame. But Jaime's followers treated him like a martyr. Cass supposed it all had to do with poverty, but she found it very offensive. She also didn't like the way they snubbed Delia, and the way, when Jaime's mother was holding the baby, everyone gathered around to touch it as if it were a good-luck charm.

After the funeral they all went off to something without inviting Delia. Cass and Lavinia took Delia and the baby back to the castle.

"Maybe you want to move out to Stanford," Cass suggested. She was standing on the drawbridge with Delia. "I'll get a place big enough for you and the baby. You could find a job in town, or at the university."

"Why?"

"You can't stay here. You're never going to meet someone here. No one lives in Wallingford anymore."

Delia turned her blunt child-eyes to her, showed her smooth forehead with the skin you can see the blue veins through at the temples, which used to scare Cass a little when they were kids and make her queasy sometimes. "He'll come when it's right. I don't have to go looking for him, I just have to make myself able to recognize him when he appears."

Delia subscribes to the "Some day my prince will come" theory, an ancient myth that hasn't lost its popularity in spite of the women's movement. It's the line Delia feeds all her female clients, even the sixty-year-olds who have been married forty years. He's out there, the perfect man for you; he is looking for you, searching everywhere; sit in the window when you go to restaurants so when he walks by he will see you. Light candles and set them in your bedroom window. Cass actually heard Delia advising a client to do this. Cass and Lazaro were in the dining room playing Scrabble and she heard Delia telling some poor female to set white candles of all different sizes in her bedroom window.

The figures glow on the computer screen like candle flames. She went off a bit there, lost her train of thought. Cass is working on a system for collecting thermal heat from the earth. Her specialty is heat transfer, minimizing entropy.

She stands, stretches, bends to touch the earth-brown industrial carpeting. She has a cubicle to herself, of translucent sea-green glass with planks of redwood along the top. On the planks are balanced pots of live plants, ferns and ivies, which flourish under special lights and are tended at night by a crew of gardeners.

Through the wavy glass partitions, she can occasionally see an arm or a head moving. She can hear the soft beeping of computers and the warbling of telephones, but she rarely actually sees anyone, even when she goes to the ladies' room or out to lunch. GeoTech encourages employees to communicate by computer or phone; it cuts down on small-talk, personal talk. It's a shock sometimes to run across colleagues in the hall; Cass tends to forget that they have faces.

She takes the program back a few steps to see where she is. Upsetting, when the mind wanders like that. Must be how Delia and Lavinia think all the time, letting the consciousness drift off in whatever direction it pleases—chaotic, undisciplined.

She must remember to pick up the laundry on the way home. She sends her sheets to the Chinese on the corner because they iron them flat and fold them square, tie them up in clean brown paper like new. She'll want to change the bedding when she gets home tonight. She always does after someone stays over. It's the smell she doesn't like, the smell of a stranger in her bed.

"I think Bubbles was disappointed that Edgar didn't show up," Lavinia tells Will in the car on the way home. "She's a little down because it's the Christmas season and things are just as slow as ever. Everything in her shop is so expensive! Seven hundred dollars for that wrought iron gate! She needs to get those people who live up in the hills in their fancy houses, the people who go to the malls, but they're not going to come into town for just one shop. If Edgar could get those other places in there, as he's always promising, then it would be different."

"According to the sign outside the mills, they are planning great things." Will turns to go under the highway.

"Seeing is believing. Bubbles invested almost all the money her husband left her to make this fancy store, and all she gets for customers are people who come to the falls and are looking for a bumper sticker or some cheap souvenir. Bubbles tries to sell them the soaps and teas instead. Bubbles could use a little encouragement from Edgar right now. He usually takes her out to lunch when she gets down like this. They have wine, and she comes back with rosy cheeks, full of Edgar's plans, but Edgar hasn't been around at all. And it's so quiet over at the mills. It used to be noisy —trucks rumbling in and out. It's hard to believe in progress when there's so little visible evidence."

Lavinia leans back and closes her eyes, thinks about the leftover cookies in her bag and how pleasant it is to have Will Appleyard drive her home in his car. He's a very nice man, not charming like Edgar Snow or Nestor, or even Jaime, not exciting, a little dull, but decent, exactly what she would have wished for Delia, someone who would settle into being a husband, a father to poor Lazaro, who needs one so badly right now.

"Do you like Delia?" Lavinia asks shyly.

"She seems very nice."

Lavinia is disappointed in Will's response. No passion there.

But then passion is dangerous. Delia's had enough passion and danger. He's balding too. Well, Delia's over thirty now, even though Lavinia still thinks of her as a girl.

Will turns into the driveway. "So you think Grand Land is a little shady," he says, "not quite honest—"

"I didn't say that!"

"You implied—"

"Gracious, no! My husband is on the board of directors."

"Your husband?"

"Nestor. I've mentioned him, surely."

"Oh yes. Excuse me. I'm a little confused. He doesn't live here, does he?"

"He—" Lavinia opens the door. "He's made other arrangements," she slides out. "For the time being."

Lavinia wonders how it will happen. How does it transpire that two people meet as strangers and somehow work themselves around to the point where they are sewing up their future together?

Hospital corners on the top sheet, the sheet folded down, two pillows in fresh cases, although she only uses one, and the quilt, a blue-and-white Japanese print. She gets down on her knees to tuck it into the frame, all around, even though she'll be getting into the bed in a few hours and there's no one here but herself to admire the effect of the neat blue-and-white quilt.

Cass leans her elbows on the windowsill, looking out on gardens, the backs of stucco houses. Who would see her white candles of varying sizes? Two fairies across the way. She pulls the blinds and switches on the news.

4

The trappings of power. Some people go after them consciously —travel to England to find the right antique partners'-desk, drive to New York for the right haircut. And then, some never have to think about those things. They are born to power. They inherit English partners'-desks from their grandfathers. They are genetically suited to rule, blessed by nature with above-average height and girth; the oversized head, hawk nose, and pendulous lower lip that makes him seem slightly dissatisfied with you and your work; the full head of hair—still, at his age!—iron gray, curling like snakes, increasing the size of his head. Well-tended snakes, of course. Everything about Nestor Bird is well tended.

Fat people are either slovenly or meticulously groomed, as if their fat comes from either a lack or an excess of caring. Nestor's fat is the latter kind, caused by an overabundance of good food, ingested over the years. His nails, large and square, are manicured regularly. She has seen on his appointment book that he also goes for massages and consults medical specialists, although he is the healthiest member of the firm, never ill, never has even a cold.

It is not easy to confront this power when you are the youngest associate in the firm, fresh out of law school, the one who is given the most rudimentary contracts to draw, the least inspiring research assignments, especially when you are also a woman, not pretty, the kind people prefer not to look at too closely, the kind who tends to draw drudge-work to herself, just as Nestor is the kind who draws power to himself.

Last time, he patronized her, sent her blushing and confused from his office, sent her back to her research. No one else in the firm will give her any credence. Instead they give her history, how Nestor is known for his honesty, how he has been involved in Grand Land since the beginning, how he is too shrewd to be taken in. They are dealing with concepts, not evidence, with what ought to be, not with what is.

Regina, however, is used to questioning what is. It's a matter of survival. If she didn't, she would accept the natural order of things, accept her own place as a gleaner of crumbs from the banquet of life.

This time she has come armed with evidence, investment contracts drawn by their own firm between Grand Land and the firm's old, established clients. The contracts are lacking certain safeguards, certain guarantees that the firm generally insists upon.

Nestor leans back in his chair, seeming as he does so to take on bulk, swell to greater importance. He is lecturing her on investments, rates of return. When the rate of return warrants—certain guarantees can be waived. The firm has a reputation for being conservative, perhaps even overly protective of its clients. To take a few—not risks, no risks isn't the right word—but when a businessman with Edgar Snow's reputation comes to Wallingford with a plan to revitalize a moribund industrial city, some safeguards must be waived because the potential benefits are so great.

What reputation? What projects has Edgar Snow completed? Regina wants to know.

He chuckles, indulgent of his perhaps overeager, but certainly enthusiastic, colleague (not pretty, but blessed with an intensity that would almost make her attractive if she were a man), his youngest and his first female associate. He hands her, with a royal gesture, his personal file on Edgar Snow. He had him checked out at his own expense. She must understand that he would never gamble his clients' money on an unwise investment.

She must know—and here he leans forward confidentially, clasping his hands on the rich, polished cherry desk that was his father's and his grandfather's before him—that he, Nestor, would be a wealthy man today if it weren't for his own strict probity. He has lived to see his clients—old school friends of his, many of them—become wealthy from the deals he, Nestor, has negotiated, and do you know these same rich clients are the ones who holler the loudest when he raises his fees to cover inflation! To cover his rising overhead!

Nestor stops himself. He doesn't want to sound self-pitying. But he does want her to understand that he was perfectly within his rights accepting a larger percentage in Grand Land than the other investors, because he introduced Edgar Snow to Wallingford, to the politicians, the bankers, the expeditors, and the money men. He used his pull in Washington to get the urban development grant, his influence in Trenton to get a low-interest state loan. He opened up the town for Edgar Snow.

"And this is why," Regina says, "I know you will want to be extra careful, be extra watchful, because of all you have at stake."

Exactly, Nestor agrees with her. He pats her on the shoulder, tells her she's doing an excellent job. She's everything a young associate should be—a little brash, a little rough, but those edges smooth out after a while. In the meantime, that's what youth is good for, stirring up trouble. She has his blessing. He even raises his hand slightly in benediction as she leaves his office.

Her calves and ankles are surprisingly good. A waste, elegant legs, when all else is clumsily put together. Donna should have them. It's the only thing about her that's not perfect. She frets about them, hides them in slacks.

Snow canceled lunch. It's just as well, gives him time to go over to the Fat Man's Cafe and collect some gossip. Baldino might be there, or even DeFelize. Nestor prides himself on keeping up with the local politicos, even though he has never run for office himself. The life of a politician is not for him. He saw enough of it when his father was mayor. Besides, he has the wrong last name. Used to be you couldn't be elected janitor with a name like DeFelize or Rodriguez. Now it's the only kind to have. Nestor doesn't hold it against them. The town used to belong to the English, then the Irish, then the Swiss and Italians, the Germans. Now the spics. That's all right. They've all been generally corrupt, except Socrates Bird, the only honest mayor Wallingford ever had.

We're not pretty and we're not rich, but we're the most honest goddamned family you'll ever meet in the history of Wallingford. Nestor chuckles. He should have said it that way to Regina. It could be the family motto.

Nestor Bird, whether living or deceased, married to Lavinia or divorced, no longer resides at the castle. It is true that his large navy velour robe hangs on the back of Lavinia's bathroom door (Will uses the bathroom when he's working in the tower. Lavinia doesn't mind. She's given him the run of the house. Since that first night, she's treated him more like a member of the family than a boarder) and there are those gigantic boots in the greenhouse which Lavinia wears over her house-slippers; photographs of Nestor stand in silver frames on an end table in the great hall;

Lavinia speaks of him in the present tense. Yet he doesn't come; he doesn't call. There is no fresh spoor. Everything is old, including the photographs. As far as Will can tell, he hasn't been in the castle for at least ten years. Either he died or he left in a hurry. If he's still living, why hasn't he sent someone over for his bathrobe, his boots, his boxes of family papers? Will has to conclude that Nestor is deceased and Lavinia, sane in all other respects, has been unable to face it.

The tower room where Will has been doing his research used to belong to the other daughter, Cass—in her photos, a dark, brooding teenager—who Lavinia says "does something with computers" in San Francisco. Cass is her full name. Nestor wanted Cassandra. The Bird family gave Greek names to their males (Zeus, Socrates, Nestor) but Lavinia wouldn't have it. She wanted Catherine. They compromised on the nickname.

Lavinia moved the original furniture out to make room for boxes of papers, leaving only a small, white, student's desk by the window, as if she knew someday someone would come to sift through everything.

It's marvelous stuff, not just marriage and birth and death certificates, but memoranda, letters—priceless source material.

Three main characters are emerging from the boxes: the two male Bird progenitors, Zeus and his son Socrates (Nestor's father), and Lavinia's own grandfather, Benjamin Tuttle. All of them are lawyers, all of their lives are bound up in the history of Wallingford. The Birds are more the establishment, Zeus being county prosecutor and eventually state district attorney and Socrates mayor for several terms, probably the only honest mayor Wallingford ever had. Tuttle is more the renegade, often attorney for the defense, arguing against Zeus Bird. The Birds are big, tall men who stand like trees, meaning they don't move around but plant themselves, letting others come to them or get out of their way. Tuttle is small, walks with a limp—no one knows why—has a pockmarked face and a large nose that gets bigger, more bulbous, in later pictures. The body stays slim. Alcoholic? Possibly.

Each case Tuttle worked on was stored in an envelope. There must be hundreds of them, closed with twine wound around two cardboard buttons. Everything went in them: receipts for messengers and stenographers, all correspondence, even records of chance encounters where the case was discussed. These records are written in black ink on square buff-colored paper, carefully dated.

Rogers—May 13th, corner Hamilton and East Street— Says Halsey's only fit for hanging. Reminded him of property rights, the repeated infractions, every year spring crop trampled, farmer's livelihood—mentioned how Halsey is good stock, trespassers bunch of drunken Dutch. May Day not Christian holiday, not American—this last struck him more than anything.

Rogers was the editor in chief of the *Wallingford Gazette*. Tuttle seemed to be testing out his defense and also lobbying for his client at the same time. It was not an easy case. A smelly old farmer, Halsey, had shot and killed a popular young Wallingford man for trespassing on his spring wheat. There was a crowd of revelers on the hill, most of them of German extraction, who had gathered to watch the sunrise on the first of May. Halsey, who had to put up with these trespassers every year, went haywire and shot into the crowd. Feelings ran so high against Halsey that he had to be kept in a jail out of town until the trial. Tuttle got him acquitted.

"I came up to see how the resident historian was getting on." Lavinia is wearing an old St. Agnes sweatshirt and a pair of flowered bell-bottom trousers. She doesn't share Will's enthusiasm for her grandfather. She never knew him. Her mother eloped to Spain to escape from his dismal house and only returned after the old man died.

"Maybe he's one of those people who are better in history than in person," Lavinia concedes when Will shows her the envelopes. Emma Phelps was a big case, with two envelopes. Tuttle was older then, successful, respected. Why would he have taken this one on? There was no money in it. Lavinia, perched on boxes, looking like a sixties hippie gone gray, agrees that her grandfather preferred the difficult, the unpopular cases. He gave himself over to them. Sometimes in the middle of preparing for a case he would take to his bed, draw the curtains, and dictate instructions to his assistant. Lavinia knows this because her poor mother was often the one who had to write down the messages for him. This strengthens Will's suspicions of alcoholism, but he doesn't mention anything to Lavinia.

Much of the Emma Phelps case was conducted from the heavily draped bedroom of Benjamin Tuttle. Lavinia recognizes her mother's handwriting in the notes, these on rectangular white paper, that went to the assistant.

"Oh dear, William, they're so fresh-looking—written in Mama's hand, and she was younger than the girls. So long ago." Lavinia pulls a crumpled tissue out of her pocket and blows her nose.

Tuttle lobbied so feverishly beforehand that he burned himself out before the case actually came to trial. Every prominent name in the town appears on at least two buff-colored sheets. Tuttle was trying to make the leading citizens see Emma as one of them, an entrepreneur wronged by her partner. She had no legal recourse and so was driven to kill him.

This was Tuttle's strategy in general, to manipulate the town leaders into regarding the defendant as someone like them who ran into a bit of hard luck. Unfortunately, Emma's victim actually had been one of them, a local manufacturer who had discovered Emma when she was working in his mill, made her his mistress, then set her up as madam of a whorehouse. Later he was attracted to another, younger, lady in Emma's establishment and was preparing to give the business over to her when Emma served her fickle partner arsenic in his rice pudding.

It didn't help the case when it came out in the trial that Emma had left the body slumped over a table in the parlor two days while business went on as usual.

Before the trial even began, Emma decided she would be hanged. She sent out for yards of white fabric and red-ribbon trimmings, planning to sew her own dress for the hanging. She must have been bitterly disappointed when Tuttle got her off with a life sentence. She had a photo taken of herself in her hanging dress.

Will hands the photograph to Lavinia. "Oh my goodness. Look at her eyes. They're hard as stones, Will."

They often look hard in those pictures, partly because of the process, the standing motionless for the image to register, and partly because of the attitude toward photography: it was a record, serious. The camera was not a toy to smile into. All the same, look at those eyes! The figure, planted solidly, framed by prison bars, is plump, matronly. The dress, draped, ruffled, bowed, is a joke. Why did Tuttle give so much to this creature? Why did he agonize over her case?

"Oh, I don't know, William. Mama didn't talk about him much, but I gathered he was difficult, suspicious, you know—uh, of the wealthy people in town. He was always defending down-and-outs. It's funny because he turned out to be wealthy in spite of himself. He had all this property in the middle of town that he originally kept to pasture his horse, and later just kept to annoy people—a big old field in the middle of town. And Mama always understood she'd been disinherited, but he never bothered to make out a will. So when he died, Socrates Bird sold the field and invested the money for Mama. I still get a small income from it. My grandfather must have turned over in his grave—to think that at his death he was one of them! He always wanted to be on the side of those others."

Lavinia looks at the photograph of Emma Phelps one last time.

"Dear, I don't know how Delia can live in that house with the ghost of this one walking around. Not that I believe in ghosts, William, but she must, if she's a psychic. Delia must see the ghost, although I've never asked."

"You don't mean Delia lives in the same house, Emma's house?"

"Oh yes. Of course. Didn't you know? But I thought that's why you were poking around there the other day. Oh my, William. That's not very good. The address is written all over these papers. Perhaps you should have your prescription checked, or even clean your glasses more often, if you don't mind the suggestion. There's a cloudiness to them."

"Ground. I'm not grounded."

"That's the bullshit you got from the New Jersey fortuneteller."

"You're very good with your left hand."

It's controlled by the right brain, the seat of lust. The right brain knows her secrets. It could never articulate them, would be unable to draw a map, but it understands the ebb and flow of her blood.

"That's the car." She jerks up, eyes glazed.

"You can't go now. You don't have any clothes on."

"You tricked me."

"I am but the instrument of Destiny."

He reaches across her body and punches up the doorman on the intercom. "Tell the driver we won't be needing him. There's been a change in plans. . . . He can bill me, tell him."

Whenever Ted is on the phone with his true love—Laura, her name is Laura—Cass stops work and listens. It's nothing personal, nothing to do with Ted (nice-looking, intelligent, but not her type). Cass eavesdrops as if she is auditing a course: Love 101.

From the next cubicle, Cass hears words that never come up

during her own blunt, bluff, one-night stands. These are subtle words, delicate and teasing, spoken in a voice softer, higher, more musical than that Ted uses when he calls Cass to discuss a problem, to verify a fact.

One time Cass followed Ted when she knew he was going to meet his Laura—at a distance, not meaning any harm. She wanted to see what this Laura, this paragon who could inspire such devotion, looked like. She had to be tall, blond, slender, clever, flawless.

Ted had arranged to meet her outside the Ghirardelli chocolate factory. They were going to walk around, pick up dinner somewhere. While Ted waited at the assigned place, Cass spied from the terrace above, searching for Laura in the crowd, for the flash of her hair as she came swiftly to her lover, and almost missed it completely, because when she looked again, Ted was leaving with a drab little female tucked protectively under his arm.

The question Cass ponders as she audits Love 101 is, Why her and not me?

"Nestor Bird?"

"Yes."

"He's alive?"

"Of course."

"Excuse me. I just arrived in town," Will explains to the tall, ugly young lawyer with the amazingly large nose and intelligent bearing. He had phoned Grand Land and gotten no response, so he has come over to the mills, hoping to talk his way in.

He was standing in front, wondering why everything looked deserted—shouldn't there be trucks, dust, noise?—asking himself if it were a holiday he had overlooked, when the lawyer pulled up and parked smartly at the curb. She's come on official business, representing Nestor Bird, whose magic name she will invoke to gain admittance. Will is welcome to tag along, although she doesn't know how much use it will be to him because much work has already been done inside.

The mills look almost untouched to Will, but he doesn't know too much about renovation. Maybe it can take place quietly behind undisturbed facades.

They beat their way through the burdocks to the side of the main building where there is a door not boarded up, guarded by a young man in a down jacket and designer jeans who is unimpressed by the letter the lawyer shows him with Nestor Bird's signature on it.

"Mr. Snow told me nobody gets in without his authorization."

"This is Nestor Bird's, an officer of the Grand Land Development Corporation."

"I don't care who he is. No one gets through these doors without an authorization signed by Edgar Snow. Now I'm not authorized to let you through except if you give me your letter of authorization, authorized by Mr. Snow himself, understand?"

"This is absurd." The lawyer's sallow cheeks brighten. She is almost attractive like this, angry. Will has a weakness for angry women.

The guard is unmoved, obdurate, cemented to the idea that the lawyer must have an authorization from Edgar Snow. She threatens to bring his name up before the board. She takes it down in her notebook. He makes sure she has the spelling right.

Will offers to buy her coffee. A drink? But the lawyer has to go back to the office and report to Nestor. Will asks her to write his name down under the guard's. In case she gets into the mill, would she mind very much calling him and taking him along?

Nestor lives. He has come back from time past into the present. He has a law firm; partners; a tall, intense woman lawyer on staff; some dealings with Edgar Snow. Lavinia isn't mad after all, only reticent about her separation from her husband. Will can understand that. His own mother never told him his father died. He overheard it weeks after the funeral. She never told him, never discussed it with him, hoping, no doubt, that Will would simply forget that there was once a father who went away on a trip and never returned.

For a while, Will took to sitting in his father's closet among the business suits and wing-tipped shoes. Then one day, he went to the closet and it was empty.

"What's this?" Nestor plants a heavy, immaculate index finger on the page from Regina's notebook.

"It's the name of the guard, the one who wouldn't let me in." She is still in her trench coat, her purse still hanging from her shoulder.

"No, this one, the other name."

"Oh! That's someone I met at the mill. He's trying to get in to see it too, for research, some history he's writing."

"What did he look like?"

"I don't know, thirtyish, baldish. Very polite."

"Nice manners."

"That's right."

Nestor punches his intercom. "Get me Edgar Snow on the phone."

What in hell was an Appleyard doing giving out Nestor's phone number, his former phone, the one at the castle? Was Lavinia living with an Appleyard? In Nestor's very home? The woman was diabolical. There was no end to her ingenious punishments. Who would have figured she would keep the house? That was her chunk, her piece. His office was ready to help her sell it and invest the money. It would have kept her for life. But no, she sits in it, letting it rot around her, living on some meager inheritance. Does the woman even eat? She haunts him. He lives in fear of seeing her on the street someday. Now she's taken in an Appleyard, with what plot in mind he can't tell.

All he wants to do is make his money on this development thing and get the hell out of Wallingford.

The intercom buzzes. "Yes?"

"Edgar Snow is out of town."

"I know that. Where out of town? Tell them I have to get to him."

"He's on a sailboat somewhere in the Caribbean, Mr. Bird."

"He has to come ashore sometime, goddamnit. Tell them I want a message left for him at his next port."

"Sailing in the Caribbean?"

Something in Regina's face is extremely irritating. Nestor has to repress an urge to throw his silver inkwell at her. Many people take vacations this time of year. The Christmas season. Nothing gets done now. Is she going away for the holiday? San Mateo, California, to see her family. San Mateo sounds like a wonderful place to have come from. He gets up from his desk and escorts her out of the room, although he'd like to throw her out. It's a long trip. Why doesn't she take two extra days between Christmas and New Year? Make a real vacation out of it.

5

Delia would have liked to go. It's spooky in the house alone at night. But she had calls coming in—booked solid from seven to ten-thirty. It's preseason anxiety.

She was glad that Lazaro went with them. He's been so remote lately, wearing his street face in the house, that she thought he would be too macho to spend the time with Lavinia and her orchids. Having Will along helped. Lazaro likes him. Will's a nice man. Too bad his cards aren't better. Although Delia's cards probably wouldn't look too good either right now. She never tells her own. It's hopeless. She always misinterprets them. She could get one of the other readers in town, but she isn't up to the drama of a Spanish reading. She feels something is bubbling under, some menace. Her clothes were tangled up this morning, the jeans under the sweater, the sweater over the jeans, and the jeans over the sweater, overlapped three times. A bad sign.

The telephone rings early—maybe Lazaro forgot something.

"Is this Destiny Ortega?" A gravelly voice—a man, a smoker in his late forties.

"Yes it is. Who is this please? Do you have an appointment?"

"No, I don't have an appointment. I'm calling about the woman I live with, used to live with, who has left me to go make a film with some jerkwater kid who thinks he can direct because he knows about lights. I want you to call her up and tell her that you don't know the first thing about the business, that it was completely irresponsible of you to go meddling in her life and my life, or I will expose you for the fraud and the charlatan that you are."

"I didn't catch your name."

"Gareth Watts."

"And this is about your friend—"

"Faye Morisson."

"Oh yes. Now I remember. How's your ankle?"

"It was my wrist, which shows how much you know. The cast comes off in four weeks."

"That's too bad. I did tell her to have the bannister fixed. Don't you find that sometimes the littlest things can swell up and become —I don't know—matters of life and death?"

"I find I usually have a pretty good grasp of what's most important. And right now, getting Faye back is at the top of my list. I'm flying down there to be with her for Christmas, and if she won't come back with me, I'll drag her off the set."

"I don't think you should do that."

"What, did you turn up a bad card? Faye told me all her cards came out upside down."

"I'm not doing your cards because this isn't a paying call, and I have a client in five minutes so I have to get off. I'm just telling you that it's not a good idea for you to go."

"Thanks very much, but since I'm not paying for your advice, I don't intend to take it."

"Wait!"

"Yes?"

"If you do go, wear boots—high, thick, leather ones, like cowboys wear."

Delia sits looking at her phone. She should call him back and tell him this was real, tell him about the chill down her back. It is important that he protect his ankle. But she doesn't know his number. She can't even remember his name. He's famous, a director, she thinks. If he's that important, the number would be unlisted anyway.

That's the trouble with the gift. You can make yourself receptive to it, but you can't control it. It sends the best, the clearest message to the one who won't heed it. That other one was about this man too. Destiny must have an especially strong channel to him.

She sits cross-legged on her bed, shuffling her cards. She isn't surprised to see the Emperor come up first. He's a ruler, an influential man; yes, she knows that. What else? The rest of the cards aren't good: spilled cups, hanging swords, cloaked figures in attitudes of despair. But the cards are dull. She doesn't trust them. It was his voice that gave her a connection. She couldn't see him, except for his feet, which were crossed at the ankle where the skin was transparent and she could see the blood pulsing through.

She forgot to lock the door when Lazaro left. She jumps up, scattering cups and swords. Jaime is at the door, very clear tonight. He wants to warn her about something, but the phone is ringing. Delia reaches through his shade to turn the latch, then hurries back to her room. Her dresses, hanging in the doorway, stir gently behind her.

Many men, probably most with his kind of schedule—the number of things he has to do in a day!—neglect their own needs, don't take the time. Not Nestor. If he has the slightest symptom, he has it taken care of. He's not one to put off appointments with the dentist; he has a complete physical examination once a year. And from time to time, if he has a problem, a nagging mental tic that won't go away, he doesn't hesitate to see a psychiatrist—not here in town but in New York; people around here are primitive, will use any excuse to talk.

He went for a consultation late this afternoon, had to cancel some meetings to do it, but his health comes first. The doctor, a big man himself, always has a decent chair for Nestor, not a couch, not something insultingly low. It's at the same height as the doctor's. They sit eye to eye, like two men. Nestor's been seeing him, from time to time, across the space of fifteen years—more, since before he left Lavinia. So the man has a file on him, no need to go over old material. The doctor is familiar with this recurring worm that comes to Nestor's consciousness every few years. He has it all down in his files, how it goes away and then comes back. This time it was brought on by the appearance of Appleyard, Appleyard in town, in his own house. Appleyard writing a history of Wallingford, trying to get into the mills, property of Grand Land.

The doctor has a big nose like Regina. Like Regina, he wanted to smell out the Grand Land thing. Why couldn't Appleyard and Regina get into the mills? He kept asking questions about Grand Land, when Nestor had come to him about this other problem, this recurring memory of a visit to the state correction facility for women.

He was young then, with intentions of being humane, open-minded, unprejudiced by history, but when he saw her eyes, small and hard as black bullets, her slack doughy face, puffy hands, ragged black nails, when the smell of her hit him in the face, he couldn't speak, had to signal to the matron to take her away.

The doctor, who has been over this story many times, tried to get him to see it as a symbol of something else, something new that was bothering him. But it isn't anything new. It's the same goddamned thing. It goes away for a while and then it comes back. There is no dulling of it, even over the years.

Nestor forces himself to drive the long way around to the office, past the mills. Dark, silent. More like a cemetery than a construction site. The crew's gone at this hour, but there should be a light for the watchman. There's a lot of material; Nestor's seen the invoices. He slows the car. Should he? Try to get into the dark mill at night? Would he end up arguing with the guard? Or tripping over something, getting bitten by a rat?

The idea of Nestor Bird, partner in Grand Land, sneaking into a mill at night—absurd. It's Regina's influence. She's too suspicious. Ugly women often are. He'll get a tour from Snow, when Snow comes back after Christmas.

"Your grandson is a big help."

"He is?" Lavinia turns to look at William over her shoulder. She's been sponging off the leaves of the Venerable One. Four buds. It will be magnificent Christmas morning for Cass, although she doesn't like the orchids, any of them, even the Venerable One.

Lavinia feels happiness swelling inside her like the Venerable's buds: Cass coming home, William here, and Lazaro. William says he's very bright, that he has the instincts of a real scholar. Lavinia soaks up William's words, repeating them to the Venerable One. She will write Nestor a letter tonight, tell him what William has said, ask him to take the boy under his wing—his only grandchild—and send him to private school. He wouldn't let Cass and Delia go to the public school, said they would mix with hooligans, that teachers were too busy disciplining to teach. Well, it's much worse now. Nestor won't abandon Delia's child. She must remind him of his responsibilities. William's words are her sign. The time is right.

· · ·

Lazaro likes Will, although he doesn't respect him because he can talk to him in the same language he uses with Delia and Lavinia, indoor talk, as opposed to street talk, man talk. Of course, street talk is Spanish and Will is an Anglo, but even for an Anglo, Will doesn't really make it as a man. His body is soft and clumsy, like he never moved into it completely. The way he walks, in careful little steps, the way he holds his arms close to his sides, even the clothes he wears, kind of mushroom-color—he's like a guy who is trying not to attract attention to himself. That's it. He walks like a wimp who's trying to get by a crowd of tough guys without getting hurt.

But it's beginning to hurt anyway. Otherwise, why would he be here? Why would he put himself up in this room, sitting at a desk that's too small for him, a girl's desk, going through every old paper, putting down what he finds on green, yellow, pink, blue, and white index cards? He says he's writing a history book, but everyone knows that he's looking for the curse.

Delia saw it in his Tarot cards. Abuela, although she's blind and has never met Will, knows about it. Everyone knows, except Will, who doesn't believe in it, who doesn't know what he's looking for in these old papers.

Even though he's cursed, Abuela says, Will brings good fortune to other people. Hugo, who's lucky himself, is dangerous for others. Abuela has never met Hugo and doesn't want to, but she has asked Lazaro to bring Will to see her.

"Bring me anything you don't know how to categorize, Lazaro."

"Here's someone with your name who married a Bird."

Lazaro thrusts a document onto the desk. It's a marriage certificate between Anna Bird and William Appleyard, Jr.

"Does that make us cousins or something?"

"No, that can't be. My grandfather's wife was Carlotta. Carlotta Jaeger. Unless this was someone before Carlotta—"

"Must have been. There's not going to be two William Appleyard Juniors in town."

"I suppose not. It's peculiar, though."

"No one ever mentioned her, no one ever said there was a first wife?"

"There were a lot of things we never talked about in my family. Look, aren't you tired? Don't you want to knock off for a while?"

Lazaro's eyes narrow, and he's suddenly very Hispanic and street-savvy. "How can you quit now? We just made a discovery. The trail will get cold if we stop now. Maybe we won't find it again."

"The trail to what?"

"To the curse."

"The curse? Oh, that stuff with the cards. Your mother told you—"

"Everyone knows it."

"Everyone" being the Hispanic community of Wallingford. They probably have a Spanish name for him that translates as "The Man with the Curse on His Family." Will has never been in a place where so many people believe in curses, second sight, portents, and omens. There are more places downtown to get your fortune read than your shoes repaired. Is it a recent phenomenon that came in with the Caribbean immigrants? It would be interesting to trace the history of superstition in Wallingford, to see if it's been prevalent in the past, to chart its peaks and valleys—maybe he'll do a separate chapter, if there's enough material.

"Here it is."

"What?"

"Here's what happened to her. The Bird who married your grandfather."

It's a death certificate for Anna Bird, dated two years after she married. The cause is pneumonia.

"A lot of people died young then, before antibiotics, vaccinations—"

"Yeah, maybe."

Will hides a smile. Lazaro suspects foul play. He's set his heart on solving some kind of mystery with these old documents. It's only later, when he and Lazaro are down in the kitchen having lunch with Lavinia, that Will realizes that Anna Bird died only a scant four months before Carlotta gave birth to William Appleyard III. He doesn't tell Lazaro.

6

$\mathcal{M}$ince pie. And apple, from green apples if she can find them. Roast beef. Yorkshire pudding. Horseradish sauce. She should have made a list. Lavinia fingers the two crisp one-hundred-dollar bills William gave her for grocery money. She put them in her pocket because she doesn't trust the clasp on her old handbag. He shouldn't have given her all that money, of course. It's her family celebration. His share is only a fifth. But he wanted to. He insisted.

"My Lord, but it's warm." Lavinia rolls down the window on the Saab. "Like a summer breeze. Going up to eighty today, that's what I heard on the news. Eighty degrees the day before Christmas! I'm afraid you overdressed."

Will is in a beige turtleneck and tweed jacket. Beige is an unfortunate color for him; he's too beige as it is, and the turtleneck accentuates his double chin.

It's windy out. Little dust devils are dancing on the sidewalk. Eddies of litter swirl up against the buildings.

"Shall I drop you off at the supermarket?"

"Oh no. I'll walk there. Take me to see Bubbles first."

Bubbles is feeling down. The Christmas season has been disappointing, and Edgar Snow has not been to see her in weeks. Bubbles hopes nothing has happened to him. Lavinia is certain he's just off on vacation, or maybe he has a new project somewhere. It's not that Bubbles has doubts, it's just that she misses his occasional presence in the shop, the reassurance that a male can bring, an illusory assurance in the main part, Lavinia thinks, although she has to admit that she used to draw comfort from being in the presence of Edgar Snow, the only male she ever saw socially aside from the odd orchid-fanatic who would come down from the city to see the conservatory. William has filled such a void! One she didn't even know she felt, the worst kind. She pats the hand resting on the gearshift. She almost kisses him in gratitude when he leaves her off at Bubbles', but she doesn't. He looked bewildered enough at the hand-pat.

"It's your next left," Lazaro instructs from the backseat. In the rearview mirror, Will can see the light striking off his sharp cheekbones. Lazaro is taking it all very seriously, this séance, or whatever it is, with his "abuela," his grandmother, Señora Ortega. Even without knowing that Anna Bird's death was followed closely by the birth of the third William Appleyard, Lazaro has latched on to poor Anna Bird as the originator of the curse.

He found a photograph of her in the boxes, a pretty, young woman, albeit with receding chin and a natural pout to her soft mouth. "She's proud," Lazaro judged. "You don't ever want to mess with that kind of woman." He has brought the photograph with him.

His abuela, it seems, is not just a fortuneteller who can see into the future and the past. She has powers to alter certain forces. Lazaro thinks she might have some influence on the curse. That is the word he used, "influence." He didn't, to his credit, or his grandmother's, promise to remove it.

Will is treating the whole thing as research for his chapter on superstition. His theory is that immigrants from agrarian cultures bring the remnants of pagan rites with them. Certain rituals that were used to manipulate the powerful and incomprehensible forces of nature are adapted in an attempt to gain more control over the powerful and incomprehensible forces of industrial society. If his theory holds, there should be an increase in ritualistic, mystical activity with each new wave of immigration. The German May Day celebration, for instance, might have had another significance for the revelers in addition to being an excuse to stay up all night and get drunk.

"Park here. It's up the street a block, but we have to get some things first." Lazaro leads Will into a small store that sells radios and detergent, depilatories, Pampers, dog food, kites.

The grizzled old fellow at the counter sizes Will up while Lazaro reels off some Spanish Will can't understand. Lazaro and Will follow as he totters stiffly through the store and out the back into a scruffy little yard, fenced in with chain-link, smelling of chickens. There are cages of them, and rabbits as well under a slanting tin roof.

Lazaro and the old man consult briefly and unintelligibly again. The old guy reaches an arm into a large cage and pulls out a young rooster. He holds the flapping wings down while Lazaro holds up another, smaller cage. He shoves the bird in and hands the cage to Will.

"You have to bring back the cage, afterwards," Lazaro says.

"This is taking it a little far, isn't it?" The bird is jumping around, beating its wings frantically against the wire. Will holds it away from his body.

"Look man, this is a powerful curse. This is a killer curse. You gotta give it strong medicine."

"But I don't believe in this stuff."

"If you didn't believe in it, man, you wouldn't be here."

A box of panatelas and a mason jar of dark rum have mate-
rialized on the counter. Will pays. One-stop shopping—everything
you need for your chicken sacrifice.

In the shop and now here on the street, Lazaro looks darker,
could be taken for a black. The boy fits in with this crowd, even
as he cuts through it with his sharp, swift stride, nodding sometimes to people he knows. No one asks what he's doing with the
balding gringo who holds a caged rooster awkwardly at his side.

The smells of garlic and cooking oil lie in the stairwell; the
rooster broods in the dark; three floors up Lazaro opens an unlocked door. "Carmen!"

Carmen appears, small and slight, definitely black. "This is my
aunt," Lazaro says. Presumably Carmen knows who Will is. She
extends a hand. Will transfers the cage to his left, thinking she
wants to shake hands, but she means to carry the cage, which
she takes to the kitchen, ignoring desperate squawks.

Out the kitchen window, a line of fenced yards with fruit trees
and dormant vegetable gardens. Agrarian. Behind the city facades,
people keep gardens and trees, chickens, rabbits, the roots of a
primitive culture.

The rooster falls silent. Lazaro touches Will's arm. He turns to
see a woman standing in the doorway. She isn't much taller than
Lazaro, but she makes up for it in her weight and bearing.

Will hears his name, but that's about all he can pick out from
what Lazaro's telling his grandmother. She appears not to be
listening; her eyes are off on a journey of their own. They travel
the kitchen, briefly scan Will's face, and come to rest on his crotch.
He moves slightly to his left, the eyes follow. Then he remembers
the woman is blind.

They lead Will down the hall: Carmen first, carrying the
chicken by its feet; then the abuela, tapping in her high-heeled
shoes; then Lazaro, with a panatela and the jar of rum. They go
into the bathroom, a long narrow room with one frosted-glass

window, a cracked tile floor, no towels, no shower curtain for the tub, only a burning votive candle and a plastic dish of water on the floor. They crowd in. Will presses against the edge of the bathtub. Lazaro closes the door. The chicken flutters feebly. Will imagines it is stupefied by blood rushing to its head, then wishes he hadn't thought about blood.

With the votive candle, Lazaro lights the cigar and hands it to his grandmother. She draws on it strongly, sucking the smoke in, letting it curl out through her nostrils. The end of the panatela glows in the semidarkness. Smoke fills the room. Will can barely see Lazaro leaning against the door. He could be miles away. Through the smoke the boy hands his grandmother the rum.

She tips her head back, takes in a mouthful, and sprays it into the air. It falls back down through the cigar clouds, a fine misty rain that sticks to Will's glasses. The sweet smell of the rum layers in under the smoke.

Carmen, still holding the rooster, advances on Will and passes the bird down one side of his body, then up the other side. Will is conscious of another odor, Carmen's perspiration. Little beads of it string across her upper lip.

The abuela, between mouthfuls of rum and puffs on the panatela, is moaning a chant, not in Spanish. It sounds African. The bird passes dangerously close to Will's face and blinks a frightened red eye. Will wonders how he can save it, how he can save himself.

"Say the name."

"What?" Will's voice is thick at the back of his throat.

"Say it. The one who put the curse on you, her name."

"Oh." Will swallows to get his voice back, but it comes out in warbles, as if the chicken is speaking. "Anna Bird."

Lazaro pulls out the photograph and sets it carefully on the back of the sink. Anna Bird looks primly off to the side.

"Now tell everyone who's died in your father's family, back to your great-great-grandfather."

Will begins with his father—whom he didn't know very well, can't really picture, only his shoes and the dark shapes of his suits in the closet—and his grandmother, Carlotta, who had her own apartment on a different floor in their building on Park Avenue. Carlotta's cook used to make him molasses cookies. He had never known William II or William I, nor did he know much more about William I's wife than her name. Will's voice trails off with "Mary Stone." The chicken burbles a blood-choked plea.

The abuela holds out her arms, the bottle in one hand, the cigar in the other. Lazaro takes them from her, and Carmen gives the rooster to the abuela, who does it so quickly that Will sees only the blood, bright and red streaming over her hands. Carmen takes the chicken and the abuela holds her hands out to Will.

"What does she want me to do?"

"You have to touch the blood. With your right hand, that's all. It's just chicken blood, man. Now cross yourself. You know, make the sign of the cross?" Lazaro shows him.

Next Will has to pull some feathers out. They are hard to wrench free, come out with a popping sound and leave a purplish-blue spot of skin on the side of the bird. He has to wad these up with blood and leave them beside the candle. The abuela is singing again as the blood congeals on her hands. It smells stronger than the cigar and the rum. Chicken blood.

Carmen is waiting at the top of the stairs. "That's twenty dollars. You should know soon if it worked. If it didn't you'll have to come back. The second visit is only fifteen."

The pale December light could be midsummer high noon; it dazzles him, hurts his eyes after the gloom of the bathroom. Lazaro stayed behind. Without him, Will feels even more conspicuous than he did with the rooster. Everyone is frankly staring at him. Will looks to see if there is blood on him, or feathers, but his clothes are clean. He is making a great effort to walk casually and maintain a straight line.

It must be over seventy degrees. He doesn't dare take off his jacket, doesn't dare stop on the sidewalk. A tinny version of "Joy to the World" is blaring from a record shop onto the street. Merchants have brought out racks of clothes. Will works his way with care around them, through the crowds. The air is thick, sweet, tropical. He can't get the taste of blood out of the back of his throat.

Will reaches into his pocket, searching for a handkerchief to wipe his forehead, and finds the picture of Anna Bird. He must have picked it up off the sink and not realized it. A drop of chicken blood has left a long, narrow streak beside her face, a sword of blood. Is this the Queen of Swords who sends the Appleyards to their deaths—this weak-chinned, slightly petulant young woman?

Will was never told how they died, only that they fell from horses. Were they riding wild? Did they break away from their companions and go splashing through a bog, ducking under branches, jumping fallen logs—laughing?! That was the best and worst part of it, the long, huge laugh, coming from the stomach, lungs, spleen, groin—bursting forth. Later they said he had been screaming. But the feeling was of laughter.

Then again, Dagne and her friends had been left far behind, up in the meadow, after his horse had suddenly bolted—stung by a bee? Or did Will actually—? It had seemed spontaneous. An urge Will and the horse felt at once.

Dagne and her friends—had he seen or imagined their faces printed with identical expressions of disbelief as Will and his horse went tearing off for the bog, as if pursued by unseen dogs (hounds of Hell) into the perilous bog, where they did not stop, would not stop for fallen logs, overhanging branches, ropes of vines?

They must have heard the laugh and said it was a scream because it didn't sound like Will, wasn't his laugh. It was someone else laughing through him. Anna Bird?

Anna Bird, at an early age, was given in marriage to the richest young man in Wallingford. William Appleyard, Jr., was married off to the daughter of the most politically prominent family in Wallingford, a much more suitable match for him than a young worker at the mill, the daughter of Swiss-German immigrants, a girl to whom he had had a youthful attachment, one he could be expected to give up when it came to the serious prospect of marriage.

Mr. and Mrs. Appleyard are wed and sent off on the Grand Tour, a gift from William's parents, who hope that a long honeymoon will give young William time to forget his earlier attachment. But when Will returns, he sees Carlotta by chance at the mill—or maybe he never intended to break things off but planned to continue with Carlotta in spite of Anna, who hears rumors but can't do anything about them, who pines, who fades, who gradually slips away and dies of a broken heart.

But before she dies, Anna Bird, on her death bed, curses William Appleyard and all who will follow him, condemns them all to early death.

Zeus Bird, Socrates—men of daylight, men of power—do not stoop to dark, circuitous means of revenge. Black magic is a method of the weak. Zeus and Socrates have other methods at their disposal if they think Anna is being wronged. Legal means. Daylight means. Perhaps they think Anna shouldn't take it so to heart. Maybe they are embarrassed at the dramatics young Anna is pulling, retiring to her bed, drawing the drapes.

Anna, abandoned in her misery, seeing the males in her family unmoved by her pain, finds someone else, hires someone—a local witch, someone living outside of Wallingford society but known by rumor as someone who deals in foretelling the future and practicing certain dark powers, a dealer in demons, like Lazaro's abuela, but evil. Anna sends a message to this person, who comes, veiled at night, in a horse-drawn cab, to the mansion of the William Appleyards, is admitted to the sickroom, where she is given her commission.

Anna's pale hand reaches up out of the bedclothes and presses something into the gloved one, a ring with rubies and diamonds, the one William gave her at their engagement. The ring, the glove, are clear, but he cannot see the face of the caller because of the veil, which is never lifted. . . .

Delia is shopping for a particular brand of high-top sneaker that Lazaro wants, when she becomes aware of Will. She finds him half a block away, perspiration streaming down his temples. Many on the street have noticed him, because of the way he walks, clutching a photograph in his hand.

Delia approaches cautiously. He doesn't see her, not in his state. If he were sitting down she would touch his head, which is the best place to begin, but she can't reach it very well, so she takes his arm as gently as she can. Still, he jumps and even cries out.

"It's Delia," she says.

Nestor watches them going into the bakery on the corner, Delia and a man, the man pale, balding, with glasses set on a round, soft, pie-shaped face, Delia the same, always the same, his golden princess.

This man is not going to win any beauty contests, but he looks decent, middle-class, a professor type, the first reasonable-looking one he's seen Delia with. Better than the hood from the gas station across the street. Balding, but he looks solid, as if he could finally accomplish the deed, lift Delia out of the slum.

Although he would like to see what they're doing in there—holding hands while they drink coffee out of Styrofoam cups?—Nestor does not go by the bakery. He never lets Delia see him. Instead he walks all the way around the block, past Delia's house, with the sign in the window: *Destiny Ortega. Palms Read. Tarot.*

She can't be making money from that. He knows for certain that she's on the welfare rolls. Once in a while, someone new comes into the welfare office, thinks Delia could be earning a living, and finds her a job, but it never lasts.

He knew she was never going to grow up, that she would never earn a living. Was it too much to expect that she would at least marry someone who would support her? One thing she had, still has, is looks. The learning disabilities aren't readily apparent, except that she's vague. At school, the sisters said she could learn but she had to be spoon-fed in easily digestible mouthfuls of knowledge. Organizational skills, none. Analytical talents, zilch.

The goddamned house looks worse than ever. He stuck his neck out to get Snow a low-interest loan from Trenton to fix the place up and Snow hasn't even done the roof. If he doesn't show progress soon, he's going to lose the loan. When's the next inspection? He'll ask Regina for the papers when he gets back.

Snow is sailing the Caribbean. Nestor is giving Donna a trip to Nassau for Christmas, a trip by herself. She says she needs time alone, to find out who she is, some bullshit she picked up from the magazines she reads. Snow calls her "your beautiful young wife." "Give my regards to your beautiful young wife," he says in that singsongy voice of his that comes through his nose. When he sees Donna he draws her to him, puts her at his side, inviting Nestor to admire how they look together—lean, both of them, and tall.

Still walking, not missing a beat, Lazaro takes out a cigarette and lights it with the lighter he borrowed from Jerry, who stole it somewhere. He pockets the lighter and exhales without taking the cigarette out of his mouth. When he's walking on the street like this and no one is looking too close, he doesn't inhale. It's cheating, but he can't let his lungs get too bad. Look at Jerry; he smokes so much he can't go over a fence anymore.

The street is crowded with shoppers but Lazaro barely sees them. He sees spaces between them, which he cuts through, walking fast. He had to return the cage. Will forgot. That's the main trouble with the man, he can't keep his mind on his business. He should have a knob somewhere you could turn to sharpen him up, like a TV. He looks like he grew up in a cage like the chickens and rabbits behind Garcia's store.

The Fat Man is in front of the house again. You never see him walking. He just appears, like he was built there, like a wall, solid as a wall, his weight never on one foot or the other but planted equally on both. Big legs. Lazaro doesn't want anything from this man, not even his money, but he would like to inherit some of that size, to be tall. If he was that tall, he wouldn't have to fight. He's seen tall guys. They just walk over and stand there, like the Fat Man is standing now, and they know that nine times out of ten, the little guy is not going to take them on. To grow to the Fat Man's height, that is all Lazaro wants from him.

Lazaro feels the Fat Man watching him. He tries to meet his look, but the man's eyes slide away. It's always this way. They never speak or acknowledge each other, and he never tells Delia that the Fat Man's been here. He takes a last puff from his smoke and flicks it into the gutter, just past the Fat Man's neatly creased pin-striped pant leg. Is it his imagination or does the Fat Man wince?

Lazaro goes into his house. When he looks out the window, the Fat Man is gone.

"Your friend was just here."

"Who?"

"Your partner, the fat guy."

"What was he doing at your place?"

Hugo laughs. He just said it to make him nervous. Hugo is in his office, at his metal desk, with the door closed so just a little light comes in the window, a window with chicken wire in it so the glass can't break. His desk is not in line with the window. He came in here because the phone rang and he knew it would be Snow, but before, he was out in front, watching the fat guy watching Lazaro.

"Don't worry, I'm not telling anyone where you are. No, I never talk to him. He was in front here because his daughter lives across the street. You know, the fortuneteller. Yeah. Nice kid. No, no trouble. Everything's great. I got it all set up. Haven't I always done good work for you? Then what are you worrying about? It isn't good for you. You've done all you can. You've delegated to me, now you should let it go. Otherwise it affects your health, you know what I mean? You could get ulcers or cancer. No, yeah. Trust me. You should try TM. Did you ever try TM? Yeah, I meditate. Sure I do. In my business, you gotta keep your priorities straight. It's all or nothing, you know?"

Disconnected. That's the trouble with those ship-to-shore phones. They're always giving out. Hugo could have told Snow a lot more. It's an interesting topic, once you get on it. Most criminals get caught because they think they are going for the easy way of doing things, but it's really the hard way, the life of crime. You have to be conscious every moment of the day and night that you are a criminal.

You can't be an amateur like Jaime: part-time saint, part-time petty criminal. Got a hole through the head trying to rob a Seven-Eleven. Hugo was just a kid, but he was in on it with them. He slipped off into the dark, ran home, miles. That's when he understood how hard crime is, the consequences.

He was just a kid when Jaime was killed, but he feels guilty—he can't help it—because he got away. That's why he feels responsible for Lazaro. The boy needs a mentor. What's Hugo going to do? Turn his back on him?

7

*m*om, *tell Will I can't go. Something came up.*

Delia hands the note to Will.

"They're probably sacrificing a goat."

"I'm sorry about that—"

"He meant well. He just didn't understand that a blood sacrifice, for a Park Avenue WASP—it's a cultural leap. At least they didn't make me drink the blood."

"Oh no, they wouldn't do that," Delia says seriously. "You have to be a saint and be possessed by a spirit."

"I don't think I'll ever qualify."

"Probably not."

"I wonder if I'll recognize Cass, without Lazaro to point her out to me."

"You won't have any trouble."

"I've seen photos at the castle, but they're old."

"You'll know her because you know us."

"You mean there's a resemblance—"

"It's the vibrations. Every family has its own. You'll just feel she's the one, and she will be."

"If we don't connect, I suppose she'll call either you or Lavinia and you can give her my description."

"Don't worry. You'll know her. Cass sends out a very strong signal."

Delia walks Will to the door and fastens the latch after him. Now why did she do that when Lazaro's not in yet? She doesn't want to unlock the door because she feels Jaime's image materializing behind her in the darkness.

Dark at four-thirty and seventy degrees. Winter twilight and summer air. Mars and Venus together in the evening sky, the moon rising between them. Smells coming, soft—chicken coops, plantains frying in oil.

She is standing, she realizes, where she used to, in the open kitchen doorway, looking for Lazaro as if he were still the child who would go exploring the vacant lots and backyards, no further than her voice could carry. She's looking for a six-year-old boy.

The phone is ringing.

"Destiny Ortega? This is Gareth Watts. I am lying in a hospital in Arizona with a very sore ankle. I was bitten by a rattlesnake on the set."

"A snake! Of course. That's why I saw your ankle. . . ."

"If I had followed your fashion advice and worn cowboy boots I would be OK. The goddamned snake would have gotten a mouthful of leather. That jerkwater director wears cowboy boots, and he's filming his disaster in the middle of a rattlesnake den. Why not? The thing I'm calling to ask you is, why didn't you tell me to wear cowboy boots because of the rattlesnakes? It would have helped if I had known the reason. I never follow orders, but sometimes I take advice if I understand the reasoning behind it."

"I didn't know."

"About the snakes, or about how I think?"

"I get feelings. I had a feeling about your ankles. I could see them while you were talking to me. They looked naked and vulnerable."

Gareth pulls the sheet over his undershorts, up to his bare chest. "Look, you're two for two. I'll send you fifty dollars if you can tell me if Faye is sleeping with this jerkwater director."

Like hanged women, Delia's dresses are turning slowly in the breeze. "I sense the presence of evil."

"So she is."

"You. You are evil. You are twisting everything she says, every thought she has. You are making it impossible for her."

"Just give it to me straight. For fifty dollars, the question is: Is she balling this guy or isn't she?"

"I can't use my powers like that."

"Like what?"

"To spy on people. I sense, however—"

"Yes—"

"—that this is a perilous time for you to be with her. Two planets are in conjunction in the evening sky, Venus and Mars, the planets of love and war—"

"Oh, Christ."

"It is a time of chaos, of conflict. The passion you feel for her increases, as well as a fierceness, a blood lust, which can rage out of control. It will be best for both of you if you separate, at least until Mars is retrograde—"

"Stop handing me all this mumbo jumbo about the planets. If you can't tell me outright, just give me a hint. For fifty dollars, is she or isn't she?"

Fast and hard, she says, "If you don't let go right now, she will break—"

Gareth drops Faye's wrist. The white marks his fingers left on her brown skin turn to red while tears make shining trails on her cheeks.

Delia covers the mouthpiece with her hand. She thought it was a ghost standing in the doorway among the dresses, but it's Lazaro. "The back door was open," he says.

Will had no trouble picking Cass out at the airport, not with her heavy, shiny hair hanging straight down, page style, the way she always wore it in those childhood pictures of her in those ridiculous doublet and hose costumes. Although she's small, like Delia and Lavinia, there is something of the jock in her stride, that slight turn of the body with each step, a little swagger, an athlete's walk. She carried her duffel bag on a strap over her shoulder. Will reached to take it from her, but she didn't let him, as if surrendering her bag to a man would be admitting to weakness. It made Will smile.

The night is still warm. It's maybe even warmer than it was during the day. Cass has her window open. Her hair blows across her face, hiding all but the line of her cheekbone. Will is trying to explain to her what fascinates him about Wallingford history.

"Is this going to be a book?"

"It's my dissertation, but I hope to get it published, eventually."

"Do you think anyone would buy it? A book about Wallingford? It's kind of obscure."

"But Wallingford is such a perfect example of the victimization of industrial cities. It's the town where people take and never give back, a classic disaster."

"I can agree with you there."

"It was literally founded on exploitation. They built the town to exploit the power in the waterfall and in the process destroyed one of the scenic wonders of the New World."

"I know. In the library there was a print of the falls before the canals and everything. I used to stand in front of it and try to figure out how this miracle of nature had been transformed into an ugly, dark thing under a bridge. The frame had a plaque on it. I think it was a gift from one of your relatives."

"My great aunt, maybe, the one who gave the library." Trying to restore the family name after her brother's scandal, probably, although Will doesn't say it. Cass pulls her hair back as they go under the highway lights and for a moment Will can see a trace of Anna Bird's profile, but the lip that on Anna looks pouty is strong and sensual on Cass.

"I wonder if it's still there. You really should go and see it."

"What?"

"The picture of the falls, the one your aunt gave."

"I should. It's the only thing my family left to Wallingford."

"The library—"

"Oh yes, the library, but look at what we took out of Wallingford—millions. We made our fortune here, exploited immigrant labor, and left, without even a hospital or a park as thanks. Or what about T. W. Woolsley? He made more money than we did and he had no heirs, so he left all his to the Metropolitan Museum in New York. The Metropolitan Museum! He'd never been inside the place!"

"What's that?"

"The Metropolitan Museum?"

"Over towards the river. Is that a fire?"

"It looks like it. Do you want to go see?"

"No, it will be a mess. We'll be in the way. I'm sure they know about it, if we can see it from here."

"There was a fire the first day I came to town."

"Yes, I think Lavinia or maybe Delia told me about it. Did they ever figure out what caused it?"

"No. I mean, they suspect arson, but no one's been accused."

"Probably won't be, either. The town is so riddled with graft."

"Another recurring theme in Wallingford's history, corruption

—apart from the reign of your grandfather, of course, Socrates Bird."

"Please, spare me any more glory stories about Socrates Bird. My father told me so much about him when I was little that I was surprised when I got to school and found he didn't share top billing with George Washington."

Will takes the downtown exit instead of the one he would ordinarily use to get to the castle. "I said I'd pick up Delia and Lazaro," he explains.

"I hear you're practically one of the family."

"I haven't met your father—"

"You're better off."

"Lazaro's a bright kid. He's been helping me on my research."

"He has brains, but they're only going to get him into trouble, unless Delia does something, fast."

"What do you mean?"

"He's a slum kid, a street kid, tough. I understand. He has to be, to survive."

"He seems very well-mannered to me—"

"Oh, he is. He has a very nice little facade he's put together, but he runs with a tough-assed bunch of kids. I know. I've seen them. Delia's seen them too, but she won't see. It's funny. My father tried to control every facet of our lives, but Delia doesn't think she can do anything to influence Lazaro. She's just watching him grow, as if he were a plant or something. She has abdicated to the slum."

Will pulls up in front of Delia's house. He's grown used to it, but now he sees it again as a dilapidated wreck on a street he'd be hesitant to walk in the daytime.

"I'll go tell them we're here." She jumps out before Will can say anything, leaving him to wait in the car. Across the street, the gas station is still open and someone is standing by the pumps, watching him.

. . .

The worst sound in the world when you are waiting for someone and it's after dark is sirens. Lavinia has a vision of them all spilled out of the Saab, like broken dolls on the road, down at the corner at the bottom of the hill, the one that William takes a little too fast, although he's generally a careful driver. She always has to restrain herself from telling him to slow down for the curve, and in the dark—Lavinia leans against the sideboard and takes a couple of slow breaths. It's a fire siren, not an ambulance, and it's fading fast. The neighborhood station turning out to help downtown, no doubt.

No one answered at Delia's. They must be on their way. Lavinia pours herself a little sherry from the decanter she put out on the sideboard. Since four this afternoon, the table's been set with the damask cloth and napkins, two beautiful little paphiopedila in jardinieres, red candles, the Spode Christmas tree plates. The tree is at the other end of the great hall. She made William drive her way out to the country to find one big enough. "You see, because of the size of the room, you need an extraordinarily large tree," she told him. She didn't say that since Nestor left, she had been making do with a three-foot spruce, mounted on a table to make it look bigger. She would buy the miserable little thing at the last minute Christmas Eve, when the trees went down in price a dollar or two, and bring it home with her on the bus.

What a thrill to get out all the old ornaments, which had been much too big for a puny little tree.

Lavinia pours herself another, smiling a little guiltily into the mirror over the sideboard. The candlelight and the worn looking-glass are conspiring tonight to turn her hair, coiled on top of her head in a braid, from silver back into gold. The gown is the one she used to wear on Christmas Eve, red velvet, with a low, Elizabethan-style neckline. It will annoy Cass, but Lavinia thinks it's lovely.

"It's just as it was when Nestor was here," she tells her reflection, seeing the great hall behind her. No, it's better, she decides. After all, when Nestor was here, the Venerable One was still young. It never would have been capable of four blossoms! She has enthroned it on a table by the door.

Tires on the driveway. She snatches up her skirt with one hand and flies to the conservatory, where she can watch them getting out of the car: Cass and Lazaro, then Delia and William, laughing and talking, pulling packages out of the trunk. Lavinia waves to them, although they don't see her. Lavinia pins up her braid, which came loose on her dash to the conservatory, and thinks that this is the first Christmas she hasn't looked out the window expecting to see Nestor.

8

The flames on the candles stretch out long like snake tongues, licking the breeze, curling toward Lazaro, who watches through lowered eyes.

"This is the first Christmas Eve I've ever had to open the window," Lavinia is saying. "But at least we won't have to bundle up in mufflers and mittens when we go caroling on the bridge."

"Another fine old family tradition," Cass explains to Will. "We open the ridiculous main doors and parade out on the drawbridge to serenade ourselves. Lavinia used to hate it, but since Nestor left, she hounds us out there every Christmas Eve in all kinds of weather. She takes care of his orchids too. She's afraid he'll come back unexpectedly and throw a temper tantrum if we're not doing everything right."

"It's for Lazaro," Lavinia reproaches Cass. "You know you girls used to love it when you were little. We owe it to Lazaro, as the next generation, to carry on the tradition."

"I think it's time we did away with the traditions, especially since they were all invented by Nestor to support his myth." Cass finishes off her wine.

"What myth?" Lazaro wants to know.

"The whole myth that the Birds are the landed gentry, the barons of Wallingford. The myth that made Nestor buy this ridiculous movie-set castle and get us to dress up like medieval nobility."

"That was fun. That was play—"

"A pretty elaborate game, a life game. We lived in a castle, after all. Delia grew up thinking she was a princess."

"I don't think living alone is good for you, dear. You brood too much. Who would ever think these things? A pretty, young woman has no business mulling over her childhood so much."

"We used to have to take the bus to get to school." Cass ignores Lavinia and directs her conversation to Will. "And there were these very tough black girls who would get on, down the line. They usually stood in the aisle because there wouldn't be any seats left, and we would have to pass through them to leave the bus. One day I was getting off and I felt this horrible jab in my leg. I screamed, and this evil fat girl grinned at me and showed me an enormous safety pin. She had it opened, hidden in her fist, so that only the pointed end stuck out. I was furious. I was only about ten or eleven, but the bus driver wouldn't listen to me. He said he didn't want any trouble on the bus. Afterward, Delia showed me her leg. It was full of wounds. That girl had been using her for a pin cushion and she hadn't ever said anything—"

"Is it true, Delia?"

"I don't remember anything like—"

"Maybe it was something like that, but you exaggerated it over time," Lavinia tells Cass.

"No, it's the truth, but what's the use. You've just proved my point, the point of my story."

"What was the point?" Lazaro asks.

"That your mother believed the myth so well that she couldn't even admit that she was being tortured on the bus. After all, princesses who live in castles and are protected and watched over by their father the king don't get poked with safety pins on their way to school."

Lazaro's eyes narrow. He's no doubt thinking that he would have carried a switchblade and slit the wrist of the hand that dared raise itself against him. Cass shivers and gets up to close the window. It smells like a fire—the one she and Will saw from the highway? But that was miles away.

They have the caroling despite Cass. It would be a shame not to use the silver lanterns that they save just for this occasion. Lazaro leads them through the carols, in the same order Nestor used to.

After the last one, "Silent Night," they usually go inside, but this time they stay on the bridge, the air is so warm, resting their lanterns on the railings. Drawbridges don't have railings, but Nestor had them built as a safety precaution. He was always afraid the girls would slip and fall into the moat, although it was only four feet down and grassy as well. Even if they had fallen, it wouldn't have hurt them, but Nestor didn't take chances with their welfare.

There are tears standing in Lavinia's eyes. Cass wants to put her arms around her, but instead she goes in to start on the dishes. Will follows. On the way he is met by the odor of burning. Didn't he hear sirens once or twice faintly during the evening? He wonders if it's the same fire he and Cass noticed on the way over.

"I don't know why I do it." Cass rinses a Christmas tree plate and hands it to Will to dry. "I'm never going to get her to realize—"

"She seems so happy, the way she is now. Do you think you should force her to accept something, in the name of truth—"

"She's only happy because she's been putting off facing the truth. Someday it's going to come and it will be too late to do anything about it. She was fifty-two years old when he left. She could have started a career, remarried—anything. Instead she's been living in limbo."

"Maybe it would have destroyed her to face it at the time. Maybe she had to keep thinking Nestor would return."

"But he was a terrible man. He used to disappear for weekends, have affairs with other women. And when he was home, he was a tyrant. This castle wasn't his game, it was an obsession. Everything had to be done just right. I would have thought she'd have felt relieved when he left for good. He was too much for all of us —too big, too strong, too tyrannical. We grew up in a lopsided house where only one person had power. When he left, there was just a vacuum. Delia and Lavinia have been drifting ever since. Maybe I have too. His voice was so strong that we're still obeying the reverberating echoes of it."

Cass's motions, as she cleans up the kitchen, are deft, precise. Maybe Delia drifts, although Will thinks she's operating on some hidden program, but Cass is definitely at the helm.

"Don't you think you have power over him too?" Will asks. "I mean, you don't have to be stronger or louder to influence another person. It's how you're placed, the place you have in the other one's life." He's thinking of the weak-chinned Anna Bird, wasting away in her bed.

From the window above the sink, Cass can see the others on the bridge. Delia and Lazaro have their arms around Lavinia. Her tears didn't send them running inside. They simply moved to comfort her, probably without giving it a thought. The lanterns, resting on the rails, make a circle of light around them.

"I wonder why she never remarried." Will's face is reflected in the windowpane above and to the right of Cass's.

"Lavinia?"

"No, Delia."

"She's waiting."

"Not for her husband to come back—"

Cass laughs and her hair swings back. "She's not that bad. But almost. She's waiting for The One. Delia thinks there is one man who is destined to come save her. It's the Sleeping Beauty complex that comes from growing up in the castle. She thinks a prince is going to appear out of nowhere and rescue her and Lazaro from the slum. It's all very convenient because she doesn't have to go out and try to meet men, get into the singles' scene and all that. She knows that one day this man is going to come riding in, cut all the thorns away, and rescue her."

"That would explain—"

"What?"

"I don't know, why she looks so calm—"

"Oh sure. She's perfectly calm. But like Lavinia, she's just putting off disappointment. She's living a dream, and it's dangerous, because she should be trying to figure ways out—"

"But someone might come. It is possible. She's very pretty. And some men might like it, playing the prince. Most women don't allow men to think that way anymore."

"Are you considering trying out for the part?"

"Me?"

"Why not? You said she was pretty."

"Yes, but—I don't think of myself as a prince."

Cass steps away teasingly, looking him over. Will finds himself straightening up, pulling in his stomach.

"Maybe not outwardly," Cass concedes. "You're not the classic image. But you're a gentleman. You're polite and you seem good. In that way, you're princely. And you have money—"

"Well, not a lot, a trust fund—"

"What looks like a modest fortune to you is a princely sum to a welfare mother, which is what Delia is."

The little group has broken up. Lavinia and Lazaro are coming back to the house, leaving Delia on the bridge. In her shabby coat, she could be a welfare mother, but her pose, with her head thrown back and her hair falling like a mantle behind her, proclaims her to be a princess in temporary exile.

"That was Marcioni on the phone," he tells her.

She doesn't look up because she is applying varnish to her fingernails. She is good at putting it on very smoothly, but it takes concentration; she has told him this.

"Marcioni," he repeats. "The fire chief."

"Hmmm?"

"This time it's the mills down in the historic district. Some of the houses have caught too. They're evacuating the neighborhood."

She puts the brush back in the bottle and looks up, not at him, but at the program on the television, a Christmas special with some comedian Nestor thought died long ago.

Bitch, he thinks, *it's our money, our investment. You should be interested in money at least,* but he doesn't say it because he knows she gets worse at Christmas time. It's harder for her then. Her psychiatrist explained it all to Nestor.

"I'll have to go over there tomorrow morning," he tells her, "before we leave." He's taking her into New York City for dinner. She likes that, dressing up, getting out of Wallingford. He'll give her the gift over dinner. She'll have something for him, a money clip—no, that was last year—cuff links, maybe. When they get back home, she will put on the pink terry robe she's wearing right now and turn on the TV and he will take a bourbon to his den. Christmas will be over.

"He says the place is gutted, completely gutted. They've given up the mill. They have to save the homes, if they can. This wind is carrying the damn thing for blocks. It's a tragedy, a tragedy."

She is looking at him now, waiting for him to finish so she can get back to her television and fingernails.

He puts fresh ice in his glass and more bourbon, swirls the ice around and pictures an iceberg crushing Edgar Snow's sailboat to bits. There aren't any icebergs in the Caribbean.

The chair at his desk has a high back, arm rests. It is upholstered in leather and of the right proportions to accommodate a man of his size. The furniture Donna chose for the living room is low and squashy. When he sits in it, his stomach lies on top of him like a weight. He has trouble turning to speak to someone, and it's difficult to get up again. He has asked Donna to find him a chair for the living room that he could sit in, but she says it wouldn't go with the other things. It would be too high; it would look like a throne, putting everyone else at a disadvantage. When people come over (they don't very often), Nestor stands to avoid the clumsiness of having to roll off the sofa to get up.

Why shouldn't people sit this way, upright? Why would someone want to throw her body across pillowing things that offer no support? If he could persuade Donna to sit in a straight chair, she might take on more will to live.

He sets his bourbon down beside the things he brought from the office to read at home: the *Wall Street Journal*, some mail, Lavinia's letter. He balances the letter on his fingers, turns it slowly, angles it down toward the wastebasket. He has never yet been able to throw her letters away unopened. It's part of her trickery. She knows he's reading them, although he never answers. She has no doubt that he cannot throw them away unread. It isn't fair of her to take advantage of his good nature.

The letter is about that half-breed bastard of Delia's. Nestor wanted to adopt it. He would have taken Delia and her baby in, but Donna wouldn't have it. She wanted her own so badly. It's just as well, seeing how the boy is turning out. Too much bad blood there. He'll be behind bars before he's twenty and Lavinia says he is showing an interest in history.

Appleyard! Appleyard is going through his papers, Bird family archives! God, she's incredible, the way she slices him up. Jesus God! Bird family archives in the hands of an Appleyard who's writing a doctoral dissertation on the history of Wallingford. Nestor's hand reaches for the phone. He's dialed the number before he realizes he can't call on Christmas Eve. Lavinia will think he's coming home. She still knows how to get him by the short hairs, after all these years, all this time. He won't be able to send a man over to seize the files until Monday. Goddamn holidays.

Nestor forms a silent apology to his father, Socrates, to Zeus too for leaving their papers in the hands of his treacherous wife. He left, they must understand, in a rush, having forgotten the papers were in the castle. He abandoned everything! He had hoped that Lavinia would sell the furniture when she sold the house, adding to her capital, but she hasn't sold as much as a hairbrush. Every year she writes to tell him how his orchids are doing and to assure him that the castle is the same as when he left it. Only this year she doesn't say it. She's too busy going on about the boy and Appleyard and the papers. She knows when she has him!

He finally has to wipe his eyes with his handkerchief and blow his nose before he gets up again to pour his last bourbon. At first he thinks it's Beirut on the television news, but it's Wallingford: aerial views of Wallingford burning, some pictures of bleary-eyed families setting up beds in the armory, a close-up of a fire fighter being given oxygen.

"Christ, it's a fuckin' holocaust," he says to Donna, who doesn't answer because she's sleeping, her red-tipped fingers spread like tentacles across her chest to dry. Nestor turns off the television but leaves the light on in case she wakes in the night.

Delia is taking off her clothes and putting them on the chair beside her bed. She doesn't fold them. She watches how they fall, as if they have a will of their own. Cass is observing this ritual from the other bed in Delia's room at the castle. Lavinia had Cass's bed moved here when she converted Cass's bedroom into the archive room, the only change since Nestor left.

Will may be right: the influence people wield does not correspond to their intrinsic strength. Cass is prejudiced because of her training. In heat-transfer studies, high energy imparts force to low energy. Strong influences weak. But look at Delia, a nonforce, someone who is unwilling to exercise control over the way her clothes go onto a chair, and yet she has a property that must be acknowledged.

Cass long ago figured out that Delia was going to be their favorite, Lavinia's and Nestor's, no matter what Cass did, no matter how bright she was, how quick, even how desperately she wanted and needed to be first. Delia would always be there, first in their hearts, without ever willing it, without even being aware of it.

And tonight. Delia had only to stand, thinking her own unformed thoughts, barely conscious that Will was present, for him to fall in love.

"What do you think of Will?" Cass says, reaching for the lamp.

"Hmmm?"

"Will. Mom's boarder."

"Oh. He's nice. Sort of muddled, you know, in his aura."

Cass turns off the light, leaving Delia standing in the dark.

Lazaro is undressing beneath his covers. Will turns away so Lazaro won't think he is watching him. He feels protective toward the boy, Delia too.

What if Will is The One? It would fit, explain why he's come back to Wallingford—to repay an old debt. That would do it, wouldn't it? Expiate the Appleyard sin. William IV comes back to marry the grandniece of Anna Bird, rescue her from poverty, rescue the family name (because Cass is probably right about Lazaro, about what he will become if he continues to live there).

Not that Will has decided to believe literally in the curse. He had a moment of weakness on the street, after the sacrifice, but he's had time to sort it through.

The great mainstream of Western thought left magic behind long ago, but pockets of belief still remain among people who hold with a simpler, agrarian culture (Lazaro's abuela) or those who, for whatever reason, have fallen from the system of beliefs they were born into (Delia). These people truly believe in curses, precognition, second sight.

That does not mean that the phenomenon, "the curse," is nonsense. It is real. It exists. The modern scientific mind has other explanations for it, however. For instance, there are psychologists, he read recently, who are studying the effects of multigenerational myths. The curse of the Appleyards could be explained as one of those.

Let us imagine the young Will Appleyard II, cruelly ignoring Anna Bird, his wife, to pursue Carlotta Jaeger. He sees Anna waste away and die, but he doesn't let it get to him—at first! Years later, he begins to brood. His conscience catches up with him, makes him quarrel with Carlotta, stop paying attention to business. He has some small accidents, and then one day he falls from his horse and dies.

This leaves Carlotta widowed, with her young son and her own burden of guilt for Anna Bird's death. Wouldn't it be natural for Carlotta to see some justice in William II's fall from the horse, to see the pattern of some terrible revenge being worked out? What if there had been a rumor floating around at the time of Anna Bird's death that she had cursed William on her deathbed?

Memories of that rumor suddenly unfold in Carlotta's mind, take root and grow. She becomes fearful for her own son's life. She may even be imprudent enough to mention the curse in his presence. Whether or not the boy ever hears directly about the curse, the idea of it seeps into his subconscious.

He's afraid of horses—huge, irrational animals—and so he

learns all about them. In his early adolescence, he takes up riding, practices daily. He learns to laugh at his timid mother's warnings. He grows up, gets married, has a son. He and his wife share a smile every time his old mother says "Be careful."

As William III, called Billy by everyone, approaches the fateful age when his own father met his death, the subconscious, the primitive part of his brain which still believes in witches and goblins, begins sending up warning signals. Billy doesn't want to hear himself thinking like a superstitious old woman about witches and deathbed curses, so he becomes passionately interested in horses again. He's obsessed by them. He goes West to ride with the men who regard horses as extensions of their own bodies, who talk to horses, sleep with them. He goes West on a vacation to a dude ranch, and then one day—nobody understands how because he is an excellent rider—he falls off his mount and he is killed.

Carlotta blames herself. Her daughter-in-law, Billy's wife, blames her as well, only because it's a relief to be angry with someone besides the dead loved one. The old lady dries up like a hard, dark nut in the empty shell of her Park Avenue apartment. When Will comes to visit, he is greeted by the cook who gives him molasses cookies, but he rarely glimpses "her," as the servants call his grandmother.

Will grows up in an atmosphere of innuendo: overheard scraps of whispered conversations among the help; his mother turning down an invitation to a birthday party for him because there will be pony rides; Carlotta's milky eyes looking away when he comes into the room. Never faced consciously, never talked about, the innuendos go directly to the subconscious, where they lodge like seeds, ready to burst into full, luxuriant growth when Will reaches the proper, the fatal age.

Not dormant seeds. That isn't quite right, because the seeds don't just lie there. They blight his life. Because the message is inarticulated, Will generalizes it. Not only does he protect himself

from horses, he never learns to ride a bicycle, or ski, or play football, basketball. He's not even comfortable swimming. The message he has received is that he is too vulnerable to participate in
life. He doesn't marry. He never has a child. He stays in school,
the last bastion of adolescence. He never even finishes his dissertation. If you don't go through life's stages, you won't get to the last
one.

Will gets up and puts his dressing gown over his pajamas. The
boy is sleeping, his lashes laid out on his cheeks, incredibly long,
something you don't realize when he's awake because he's so active.
Will pulls the blanket over Lazaro's shoulder, small and bony.
Again, when Lazaro is awake you don't see the fragility. His *machismo* covers it.

He'll buy them a house near the university, with a swimming
pool, and a basketball hoop over the garage for Lazaro. He can't
quite see Delia as a faculty wife—no matter. They will make their
own friends, or not. They'll be an island. Delia can tell fortunes
over the phone. Will can teach, and Lazaro will grow up middle
class, have a chance in the world.

Very carefully so as not to wake Lazaro, Will lets himself out
the sally port and stands barefoot on the broken pavement. It
smells like rain coming and a fire somewhere, wetted down.

Chicken blood might have done it for him if he were a simpler
man, but it's going to take more than animal sacrifices and African
chants to drive the curse out of the throne of the subconscious. If
he gives his life, devotes it, to Anna Bird's grandniece and her
great-grandnephew, rescues them from poverty, and in Lazaro's
case, possibly crime, will that do it? Repair the damage his grandfather inflicted on the family?

The clammy air comes against his cheek like an old woman's
hand. He pulls away and retreats inside the door.

9

Jeez, Christmas Eve. Goddamned bastards . . ." Marcioni is tramping around inside of what's left of the Appleyard mills, thoroughly enjoying himself, all the while complaining. What monster would set a fire Christmas Eve? As if arsonists were sentimental enough not to work on holidays. Like the Hessians when Washington attacked—"What, on Christmas?" As if evil weren't irresistibly drawn to times of innocence and feasting. Who's he kidding, Marcioni, complaining about having to leave his family? He's tickled pink. What man wouldn't like an excuse to get out from under all that family, all those little ceremonies the women concoct to keep you coiled up in the shell of domesticity, trapped, until it's time to go to work again, back to the job where you are safely incarcerated until the next holiday. Look at Marcioni in his fire hat, his raincoat and boots, giving orders, turning over blackened beams. He loves it.

They give Nestor a fireman's hat, and a coat too. Edgar Snow's buildings burned, the crown jewel in his plans for renovation, and Edgar is nowhere to be found. Nestor had to come out to watch the investigation, although he has no idea of what to look for. Of course it's arson. Any damn fool knows it, knows it's the work of the street urchins, the same scurvy bunch that scrawl obscenities all over town, the same ones who started the other fires, the misfits, the bottom of the barrel, the social savages, the underclass.

Not that Marcioni and his men are going to find anything. They're making a show of tramping around so they can go off and have a couple of drinks before returning to the bosoms of their families.

"I thought there would be more here—you know, Nestor?" Marcioni has blue eyes (where did a dago get blue eyes?) and a smudge of carbon on one cheek.

"More what?"

"I don't know—more pipes, insulation, building materials. The mill's basically the way it was when Snow took over, as far as I can see. I thought he started construction a long time ago."

"Dan, look at this." The men have clustered in a back corner. Marcioni tramps over in his boots. Nestor picks his way.

"Yeah, yeah. This is where it started." Marcioni directs the men to put some material in bags. "Naphthalene, looks like a couple of barrels of it," Marcioni tells Nestor. "Why would they need naphthalene?"

"Must be some old barrels they hadn't cleared out yet," Nestor says. "The mills were used for storage, warehousing a lot of different things before."

"Maybe. I'd sure like to see Snow and ask him a few questions, like how come he left those barrels here and what his security guard was doing last night."

What everyone was doing last night, drinking. Marcioni was too and all the men, which is why the fire got out of hand. Marcioni, having failed as fire chief, wants to try his hand at being a detective.

Rain is sifting down through the blackened, broken roof, not heavy, but heavy enough to help Marcioni decide the investigation is over for the day. Nestor hears someone saying that the Gallway on Hamilton Street might be open.

Nestor is going to stay for a while. The police guard is bivouacked in his car. Nestor can call him if he needs anything, Marcioni says. Nestor waves him away.

No new plumbing, no flooring, no partitions, no building materials. Nestor does not need to see the files to be able to picture the contracts Snow signed with various construction companies. What about the cement mixers that were standing conspicuously around for a couple of weeks? What about the trucks, coming and going?

A grackle drops down through the blasted roof and perches on a charred beam, fluffing its feathers to dry. The rain is coming steadily now, falling into black puddles left from the fire hoses, adding to the stink of wet ashes. The old looms, the ones Snow hadn't removed yet, or never intended to, stand like twisted, charred skeletons of prehistoric monsters, relics of the industrial age.

"Bare ruin'd choirs . . ." he thinks he hears, like a groan, or maybe something giving way. He remembers other roofless walls, a cathedral he discovered in France, on his honeymoon. He'd seen the spires among tall oaks on the hill the evening before and the next morning, leaving Donna still asleep at the inn, he hiked up there following sheep trails past giant hand-hewn stones lying in a pasture, until he came to a fallen doorway where he stood and saw the sun coming up and swallows dipping in and out through gothic arches.

Nestor unfolds his handkerchief and clears his head. The brain is a treacherous organ, to unearth the memory of a happy time— yes, he was happy then, or pleased with himself, for seeking out the ruin, walking the distance, for having a beautiful young pregnant wife waiting for him—and turn it into something that could tear the heart out of his chest. He doesn't know whether to laugh or cry, at how, when he saw the rising sun held for a moment in the frame of the rose medallion window, he'd taken it for a sign that his soul had been washed, that he was beginning anew.

He never learned the history of that cathedral, whether it had been burned, or destroyed by men, or had simply crumbled from neglect.

How many years does it take a ruin to get that clean? How many years before the black beams are scoured down and the putrid stink lifted away by the wind?

In how many years will the organic matter of his mistakes, the decaying scent of his lust and greed, be washed away so that the pure bones of his good intentions stand clear? Or will they? What if his frailties have penetrated to his very skeleton, twisting it out of shape? Maybe he will be remembered in history—the one Appleyard is writing—as the man who sold out his friends to a con man from New York. The man who left his wife and children to marry a girl his daughter's age. What if Nestor Bird, with all his work and good intentions, the last in the line, comes out a blot that sullies the family name?

Zeus and Socrates weren't blameless either. There were certain things they had to do. Private matters. Hidden in those boxes of papers, no doubt, certain clues. Last night Nestor was in a fever to get those boxes away from Appleyard. But this morning the matter seems dried up and old, a nasty, etiolated bit of shame compared to this new juice-bag of scandal about to burst all over Wallingford. He'll do well to stay clear of Appleyard. Let him rattle old skeletons—better that than exhume fresh corpses.

Why couldn't Snow at least have made it look better? He didn't even try! There were bricks. There were cartons of plate glass. Nestor remembers now. Where did they go? Cheap bastard carted them away before the fire, wouldn't even spend the money to make it look good.

"Did you call me, Mr. Bird?" The police officer, whose name Nestor has forgotten, is standing in the entrance.

"What? No."

"Oh, I thought I heard you, or voices. I wouldn't go too near that wall, sir. It might collapse."

Nestor's shoes are wet and black with charcoal. How the hell did he get over to this side? He's got to get a hold on himself. It's going to be very important, in the weeks to come, that he doesn't crack, that he maintains his equilibrium. He allows the officer to take his arm as he picks his way to the door with the slow caution of a mastodon trying to inch itself back from the edge of a tar pit.

Appleyard is writing his history, but he isn't engraving it in stone. Books rot too. Maybe something will happen—a sudden freeze and then a nuclear bomb will drop and all that will remain of Nestor Bird will be these tracks in the ashes, to be read by some other being a millennium from now: "He was a tall male human, big-boned, larger than most, a chieftain probably, someone who walked on the earth with authority and dignity."

Her heart sees him first. Before Lavinia realizes who the heavy man is being escorted by the policeman through the rubble to his car, a deep red Cadillac, too shiny to be here amidst the wreckage, her heart speeds up. How old he looks, and beaten. Cass and Delia, sharing an umbrella, haven't seen him. She doesn't want them to, not the way he looks now. The officer closes the door, and the Cadillac noses its way through the crowd.

They have all come to view the ruins and bring blankets, food, clothes. Lavinia had some blankets to spare. Cass wouldn't let her bring clothes, said they were twenty years out of date—as if that would matter. Now they are standing with the others under umbrellas, watching the rain mix with the ashes. It's odd that it should feel so pleasant, in a solemn way, to be standing here with hundreds of others, roofed over with umbrellas, and so comforting to be one of this many people.

This is new for her—seeing Nestor this way, at a distance, as if he were someone unknown to her, an important man in the community, allowed privileged access to the ruins, but sad, a man bowed down by his own troubles, troubles Lavinia doesn't know or share. Cass and Delia, standing beside her, did not see him. It's almost as if she didn't either, or if she did, he was someone she didn't know, had never known.

Will has to leave. He promised his mother he'd spend Christmas with her. As Lavinia works her way back through the crowd, following Will's beige trench coat, she sees Carmen and the Señora sharing a large black umbrella. She catches Carmen's eye and they nod. Why would a blind woman come out to see the ruins of a fire?

"It's Mrs. Bird," Carmen tells her mother in Spanish.

"Who's with her?"

"The man with the curse. And the two girls."

"Lazaro's not there?"

"No."

"Take me home. This place is heavy with bad spirits."

There was a murder in Lazaro's house a long time ago. Lazaro's great-grandfather—no, great-great—collected a lot of stuff about it, but Will hasn't let Lazaro go through it because the murderer was a prostitute. Will's kind of like a little old lady sometimes.

They all went down to look at the fire. "Don't you want to come, Lazaro?" Lavinia kept asking, like it was a circus, some treat for him to see. He does want to, but alone, not with other people who can watch him seeing it, because he doesn't know what his face will do. Laugh maybe, or cry.

Nobody died. It went on all night. He heard it through dinner, roaring like a wind, crashing like big trees coming down in the forest, a volcano of flames. He saw it spreading out on the horizon when they went on the bridge to sing. He heard it hissing quietly under the misty rain that began in the night.

The murder is in these envelopes, which Will keeps hidden under the rest, like a sex magazine, so he can bring them out when Lazaro's not around. There is good stuff here, but it's hard to get used to the different handwritings and the way they talked—like another language—with big words, a lot of legal words. You have to understand that most of the time this great-great-grandfather stayed in bed with the curtains drawn. He was a wino. He wrote notes, instructions, to his assistant, some dude who had to lie to everyone that his boss was sick and everyone in town knew the real story.

This assistant's name is Ferkin, which is a good one because Lazaro can see him freakin' when he goes to see Hot Emma in her cell. He calls her a Hell-cat, a sorcerer, a harlot, the embodiment of evil. All she wants of him is twenty yards of white cotton dimity to make a dress. And satin ribbons, red, yards of it. She's counting on a spring or summer hanging.

Ferkin writes three long letters to the Great-great giving him the rumors on the street about Hot Emma being a witch, a diviner of fortunes. Ferkin thinks they are going to bring this up at the trial, Emma's reputation as a "disciple of Satan," someone "versed in the black arts."

The Great-great tells Ferkin to keep his shirt on. Emma was in the habit of reading palms when business was slow, that's all. She was pretty good at it. The Great-great tried her more than once. In fact, many of Wallingford's prominent citizens have sampled Emma's talents at fortunetelling, as well as her other talents, of course.

Zeus Bird is above every weakness of the flesh except gluttony and pride. He'd do anything to protect the reputation of his family. He knows if he brings up the rumors of witchcraft, sorcery, black arts, the defense will have an opening to bring Anna Bird Appleyard's name into the testimony, and Zeus wants to keep that issue well buried. Zeus knows there were whispers at the time of Anna

Bird's death, about Emma Phelps. The Great-great doesn't think Zeus is going to give the rumors a chance to be immortalized in the court record.

Lazaro jumps up. There's a noise coming from one of the boxes, like writing—the dead hand of the Great-great is still writing, plotting, recording. Doesn't the message Lazaro is holding right now feel crisp and new, as if the Great-great finished it just now and gave it to Lazaro to deliver to Ferkin. Lazaro knows exactly where to find Ferkin and what he looks like: pale-blue eyes, light-brown hair, flakes of dandruff on a brown wool suit; his desk is dusty.

The dead hand of the Great-great continues scratching in the bottom of the box. Lazaro creeps up slowly. His hands open and close at his sides without his wanting them to. He forces them into fists and kicks the box hard. It flips over, spilling out papers and one gray mouse, fast as a shadow, streaking away under the radiator.

Lazaro hits the stairs, never even feels them, doesn't feel anything until he's outside, standing on the crumbling blacktop and senses the prickle of rain on his arms.

10

Her clothes have fallen into an unusual configuration during the night. Delia has never seen them like this before, scattered across the slipper chair with abandon, one arm of her sweater outstretched, the other folded over the top, and the jeans, half off the chair, one pant leg bent as if ready to spring. Her bra is hooked onto the sleeve of the sweater and her socks are under the chair.

Delia sits back on her bed, her robe wrapped tight around her, watching her clothes as if they might do something more to reveal their message.

She overslept. She had calls until midnight. It's the postholiday discontent. People want new jobs, new lovers, to lose weight, to find money. Everyone wants money. Delia has raised her fee to thirty dollars and she's getting more calls than ever. If this keeps up, she could move to a better place, put Lazaro in private school. But she can't count on it continuing. There's a mysterious vogue to this. Now it's "in" to call Destiny Ortega. Next week it could be out.

The president of the International Psychics' Society called to invite Destiny into the city for lunch. Delia had never heard of the society, but she accepted anyway.

Delia pulls on the socks she wore yesterday. Lazaro has left for school. She hopes he dressed warmly enough. The temperature dropped in the night. It looks like snow.

She stirs herself up a cup of hot bouillon and takes it back to her bed. It's worthless trying to tell the cards for herself, but she puts them out anyway.

The Tower. It's not necessarily bad. She knows that, but all the same, for the first card to turn up the stark tower in flames, lightning striking at the crown, people falling helplessly to their doom. Delia quickly turns up the next for elucidation. Page of Swords, Lazaro's card, the young page grasping a sword, alert for enemies. The next is the two of Pentacles, reversed. A letter, or exchange of letters, perhaps concerning Lazaro. Queen of Pentacles.

Delia sips her bouillon. Never has she turned the Queen of Pentacles up for herself. Of course, it could be a mistake, although she did everything correctly: shuffling, cutting with her left hand. But you can never tell, doing it for yourself. Queen of Pentacles. Security, liberty, generosity.

What could it mean, beginning with the Tower and ending with the Queen of Pentacles? She tries to imagine what she would tell a client if these cards came up, but she can't because so much depends on the client and the wordless communication that goes on between them across the cards.

Delia shuffles the deck and puts it away. She retrieves her clothes from the chair and pulls them on, adding a wool scarf around her neck to keep out the cold.

She hears the mailman on the front porch and the squeak of the letter flap in the door. Checks from clients. She takes them into the dining room to see them better. Two are from Los Angeles, both new clients, both thirty dollars. Amazing that people will actually pay her new price without even questioning. The third is from Arizona. Fifty dollars. Gareth Watts. Delia has to think for a moment, then she remembers the angry man. But why did he send her this?

The check in her hand, Delia stares out the window and sees snow falling in perfectly formed individual crystals.

Will notices the snow falling past the iron grating on Bubbles' shop window, but it seems inappropriate to mention it while Bubbles is grieving over the tragic disappearance of Edgar Snow, whose rented sailboat and native crew came back to harbor in St. Croix reporting that their employer had gone scuba diving off the side of the ship and never resurfaced. As there was no other scuba equipment on board, nobody could go after him. The crew is vague about the position of the boat at the time. It is likely that Edgar Snow's body will never be recovered. The story was in the *New York Times* this morning, in the B section. The article described Snow as a flamboyant character, an expert diver and sailor, a real estate speculator, and the head of several investment funds.

Something has happened to Bubbles' face. It has taken on cracks and fissures that were never there before, dark rings under the eyes. The eyes aren't lavender—or were they green?—but leaden, the color of a winter sky. Even her hair has changed texture, from smooth and shiny to rough and wiry, with a suspicion of darkness lurking at the roots. Will feels he shouldn't be here with Lavinia and Bubbles, that this is a time when women need to be alone. He excuses himself and walks out into the first snowfall of the year.

The old man (Regina finds herself thinking of him as "the old man," but she never did before) has lost weight, or at least, his beautiful blue suit seems slightly large and the skin on his face is looser, hangs in folds under his eyes, around his mouth.

The fire, the disappearance of Snow, have hit him hard. Since she came back from vacation, Nestor has taken Regina into his confidence in this matter, alone, out of all the firm. Soon everyone will know.

"Snow bailed out," he told Regina. "He's not spreading his money around; he's keeping the lid on. It's all going to come to the surface. It will be a matter of days. I want to see what, if anything, we can salvage out of this, if there's any way we can protect our investors. What I have, personally, isn't much, but I'm prepared to give it all if necessary." He wants Regina to find out how deep the corruption goes, and do it quickly. There's bound to be at least one reporter from the *Times* on this. If there isn't one from the *Wallingford Gazette*, then they're even bigger fools than he thought.

The results from the investigation were bad. Water pipes to the hydrants were clogged with plaster. The men had to join hoses and use a hydrant two blocks away, losing precious minutes. There were barrels of naphthalene on the site. Damn thing went up like a torch.

"Have they discovered who actually started the fire?" Nestor waves an immaculate hand past his face. "Some local kids, they're pretty sure. They're asking around. They'll get them, not that it will tell us much that we don't know already. Edgar Snow—I only wish he has been torn limb from limb by sharks."

Nestor pictures Snow's tooth-raked, limbless body rising in a pool of his own blood, a carmine blob in the turquoise Caribbean, his mane of white hair spreading in a nimbus around his tortured face. He grunts in satisfaction and catches Regina watching him.

"I'd like to start by going to the scene of the fire," she says.

"You won't find anything there you can't read in the report."

"I'd just like to."

Nestor shrugs. "Be my guest."

·   ·   ·

The snow around Our Lady of Tears is trampled into slush from the feet of those coming to donate food, clothing, and blankets, and the feet of those coming to carry them away. A large poster has been erected in the churchyard. There will be a benefit concert for the fire victims.

The peculiar myopia of the historian has prevented him from seeing the vitality of this community. He saw the ghosts of the Irish and Italian immigrant workers and never noticed what is still going on. Undoubtedly, just as in the past, whole villages are migrating here, one or two bringing over more, then more, all allied and interconnected.

Will, brushing past the people waiting to get into the church, tries to read their histories on their faces wrapped in woolen scarves against the snow, but he fails. He hasn't learned to interpret the clues of the present.

It's uncanny how the borders of this fire duplicate those of the fire of 1902, which began in a railway shed, close to but down-wind of the Appleyard mills. Then, of course, it was the wealthy who lost their homes, capitalists of Northern European stock. You wouldn't have seen them coming around with wheelbarrows to salvage whatever they could from the cinders. Many of them had second homes in New York City and probably weren't even here the night the wind blew flames across tree-lined streets, devouring Victorian gingerbread, lapping up ornamental gardens. Instead of rebuilding in town, the homeless rich set their new residences up in the hills. This time, they did not display their houses but hid them at the end of long, winding drives.

Time was running out for the old mansions anyway. The auto-mobile was coming, and in ten years everyone would have been leaving for the hills, getting away from the pollution of their own factories. The fire merely accomplished in a single stroke what would have taken twenty years. Instead of each mansion making its own trip down the social ladder, being partitioned into apartments, having smaller houses squeezed in on its lawns, all the houses died in their glory, gone so fast that people must have thought they dreamed the streets with the arching elms, the iron gates, the mansard roofs. Only the photographs bear witness now, finely detailed, made from platinum plates.

It has something to do with the wind, probably, the reason why this one followed the path of the other. The fire fighting equipment was better this time, but the houses were closer together. There was no subzero temperature to fight as there was last time, but water pressure was low and certain pipes were clogged. Hydrants by the mill, where the fire began, were not working.

It's the last chance for them to rescue their treasures out of the ashes before the wreckers and earth movers come in. Family albums, wedding pictures—Regina knows what they're searching for. All immigrants are alike. She looks for a clear place to park and sees Will Appleyard, standing with his back to the destruction.

Regina honks her horn. Will comes over to shake her hand through the open window. "I was admiring the view of the river. There was never any way to see the river, before the fire."

"Isn't it incredible that no one had the foresight to set part of the riverbank aside for a park?" he asks as she locks the Toyota. "It would have been so easy, after the last fire."

"It would seem so." She's irritated with him for thinking about parks when he should be mourning the destruction of wedding pictures and christening dresses. She decides it's a class failing, not an individual one. "I can get you into the mill now, or what's left of it, if you want to take a look," she offers.

There's a new guard at the mill, a black woman, with a face Will thinks he knows from some other context, but one so remote that he can't connect the two. She neither avoids his eyes nor gives any sign of recognition. Perhaps he's mistaken, suffering from déjà vu. Regina has only to mention Nestor Bird and the security guard lets them through, warning them to watch where they place their feet.

The snow has blown in through jagged black gaps in the roof, etching white lines over the charred machinery, shrouding fallen beams. The two women are making a slow tour of the inside. Regina, gawky next to the diminutive guard, is bent over her notebook. With their low voices murmuring, they could be nuns doing stations of the cross. Will stands in his great-grandfather's temple, inhaling frozen ashes and falling snow while the sun breaks through the clouds and strikes the wall at the end of the mill. The bricks glow golden rose like a Renaissance fresco. "Look!" he cries. "The color of that wall. Incredible."

The other walls too, Will notices, even though they are in shadow, possess the color. The heat of the fire must have glazed the bricks this miraculous hue.

He expected, when he finally saw the mill, to find it haunted with the sounds of machinery and the voices of workers; instead he sees an evanescent convergence of blazing pink wall, white snow on black beams, and women watching the sun against the bricks: the present, only the present, without future or past.

Snow has piled up against the dining room window, marked at the top by a thin black line of grit.

Some coffee spilled when Delia set it on the table. She went to the kitchen to get a sponge to wipe it up, and now she seems to have forgotten what she was doing there. *The sponge*, Will feels like prompting, but he doesn't want to embarrass her. Delia's hands flutter over the countertop, as if she's hoping they will remember and light on the right object, but they don't. She puts them into the pockets of her dungarees and comes back to the table, sees the spill, remembers, and goes back, this time successfully, for the sponge.

Her hand, too small to cover the sponge, pushes it across the table.

A fat black fly is methodically trying to bash his brains out on the window pane.

Will has come to propose marriage. What seemed clear on Christmas Eve has furred over. Somehow, the image of the princess on the drawbridge is becoming confused with this woman, in all her contradictions, who is trying unsuccessfully to wipe off her dining table.

Marriage in the abstract was a fine idea, but when he sees Delia here before him in the flesh, it descends into particulars: going to bed together at night, getting up in the morning and having breakfast. It's the fly, the suicidal fly, that is distracting him, paralyzing his imagination. He cannot imagine being married to Delia.

The fly has fallen on its back and is beating its wings frantically, trying to right itself. Will wonders if he should help it up.

"Hi, Mom. Hi, Will." Lazaro comes in, changing the current in the air, saving the fly, which takes off in search of a new window.

The hanging dresses rock back and forth in the cold breeze. Delia wraps her muffler close around her neck. "You're going to see Abuela tonight?" she asks Lazaro.

"Yeah." He goes into the kitchen and comes out with a couple of cookies in his hand.

"What time are you coming back? Not too late, I hope."

"I'm staying over," he says through a mouthful of cookie. "It's a party. Abuela's giving it for me."

"On a school night?"

"I'm gonna do my homework now. Don't worry about it."

Lazaro closes his bedroom door. Delia studies it, as if there is something to be divined from the pattern of cracked paint. "He's in trouble."

"In school, you mean?"

"No, I don't know."

"Have you called the school?"

"I wouldn't know who to call."

"His advisor, or the guidance counselor—" Will checks himself. He sounds like Cass. He feels the way she must toward Delia, frustrated, hopeless. Delia doesn't know about guidance counselors, how to use conventional means of communication. She relies on "vibrations." Will wonders if Delia could use a psychiatrist, but he doesn't see how it could work. Her thoughts are pre-Freudian, medieval.

"I'll call, if you want—"

She consults the paint cracks again. "It isn't school. It's something else."

Will looks down at the table so she won't get him reading paint cracks too.

"Could we go to your mother's in New York, if there's trouble, if we need to get away?"

This is the time to tell her about St. Louis, the house with the basketball hoop on the garage, but the words don't come out. She's looking at him. Can she read thoughts?

"Will? You told me your mother has lots of rooms in her apartment. Would she mind? Just a few weeks?"

Will pictures Delia and Lazaro, Delia's dresses, the Tarot cards, all moving into his mother's over-furnished immaculate apartment.

"You have such a nice smile, Will."

She says she knows she and his mother will get along fine; it's only for a few weeks.

Not until later, after Will and Lazaro have freed his car from the snowbank, and Will has dropped Lazaro off at his abuela's house, does Will recover from the confusion Delia threw him into. He didn't actually say she could live at his mother's, or did he? Turning to go under the highway, he suddenly pulls over to the side, risking getting stuck in the snow again. He could go back and explain about St. Louis to Delia, about faculty wives, but he's afraid of what he'll find: another fly, a disturbing movement of dresses in the doorway, something else to cloud his mind, get it going off in weird directions. He carefully steers his way out of the snow and surprises himself by turning onto the highway—eastbound, for New York City.

"You're not afraid to walk in Dublin at night?"

"No. It's Hispanic, that's all. It seems safe enough."

"It isn't, but there's a good Italian restaurant here left over from better days. Family run. Fine people. Florio's. Ever been there?"

"No."

"It won't be around much longer. The kids are third generation, like you. They're all going to Harvard Business School or getting law degrees."

Regina has to press up against Nestor to let a woman pass on the snowy sidewalk. The woman is carrying a cage of some sort wrapped in a towel. It's the security guard at the mill, but she doesn't recognize Regina. Regina wonders what kind of life the guard leads, here in the barrio Nestor calls Dublin, and what kind of mission she's on, carrying a cage through snow-covered streets.

Nestor, instinctively responding to the contact of Regina's body, puts his arm around her waist. The former ladies' man still lives somewhere inside those two hundred and sixty pounds of aging flesh. Regina pulls away. Perhaps her homely face isn't protection enough from Nestor, whose wife, they are saying in the office, has been away an unusually long time.

If anyone had been watching them lately, he would think they were having an affair, the way Nestor speaks to her several times a day, dragging her off to restaurants for lunches and dinners. Maybe he doesn't know how to relate to a woman as a colleague, so he treats her as he used to treat his mistresses. Apparently he was quite the roué in his younger days.

Florio's has an interior that both infuriates a third-generation heart and makes it melt with homesickness: deep, red banquettes; flocked wallpaper; framed technicolor wedding-pictures; oil paintings of romanticized Roman ruins.

A florid-faced maitre d', with the build of an ex-bodyguard, gives Nestor a secluded corner-table.

"The thing about Snow"—Nestor stops to motion for another bourbon and ice. Regina is still nursing a Campari and soda—"Goddamned Snow," he continues in a lowered voice, "was planning the fire from the beginning. He was going to pocket the money for the renovations and then burn the evidence and collect the insurance. I bet he was even behind those other warehouses that burned around town in the past year or so. He was setting the stage, establishing a wave of arson." Nestor swirls the ice in his glass.

"But, he decided he didn't want to take the risk, so he jumped ship with a tank on his back, probably had another boat waiting to take him on board. In the unlikely event that the insurance money does come through, I'll bet you dollars to donuts he's set up a way so it filters through to him, to wherever he's hiding out down there."

"Then that's the way we can find him. We can find out who gets the money from the insurance and trace him that way."

"I don't want to find Snow."

"Don't you want to bring him to justice?"

Nestor smiles at her choice of words. "I don't want to bring him to justice. I want to cut him into croutons and throw him to the sharks. Goddamned son of a bitch. But what's the use, darling? I don't have to tell you that I'm tied to him, that I am personally responsible for his state loan, his bank loans, not to mention the responsibility to the investors. They can sue me. What am I talking

about? You think I'm worrying about the money? It's the dishonor,
the dishonor." This last word rumbles in his blubbery chest.

"But isn't it better to take the honorable way and make a clean
breast of it? Hire a private investigator. Have him traced, bring
him back—"

Nestor waves a hand in front of his face. "Listen, Regina," he
leans his jowls toward her. "I want to tell you something, strictly
confidential."

Carmen knew very well who they were, the woman lawyer who
works for Nestor Bird, and the old man himself, and she could
guess where they were going: Florio's. Why else would two outsiders be walking through the barrio at the dinner hour? She had
also recognized Appleyard at the mill, but she didn't say anything
because she is used to being overlooked. Her race and poverty
make her invisible to the outsiders. She has nothing to gain by
making herself known to them. It does not surprise her that these
faces are turning up, crossing and recrossing her path. Mama is
bringing the forces into play. It is expected that these people will
be drawn in tighter, anyone who by blood or circumstance or sympathy can offer protection.

Carmen adjusts the towel to keep the draft out of the cage.
There is so much to do, much to buy. They've been cooking for
days, a whole case of rum delivered to the house—the expense.
But Mama would give her life savings, her own life and Carmen's
too, Carmen knows this, to save the boy, the only one of the one
who died.

Carmen climbs the stairs, holding the cage high. It's her third
trip out tonight, but she isn't tired. She is never tired, because she
is fierce. The fury doesn't abate with age; it grows, giving her
strength, giving her more and more energy.

Mama hears her angry steps and opens the door. She is splendid, dressed in a robe and turban, golden wings painted over her wild, unseeing eyes. Mama has no fury. She is royalty. She does not meddle with other kingdoms, never feels the pain of humiliation.

Mama holds the cage while Carmen takes the doves out and puts them in the special cage hanging from the ceiling. One settles himself on the perch. His mate fluffs her feathers and looks out with meek pink eyes.

The furniture has been pushed to the edges of the room, the carpet rolled up along one side. Borrowed card tables lined up side by side, covered with lace, recovered with heavy plastic, hold platters of food, gleaming bottles of soda and rum. Santa Barbara is dressed in beads and charms; green bananas, corn, and okra are at her feet. Carmen brought in buckets of dirt and set candles in them. She hung bright rags from the ceiling, silk neckties. In the dark hallway, where she didn't see him before, is the boy. When she is away from him, Carmen wants to hate him, but when she sees him, tears come into her eyes, she loves him that much. He is so pale and thin, she could hold his arm up to the light and see through to the bones. Yet there is something hard too, deep inside, that the light has to go around. She holds him for a minute in the hall; he wraps thin arms around her while she pours angry waves of love over him, over his smooth, unknowable center.

Three hover around the chafing dish, the captain and two acolytes, whipping clouds of steam, preparing Nestor's zabaglione. They have been in constant attendance all evening, and through it all— the laying on of fresh silver, the pouring of wine, the supplying with bread, the grindings of pepper—Nestor has continued his low, urgent confession, ignoring the waiters as if they were deaf-mutes. Initially Regina was flattered to be his confidant, but now she understands that it is precisely because she is young, female, ugly, and powerless that he is using her to hear him out. She is one step better than the empty chair. In fact, when she left to go to the ladies' room and came back, Nestor was still leaning forward over the table, as if he had continued even while she was gone.

The confession concerns his enormous sexual appetite, something he picked up in the war, like a disease. He came home knowing he could never marry because he would never be faithful to one woman. He came to lay it out before Lavinia, who had been waiting for him all that time, for him to come back and marry her because they had, before he left—well, it didn't matter, really. She could have found someone else. It's not as if they were Greek peasants even back then, where you have to show a bloodstained sheet on your wedding night. Anyway, he told her everything. Nestor was not raised to be a cheat, a liar.

Then Lavinia, with all the cunning of an orphan (she had lost her father during the Spanish Civil War; her mother had died of cancer while Nestor was away), with all the subtlety of her Spanish upbringing, made the move that was to lead him down the road to his doom. She forgave him.

"I didn't ask her for forgiveness, goddamnit!" Nestor's fist banged down on the tabletop. "I came to tell her what it was like. I wanted to give it to her straight, and she turned it all around. She forgave me because of the war; she was certain I would be a good and faithful husband. She even convinced me for a time, although somewhere I knew it wasn't true. And that was my undoing."

Nestor drains his wineglass. "Never underestimate the power of the weak." Priapic tendencies had returned, stronger than ever, after Nestor's marriage. He stayed out late, took afternoons off, even disappeared for weekends. Lavinia never complained, never asked, never *acknowledged.* Nestor even heard her—when his excuse had been too lame, or when he had simply declined to offer one—making up stories for the children or friends, about how he had suddenly been called away on business.

The more debauched he became, the more Lavinia clung to her ideal, her first lover, the boy she knew before the war. He became more reckless, "trying to make her see, so I could see." Finally, at his lowest, or his highest, or his most desperate point, he fell in love with a classmate of Delia's, "seventeen years old, in a Saint Agnes jumper and lace-up oxfords." She was second-generation Polish, the only daughter of socially prominent parents.

He was responsible even then. Before he began taking her to out-of-town motels, he sent her to his friend the gynecologist who inserted a coil and informed him, by the way, that she wasn't a virgin, not that he cared. He preferred it that way, but she did lie to him, an indication of character.

He was madly in love. He doesn't know what came over him, some mid-life thing, no doubt. He took terrible chances. Lavinia, predictably, rose above it all. The girl, unpredictably, got pregnant. The family, supposedly good Catholics, wanted an abortion, but Nestor wouldn't allow it. "That might have been my son, the one to carry on the family name. I couldn't let her."

Nestor went to Lavinia, explained that he would need a divorce so he could marry the pregnant schoolgirl. Instead of anger, Lavinia showered him with pity: poor Nestor, to be trapped by a shallow, scheming girl, to be ousted from his home and loved ones! She vowed to remain true to him, just as she had during the war, until he came back.

The waiters wheel the chafing dish away, leaving their offering behind: two long-stemmed goblets filled with foamy cream.

Nestor picks up his spoon. "She miscarried after four months. She didn't want to go home, or to go to school. All she wanted was to get pregnant again. That didn't happen."

Nestor drives his spoon into the middle of his dessert and begins to eat, letting the stuff slide down his throat without tasting it.

Regina, occupied with organizing the few crumbs that the waiter missed when he brushed off their table between courses, hears

Nestor droning on, between spoonfuls, about how Donna doesn't care for him, just uses him to pay the bills, how she conceals things from him, how he doesn't know her friends—

"But listen to this," he commands. Reluctantly Regina lifts her head, and his eyes lock into hers, forcing her to remain.

"I have never once cheated on Donna. It's remarkable, isn't it?" He wills her to nod assent. "My sex drive plummeted." His hand hits the table with a bang. Waiters, alerted, turn. Regina imagines a fat penis losing its erection. "Because she has no illusions. I don't have to wrest my true self out of her ideal image of me. Now you understand what that woman did to me."

"Lavinia?"

"Yes, of course—Lavinia. She forced me into a life of duplicity. I was raised to be an honest man. It's a family tradition. Lavinia forced me to be a cheat and a liar. Furthermore," he raises a finger as if Regina were about to interrupt him, which she is not, "I think this is what led me finally into Snow's trap. I allowed myself to be seduced by him because I had lost the habit of strict probity." Nestor spoons more yellow dessert into his mouth.

"Now, investigation into Snow's activities is going to implicate me. And he's messed up a lot of things, not just Grand Land. I've been scratching around. Those Caribbean vacations for instance, you don't need a trained dog to smell out what's rotten there. If they get him back, there are going to be fresh indictments for years, and every time, Grand Land is going to come floating to the top like a dead fish." Nestor has pushed his empty goblet, with tracks on it where he has scraped against the glass, to one side, and he is looking at hers, untouched in front of her. Regina sticks her spoon in it.

"I don't want to be involved in a cover-up." Regina means it to come out strong, but her voice betrays her, lilting at the end, an invitation to be convinced.

"Of course you don't. Are you going to eat that or not?"

"I—I'm not hungry."

"Do you mind?"

She takes her spoon out and hands the goblet over. There is something about this man, the power and bulk of him, or his assumption that she will go along, that makes him impossible to resist. She can't even deny him her dessert.

She's not going to falsify records, numbers, she manages to stipulate. He wouldn't dream of being involved in something that low, he protests. He is merely not going to facilitate the investigation, not do anything to speed it along.

"When they find the arsonists, which might be any time now—" Regina says.

"That could be a problem, depending on who they are and how much they know. By the look of it, they weren't too professional. Snow is such a cheap bastard. He probably got kids, locals culled from Wallingford's vast reservoir of juvenile delinquents, who would do it for five bucks and some marijuana, no questions asked."

After Nestor has walked her back to her car, in the garage near the office, Regina wonders what the connection was between Nestor's long confession and the Snow matter. Something was missing in the narrative. She's seen Donna a few times. She has a pretty face but there's no life in it. And her ankles are heavy.

11

—————

Yu should get into past lives."

"I never had much luck with that—"

"Or communication with the deceased."

"I don't really—"

"How about astrology, doing charts—"

"It's too complicated. I never understood all those planets—"

"But the Tarot is so limiting, and a little tacky, for the caliber of client you've been attracting. If you could expand into past lives, you could give hour-long consultations. You could charge a hundred dollars, easily."

"I could?"

"Goodness, yes. The people you've been doing prefer to pay a hundred dollars."

"Do you charge—?"

"It lasts a full hour, of course. And you make a tape of the consultation to present to the client at the end. And then follow-up calls for free."

"A hundred dollars—"

"You could just as easily ask a hundred, with the clients you've been attracting."

"I could?"

"My God, yes. You've tapped into some interesting groups, and you've done well by them."

"How do you know?"

The president of the International Psychics' Society, whose last name Delia's forgotten but who's insisted she be called Evelyn, laughs, and Delia can't help laughing with her, she has such an easy way about her. Evelyn reminds Delia of a butterscotch sundae, with her creamy plump skin, her golden hair—fake, of course, at this age, but nice just the same.

"We're a gossipy group. Very gossipy, I don't mind telling you, and we call each other constantly. And we visit. I'm leaving next week for Brazil to visit a member, marvelous woman, who does past lives. We are the *crème de la crème*." She bends over her plate to take in a forkful of fettucini with white truffle sauce. "We're the ones who are quoted in the columns, who get flown places for premieres and opening nights," she says through her fettucini, gesturing with her fork.

Delia wishes she could keep her mind on what Evelyn is telling her, but she is too worried about what lunch will cost in this expensive restaurant and too concerned about Lazaro, who spent the night at the Señora's. She should have called this morning to make sure he went to school, but Carmen would have been nasty.

"What keeps you in New Jersey?"

"What?"

"Why do you live all the way out in New Jersey? Does your husband work there?"

"My husband died."

Evelyn reaches a freckled hand across the table to rest on Delia's. "I'm sorry." Green eyes flecked with gold liquefy in sympathy. "I too lost my husband some years back. In fact, that is what moved me over to the spiritual side. It's often the way, I think. The death of a loved one . . . I have a charming friend, a French woman who lives outside Paris, who had the same experience. Her husband died young, but, refusing to believe he was gone forever, she developed her powers for contacting the dead. Now her husband serves as a medium and she gives regular séances for certain officials high up in the French government."

"Your friend is also a member of the society?"

"We all are, my dear. And we would like you to be."

"How much does it cost?"

"Nothing. No dues. No newsletter, no mailings. It's a perfect psychic society because we simply tune in to each other. There's no membership list, no voting. I'm currently president, but that could change, evolve into someone else as president, or there might be three or four."

"I guess I could join then—"

"Of course. It's only to your advantage. No one refuses."

Delia should move to New York, Evelyn says. She is wasting her good looks conducting her business by phone. She could easily do three clients a day. Three clients a day at a hundred dollars per! Delia can't do the arithmetic, but she knows it would put her way ahead of what she's getting now. Would it be enough to afford the rent here, maybe send Lazaro to private school, have a credit card like Evelyn, who pays the bill as if it's the most natural thing in the world?

They part on Madison Avenue with hugs and kisses. Delia can feel Evelyn's body heat through her fur coat, something cream-colored with golden spots—lynx, perhaps? In spite of the cold (it dropped to zero in Wallingford last night and must be no more than ten degrees out even now), Delia decides to walk to Port Authority. The cab ride to the restaurant cost her five dollars. She doesn't want to spend another five getting back, and she isn't certain she could find her way by bus. She has a terrible fear of being on a bus that suddenly takes a wrong turn and whisks her far out of her way. Better to walk, and that will give her time to calm down after lunch with Evelyn.

It never occurred to Delia that she could make money, that she could be the one to move them out of the place where Jaime left them. But today, talking to Evelyn, walking on Madison Avenue (which has no snow, not any, whereas the walk in front of her house is covered, crusted and icy), it seems possible; in fact, it seems right.

The signs are propitious: the way her clothes have been in the mornings, springing to leap out the door; the way Will offered his mother's apartment to her; even Hugo, yesterday, came bursting in, demanding that she and Lazaro go with him to Florida. He had their tickets in his hand. He pulled a suitcase out from under Delia's bed and began stuffing her dresses into it, said she had to get out for Lazaro's sake, that he would marry her down there, that it was all arranged.

He was so positive, so forceful, that Delia became confused and thought for a moment he might be The One. She asked him to let her see the palm of his hand, the strong, clever hand of a car mechanic.

"Well, what do you see?" he asked when she turned it over quickly and laid her hand on top.

"I'm sorry."

"What? What did you see?"

"You're not The One."

"Look, there's going to be trouble. That's all I can tell you. Lazaro is—you can't understand because you're like living in your own world, OK? It's like, you know how certain people are born color-blind, like red and blue are the same color to them? Well, you were born with eyes that can't see certain things, OK? You can look right at them and not see them. It's like, to the person who is color-blind, red and blue don't exist, OK? You understand what I'm saying?"

What she understood was the way Hugo was standing, as if he were trying to surround her with his body, to carry her away, her and Lazaro.

"Don't worry," she told him. "I feel it, that the time is coming near for us to go away, but not with you. You aren't The One."

"The time isn't near, it's now, and I'm sorry if I don't look like the prince you've been waiting for, but you can't afford to sit around dreaming. For Lazaro's sake—"

It's Lazaro she's thinking about. Hugo can rescue Lazaro, but only for a short while. What happens when Hugo's life line ends?

Delia clutches her coat around her (the camel's hair her parents bought her for high school; the fuzziness has worn off and it lets in the cold). Maybe Evelyn is right. Maybe Delia is the one who can pull them both out. Perhaps what she's been waiting for all along is not someone else, from outside, but for her own powers to develop, so that she could be strong enough to get them out.

Walking with her head down against the wind, she collides with a young woman. "Oh, sorry!" they say in one breath. Her hair, long and dark, trails across her face, which is beautiful, filled with tears. She pulls her scarf around her head and rushes on, pursued by an older man with longitudinal creases in his cheeks. He walks with a limp (newly acquired, Delia can see, because he's impatient with it). He shoulders past her, his eyes fixed on the back of the beautiful girl.

"Let her go," Delia transmits, but he continues hobbling up the street, with his tanned, arrogant face, his humble, wounded leg.

The light hurts his eyes and the noise goes around inside his head like an empty oil drum. His abuela made him go to school. She thinks school is a holy place. If you go in enough times you come out white and rich. Good thing she can't see. Good thing she can't know.

Carmen would have understood what he meant, but she had gone to work early, the early shift. "I can't go to school like this. I'm too weak. I'm sick. They'll kill me," he told Abuela, but she shooed him out the door with smiles and pats. She hustled him out along with someone else, some kind of cousin who had fallen asleep in a corner and forgotten to leave with the others.

So far, amazingly, no one has messed with him. It's because he's keeping quiet, laying low, and wearing a mean look. Or maybe it's Chango, his sacred leopard. Maybe Chango has decided to protect him, like last night when he let him pass the burning torches over his body and he didn't even feel them. He swallowed fire. Carmen handed him the torch, and he put it down his throat, ate it right up, swallowed its hotness down into his stomach, where it burns still.

A lot of people came up to touch him and look at him, the Followers, Carmen said, the ones who used to come to his father for advice, who used to bring him things. It's embarrassing now to think about it, but then it seemed like a natural thing to have all these people wanting to touch him, like Chango was sending everyone power and luck through Lazaro's body.

The bell goes off inside his head, jangling his brain. Everyone pushes by. Lazaro gets up slowly, old-man slow, stiff from dancing for Chango all night, dancing to the drums and the ancient African words Chango loves. Who knows what they mean? Abuela maybe.

The teacher is looking at him because he's the last one to leave, getting up from his desk like a slow old man. "What do you want?" She's a little thing, in a brown suit, scared, he realizes, of him. It's the first time a teacher has ever been afraid of him.

"Nothing." He feels a grin coming on his face, not his but Chango's. It's the kind of grin that might hurt you or let you alone. "I'm sick."

"Do you want to go to the nurse?" Her voice is sharp.

"No, just—you don't have an aspirin, do you?"

She looks at him, trying to decide if he's telling the truth. She's a little thing, but he's still smaller. Keeping her eyes on him, she opens her desk drawer and pulls out a bottle. "Here. Have a Tylenol."

Lazaro saunters up to the desk, feeling better already. "Thanks."

Chango. The spirit of Chango. That's why he feels so lousy. It isn't the rum, the cigars, it's Chango burning in his stomach, drying out his mouth. His legs, his arms, shake in Chango's invisible hot wind, and his brain aches from his searing breath. But he has the power. Did you see how the teacher looked at him? Walking down the hall, even the bad spots where the guards don't come, no one messes with him. They clear a space when he approaches. Look out. Here comes Chango's child.

Used to be, before today, he wouldn't leave the school without protection. He'd hang back waiting for a group of bigger guys he knew wouldn't hurt him, and he'd attach himself to their group, to get him through the streets. Today he strolls out, a cigarette in his hand as if ready to light up as soon as he gets out, but he won't because with Chango's fire still burning in his belly, he'd vomit at the smell of smoke. He goes right by and no one challenges him. They leave him alone because they see it, the fire at the back of his eyes.

"I can't let you take me out, William. I haven't cooked your dinner all week, and you paid me for the groceries—"

Lavinia's already tied on her apron and is rushing around the kitchen opening and closing cupboards. He should have called but he didn't know. At the last minute he realized he couldn't spend one more night at his mother's apartment, feeling misplaced or displaced, definitely in the wrong place.

Lavinia was at the sally port before Will had even turned off the ignition, welcoming him home, taking him by the arm. Will kissed her on the cheek, surprising himself and her, and embarrassing them both a little—a contrast to the premeditated pecks he and his mother had exchanged upon parting. ("Well now, that was a nice visit, certainly not expected. Come again, Will, but do call first. Mrs. Jivinsky likes to be warned. . . .") Mrs. Jivinsky, his mother's housekeeper. When Will isn't there the two of them live like friends (two small tables, two armchairs pulled up in front of the television so they can watch their favorite shows while they eat). He wonders why his mother and Mrs. Jivinsky think they have to go through the charade of mistress and servant when he's in the house.

Will finds he's grinning openly at Lavinia flying around the kitchen, trying to come up with something besides cookies for dinner.

"William dear, look in the cabinet by the dining table, where I keep the whiskies, and see if there's any dry vermouth."

Tuna. She has tuna. If you have tuna fish you can have dinner. She had to send Will out for a moment so she could think. It was puzzling and disturbing the way he left so abruptly—when was it? Tuesday, after seeing Delia. He had seen Delia and he had left. Had he asked her to marry him? Delia didn't seem to think so, but then, Delia often misses things.

Rice. And saffron. Saffron that she bought on impulse after Will had given her grocery money. It's such a luxury but it reminds her of Spain. If she can find an onion she's in business.

"Vermouth! I thought we had some. Let's have a small glass to celebrate your return, shall we, William? And I'll use the rest in the paella."

In fact, it's tuna and rice, but it tastes wonderful. They eat it at the kitchen table, which Lavinia has set with a linen cloth and candles.

"What's the spice in here?"

"Saffron. This is a corruption of something Mama used to make in Spain. Poor man's paella. We weren't poor for Spaniards, but for Americans in Spain, we were. Genteelly poor. Living in the castle with Nestor, having everything, always felt temporary to me—everything new, nothing patched. It never felt quite real. Isn't that a funny thought, William? I guess whatever you grow up with is what always feels like home. You always try to get back to it, like those eels who live in the rivers in Belgium, who suddenly have to go swimming all the way back over the Atlantic Ocean to spawn in the Caribbean because that's where they were born—look at me, a dotty old woman rattling on about eels. William, you must wonder why you ever came back. You didn't just come to pack your bags, did you?"

"No, not at all. I'm sorry. I left suddenly, didn't I? It was my research, things I needed in New York. But I was just thinking how at home I feel here. Isn't that strange?"

Lavinia ducks her head to dab at her eyes with her napkin. William can just reach out and touch her heart sometimes, but he's so exasperating! Of course he's at home here. This is where he's meant to be. But why can't he see it? Why can't he get on with it and marry Delia?

"I'm afraid all I have is cookies for dessert, William dear. And not those nice ones from the Italian bakery. These are supermarket package things. But tomorrow, maybe you'll drive me to town and I'll stock up, since you're going to be here awhile."

She dresses in black: black and white bandanna around her forehead to catch the sweat; black leotard and tights; black, cutoff T-shirt on top. Around her waist is the sweat-stained weight-lifter's belt. It's the image of herself she is most familiar with, because the weight room is a narcissist's paradise with three walls of mirrors. The fourth wall is plate glass, inviting passers-by in as audience.

By unspoken agreement the regulars this year are dressing in black and white. Once in a while a newcomer stumbles in wearing magenta sweats, but everyone quickly conforms—all those mirrors.

It is not vanity that keeps Cass checking the mirrors. She watches her body with professional detachment to see that knees are over feet, abdominals held in, glutes tight. Each muscle is properly worked in the correct sequence: a general warm-up for the large muscle groups and then down to the particular, the deltoids, pecs, biceps, triceps, the lats.

"Cass! How's it going?"

"Hey, Charles."

He massages her shoulders with his lifting gloves still on. They trade comments, a little bonhomie, but that's as far as it's going to go. Charles might like to take it further, but Cass is staying away from anyone who could be bisexual these days, because of AIDS. That eliminates most of the good-looking men in San Francisco, almost everyone at the gym.

"You're hard as a brick back here." Charles is pressing her trapezius. "This is where you carry all your angst, like you're tensing up before someone hits you. You weren't an abused child, were you?"

"Only psychologically."

"Like everyone else." His hands are strong, but gentle and methodical. Cass longs to give in to them, but she can't because she doesn't know the price. Everything you take must be paid back in kind. She doesn't know what price Charles will ask.

"Thanks." She shakes her shoulders. "That feels a lot better."

Cass puts one knee on the bench and brings the ten-pound dumbbell up smartly to her shoulder, exhaling as she brings it up, inhaling as she lets it down. Delia is moving to New York. She seems to think that Will's mother can put her up until she finds her own place. Some woman named Evelyn told Delia she can make a hundred dollars an hour. Delia thinks Evelyn is going to help her get started. It's difficult to know what exactly is going on with this Evelyn, who is president of something called the International Psychics' Society and whom Delia has confused with her fairy godmother. "What's she getting out of this?" Cass wanted to know. "Why is she taking you out to lunch and making you a member of her society? Why should she be helping you? You're in competition, after all."

"She's helping me—" Delia's voice went vague. Cass was taking a line of reasoning Delia couldn't follow.

"What's in it for her? What does she want you to do for her?"

"She wants to help me. That's the way she is."

"She's just good." Cass meant it sarcastically.

"That's it!" Delia's voice brightened, as if Cass had finally grasped a point Delia didn't have the words to put across. "It is her nature to help. It gives her pleasure. She has a golden aura, Cass. It's beautiful to see."

Cass rests while Charles uses the bench to do his chest press. The veins stand out on his forehead when he does this, making Cass think of how he would be in bed—appealing and funny, probably.

Delia believes that people are good, that they want to help someone—help her—for the sheer joy of it. The laws of thermodynamics, I and II, don't exist for her.

Will, for instance. Delia is full of plans to go live in Will's mother's apartment in New York.

"Are you and Will getting married?"

"Oh, no. I'm just staying there until I can afford my own place. Do you think I'll be able to afford it? If I see three people every day for five times a week, at a hundred dollars a session. What does that work out to? Could I get an apartment for that?"

"Then Will hasn't asked you to marry him?"

"No, Cass. We're friends, that's all."

"He's offering his mother's apartment, and his mother has agreed, just because you're a friend?"

"Because Lazaro has to get out of Wallingford."

Of course Lazaro has to get out of Wallingford, but what's the urgency? What happened? Delia couldn't say. Some vibration she's picking up, or maybe her clothes told her—

"What's wrong? Did you pull something?"

"I'm thinking about my sister."

"Family." Charles grins, showing perfect white teeth. He doesn't look like an AIDS victim. Maybe if he wore a condom—

Cass drops to the floor for push-ups. Is Delia's view, that people help each other for the fun of it, saintly or selfish? In a way it absolves her from ever having to pay back. What if it's a convenient and willful refusal to see?

"Don't you see," Cass told Delia, "he's offering his mother's place because he's in love with you. Men don't protect women because they like to be gallant. They do it because they want to sleep with them. It's biological."

Delia said she didn't think Will thought about those things. Delia with her Latin husband, his quick hands. She doesn't pick up the more subtle signals, like the way Will's eyes sneak over your body, against his volition—clouded, inward-looking eyes, indicating trapped reserves of passion.

"Are you using that bench?"

An Oriental man with a black T-shirt is looking down at her. Cass gets up and shakes out her arms. "No, go ahead."

Charles, leaning up against the double shoulder machine, is chatting with a boy in lycra black-and-white tights. The boy has dyed his shoulder-length hair black. Cass wonders if everyone at the gym will start either dyeing their hair black or bleaching it white.

They almost seem to be doing a dance together. Charles's hands come together and push something aside. The other boy takes up the gesture and executes a variation, his hands spread wide. The mirrors repeat their movements, flowing from one to the other, the nod of a head sending waves to the other head, which bobs in response.

"Why are you always looking at the edges?" Delia asked her at Christmas.

"What?"

"The edges of people, their boundaries. You think of people as entities, wrapped up in their skins—"

"Of course they are wrapped in their skins—"

Delia shook her head impatiently. She has trouble expressing herself, always has. She was in an old shirt of Jaime's, sitting cross-legged on her bed, looking more like a kid than a grown woman. Cass was already under the covers. Her lamp was on. She was trying to read.

"What I mean is, you don't see the connecting streams—"

"Streams."

"Of energy."

"I hate this kind of psychic babbling. You know that."

"But we're all connected, don't you see?"

Cass shut her book and turned out the light.

"We are points in a web," Delia's voice continued softly in the dark. "We're just like knots where the threads connect. I look at the web and you only consider the knots."

Although Charles's back is to her, Cass can see his face in the mirror, how it is taking in points of light from the other boy's face, and increasing them, sending them back. Both faces are glowing with the pleasure of energy exchanged.

Charles is definitely gay. Cass turns her back on both of them and does some work on her deltoids.

12

———

Lavinia and Bubbles have been helping out at Our Lady of Tears most mornings, showing the people left homeless by the fire how to fill out claims for emergency aid, petitions for temporary housing. Lavinia, with her rapid, slurry, Puerto Rican Spanish, is very good at this. But even Bubbles, with no Spanish at all, is managing well with hand gestures and a lot of expression. Afterward, they both go to the store, where they have sandwiches and share a pot of tea. Bubbles says the day has been going faster since she's been working at Our Lady and opening the shop at one instead of eleven.

Lavinia took the key ring to the Señora yesterday, the only time she's actually requested a reading. Bubbles asked her to. She's been giving Lavinia anxious glances all morning, looking for hints as to what the Señora said. Lavinia still doesn't quite know how she should put it to Bubbles.

"Chaotic?" Bubbles sets down her teacup.

"In a cosmological sense," Lavinia tries. "The word she used is one you use for nature, for instance—a blind, disturbing power, not necessarily malicious."

"But chaotic. She must have the wrong person, Lavinia. You know Edgar. He was the soul of organization, his shoes always polished, shirts impeccable."

"Maybe she simply meant energetic," Lavinia says, although she knows it isn't true.

"Did she say he is still alive?" Bubbles leans forward into the light, where Lavinia can see that she has bags under her eyes. She longs to rest a hand on her shoulder and tell her that it's fruitless for a woman her age to be in love, and with Edgar Snow, who according to the Señora might do harm or good but whose purposes are as whimsical as a god's. She wishes she could lie, but how can she when Bubbles is fixing her lavender contact lenses on her with such need and trust?

"She says he is." Lavinia's own chin trembles to see Bubbles' eyes fill up. "But he's in danger."

"Oh dear!"

"He's always in danger. It's part of his nature."

"What kind of danger?"

"She didn't say." But again, the words the Señora chose implied. And Lavinia didn't ask. She regretted bringing up the whole topic with the Señora, who looked worn out. Lavinia seemed to have come in the middle of housecleaning. The windows were open in spite of the cold. The parlor rug was rolled up, and the plastic-covered chair Lavinia sat in, still wearing her coat, was wet from being wiped off. Why two perfectly neat women should need to tear the house apart to clean it, Lavinia didn't know. Carmen must have a thing for cleanliness. It couldn't be the Señora, who can't even see. All through the session, Lavinia could hear Carmen slapping the mop around in the kitchen.

The Señora didn't want to be read to. Lavinia had the feeling that she couldn't wait for her to leave, but when she did get up to go, the Señora took her hands in both of hers. "I want you to do something for Lazaro." She called Carmen to bring some candles. They were cheap things, wax poured into heavy glass, and they were perfumed too. Lavinia is supposed to light them at night for Lazaro's sake and recite the Twenty-third Psalm.

"When am I supposed to do all this?" Lavinia asked.

"You'll know," the Señora said, in a way that made Lavinia go all goose-pimply. She's hidden the candles in the conservatory, behind the peat moss.

The look in the Señora's poor blind eyes haunted her all night. She kept thinking of Lazaro: how he looked when he was just born, those tiny brown fists; how, when he learned to walk, she used to worry that he'd fall off the drawbridge; how she had ached for Nestor to see him; how perfectly beautiful he was.

How can she worry about Edgar Snow when she has Lazaro to think about?

"Here's your key ring back." She presses it into Bubbles' hand. "Don't let it go on years and years—the thinking about him."

If he hadn't seen her on the street, he would have been all right. It was meeting her by chance that tore him up. Tore him up! She has a lien on his soul. An actress, young, just another actress. They all have those supple bodies, quick heads. They all glow from within and laugh from the diaphragm. Why this one?

It's no good seeing people when he's like this. He had to cancel everything. He was planning to stay home, but that is the worst place. Her clothes are still in the closet, along with her smell. He could go crazy at home.

He would have walked it off except the ankle still hurts. The car is good, a beautiful machine that complies instantly to your command. Only it doesn't feel that way, not the way it usually does when he is driving. Today it is not as if he is driving the machine, but more as if the two of them are obeying an outside impulse.

This used to happen to him when he was young, only then it would be on foot. He would leave his door, no idea where he was going, and walk for hours, days even. His mother didn't worry, she was used to his rambles. She never even asked where he had been, and most of the time he couldn't have told her. It's like it was then.

His ankle hurts just a little when he presses down the clutch, reminding him of Faye. She would be astonished to see him crossing the George Washington Bridge with no destination in mind. She used to complain that he had no spontaneity. She didn't understand how the powerful must protect themselves. They have their few restaurants where they are known and their privacy is respected. They have their friends on the same social level. It doesn't do to take on friends who don't have your power. It makes them giddy; they can harm you.

It used to bother her that he scheduled her in—six o'clock every evening, most evenings. It made sense. There was still time to dress afterward and go out to dinner. It wasn't so late that they were too tired. The housekeeper had gone home, and the light was beautiful then. "But always at six . . ." She complained. He surprised her at two. She never knew he had written it in days ago: 2:00—Faye.

Faye does not understand how necessary the schedules become. When you rise in power, you do not become less needy of the appointments, the waiters who know where your table is, the hotels abroad where the staff remembers what room you like and what paper to bring you in the morning. You need them more. "You are young," he lectures the empty seat beside him, which if he doesn't look at it directly can be made to hold the form of a young actress. "You are used to being ignored. You have built up a shell against the slights of others. They may not know that you are the greatest talent of your generation, but you know it. You keep that knowledge close to you. You hug it tight, and you don't care if someone's assistant keeps you waiting in the outer room, if there isn't a table free for you at Jam's. But the powerful lose that shell from lack of exercise. They become tender and vulnerable. They could not bear it if they were to walk into—what if I went to that little Mexican place you always want me to try—"

"Lucy's?"

"What if I walked into Lucy's and the kid who gives out the tables didn't recognize me? What if he looked at me and saw a middle-aged, middle-management type and made me wait for an hour at the bar?" Of course she laughs, that marvelous, loose, bottom of the rainbarrel laugh.

If she could see him now—in New Jersey. In the heart of the land of the great unwashed, where nobody knows his name, stripped of the trappings of power, except for the car, of course. It is not an anonymous car. Gareth Watts means nothing in the backwoods of culture, but Jaguar is recognized everywhere. In fact, as his own name diminishes in luster, the car takes on more. It has the power to turn heads out here, in these broken streets. When the hell did it snow? It must have snowed in New York too, but he doesn't remember it. A week ago, could be; the snow looks old, decrepit, slouched up in the shadow of buildings, bleeding into gutters.

From the highway, he saw a whole area burned to the ground, as if there'd been a war. Race riots? It looked recent, but he couldn't remember anything in the news. How he's lost touch—not good. Weeks have passed. He pulls into a gas station to fill up and get his bearings. It takes him a while to realize it's closed, although why it would be, in the middle of the week, he doesn't know, unless some obscure New Jersey religious cult has a holiday today.

Coming out, he sees that the house across the street is the one he wants. Piece of luck, a good omen. There is no reason in the world why he is going to see a fortuneteller in a bombed-out corner of New Jersey. No one else in his position, of all the people he knows, none—not even writers he knows—he can't imagine any of them doing this. It is his upbringing in Wales that sets him apart. The stories about him make a lot of this, his rural Welsh childhood, his sense of adventure, his eye for the bizarre, bordering on the mystical.

Better set the alarm in the Jaguar, in this neighborhood. When he turns the key, the two doors and the trunk lock simultaneously with a solid clunk. Snow falls into his hand-sewn Italian moccasins. He negotiates the slippery walk like an old man. His ankle remembers the snake, and his arm cringes, recalling an awkward tumble. Is he wise getting so close to a witch who seems able to harm him even as far away as Arizona? The Jaguar waits serenely beyond the dirty snowbank, promising to take him home whenever he commands. He rings the bell. It doesn't work. At least, it doesn't look like a working bell, and there was no sound inside. He knocks.

The door opens on someone very young, a child, he thinks at first, until he sees faint lines at the corners of the eyes and around the mouth. It is a small woman, in a sweater and baggy jeans, thick wool socks, and clogs, with a frizz of dishwater-blond hair and no makeup at all. Extraordinary eyes.

"Are you Destiny Ortega?"

"Yes."

"I'm Gareth Watts."

A silence.

"You don't know who I am?"

"I'm sorry. Did you have an appointment?"

"I find this incredible that you don't even remember—"

"I'm really sorry. If I don't write things down—but it's all right. Come in. I don't have anyone here now."

The first room has brightly painted plaster saints in it. She considers going in there with him, but decides against it and seats him on a chrome and vinyl kitchen chair, circa 1955, at an oak dining table that could use a good sponging off. The window looks out on a snowy patch of ground and someone else's back-porch clothesline. There's a small kitchen to his left, with dishes piled in the sink. To his right is an open doorway with dresses on hangers suspended from the molding.

She takes a chair opposite him. The sun backlights her cloud of hair, throwing her face into shadow. She takes up a pack of large, well-worn cards and begins shuffling them, clumsily, because her hands aren't big enough to cover them.

She has him cut the cards three times with his left hand, and then she lays the top thirteen in a circle, the last one in the middle. She rises in her chair, the better to survey the entire layout. She smells warm and sweet, not perfumey, but clean, young—the nose, the stupidest sensory organ in the human body, sends an extra supply of blood to his groin.

"You have placed yourself in the path of certain powers, ancient forces that are working in diverse ways. . . ."

He is fascinated with himself, the way he is laying himself open to this—crap she is giving out. How could Faye—even Faye, who isn't the world's greatest skeptic—have believed her? All actors are credulous. They believe in fate because they have so little control over their own careers. Even Faye must have seen that this is a bunch of generalizations that could be applied any way you choose. If anyone he knows could see him now, bending over these gummy, medieval cards. The image tickles him. And those dresses hanging from the doorway—for what reason? She can't wear them, can she? Perhaps they are instead of a door, hung there in place of a door.

As the snow melts in slow drops from the gutters, she announces the cards and their meanings in terms so vague he loses track and possibly falls asleep, because when the siren starts on his car, he leaps up, his heart jumping. Before he can get to the front door, it opens and a kid bursts in.

"Is that your car?"

"What happened?"

"Nothing. I was looking at it, that's all. It went off."

The car is fine, no damage. As soon as he puts the key to the ignition, the siren growls down. He sits there, breathing in the leather, letting it seep into him again, the feeling of who he is. He lost it inside with the fortuneteller; something about the chairs, the dresses in the doorway, reminded him of poverty, anonymity, and the absence of hope. It frightens him to think of where he might have gone if the car hadn't called him back to safety.

"Is everything all right?"

She is on the sidewalk with her arm around the boy—it must be her son. Gareth thought he was black at first, but he is something else, some other mixture. His hair and skin is like his mother's with just a drop of coffee added. Gareth has seen kids with this color in Abruzzi in the summer, suntanned and bleached-out hair so they're all one color. Only his eyes, a deep, somber black, make Gareth think of Africa, African blood. He's small and fine-boned like his mother, but while her movements seem filtered through a haze, his are sharp, defined, lightning quick. Something Latin there, and in the stance. *Machismo.*

"Aren't you coming back in?"

Gareth looks at her a moment, wondering what she's talking about.

"The reading. We weren't finished."

"No, I should be getting home."

"But—"

"Oh, yeah, right. I forgot. How much do I owe you?"

"It's not that. You left your jacket inside."

"I'll get it." The boy leaps up the stairs, and Gareth's heart turns over, remembering Faye, how she moves.

"Look, I really came to ask you a favor. Something you did. I see now that you wouldn't have done it maliciously, I mean I'm sure you believed in what you were saying, but you told the lady I live with to leave me and it's tearing me up. If you would call her and explain that you made a mistake—"

"I can't. I'm sorry. I know you are suffering right now, but—"

"What if I gave you five hundred dollars—"

"That's not ethical. I'm a member of the International Psychics' Society." She's come over to the car so that they are speaking over the top of the Jaguar. "I know it has been very painful for you," she says in a different tone, "and I'm sorry you've had to suffer, but it's already getting better. You know this and it frightens you. You feel lost without the passion, but you will see that you are better off without it. You are healing now—"

He doesn't see the boy until he is beside him.

"Nice jacket too," he says softly. A slim brown hand lingers on the suede.

Gareth pulls on the jacket and slides back into his car. The kid's eyes go black with longing. "Want a ride?" Gareth hears himself say.

Delia doesn't mind if he goes for a ride in the car. How could she deny Lazaro? She wasn't surprised to see the man from Madison Avenue here on her doorstep. His face was too significant for her not to see it again. They had to meet eventually because the psychic channel between them is clear and strong.

The scent of his suede jacket is still in the room, the smell of power, wealth, sensuality—something Destiny never read in the vibrations over the phone. Destiny, like Delia, is an old maid who lives with only a ghost of a man. Delia and Destiny couldn't comprehend these qualities over the telephone. They needed the smell to open their eyes. Now they understand.

· · ·

Delia is bending over the cards exactly as she was when Lazaro first came in—only an hour ago, maybe, but it seems like more because of all that has happened. An hour ago he was wondering if he would ever get to ride in a Jaguar, and now he's been—all over, even past the Fat Man. Lazaro put the window down and yelled to him. The Fat Man looked. And Lazaro laughed.

"Who's that?"

"My grandfather."

It's an amazing car, with real leather seats and a working clock, a telephone that Gareth used to call someone in the city. It was like riding inside of money.

"Oh—here, Mom."

"What's this?"

"It's a fifty-dollar bill. He said to give it to you. Why don't you turn on the lights?"

"For what?"

"To see. It's dark in here."

"I mean the money."

Lazaro flips the switch. His mother is hunched over the table, looking at the crisp bill as if she expected it to talk, like the cards.

"For the reading. I told him it was too much, but he made me take it. Was that OK?"

She folds him into her. He smells of cigarettes, from the car, probably. He and that man had cigarettes.

"Let's take the fifty dollars and go to dinner at Florio's."

He could think of lots better things to do with fifty dollars, but she looks so excited and happy, in a way Lazaro has never seen, that he agrees. He goes to the bathroom to clean up, and when he comes out, she's in one of her dresses, the one with fringe on the sleeves and the hem. It comes down only halfway to her knees. He never sees anyone dress this way, only in the reruns on television, but he has never told her so. He figures Delia has a special license to dress strangely. It has something to do with being Anglo, or having second sight.

Later, halfway through the mozzarella in corrozza she and Lazaro are sharing, Delia will realize she didn't see Jaime at the door when they went out.

13

---

avinia says they chew up her dish towels for their nests. They scamper through the walls at night. They've even been sampling the family archives. There's a small round hole in the bottom of this box, and some of the letters are chewed.

It was mice that woke him, knocked something over on the shelf above his head, and he sat straight up, full of adrenaline. He must have been thinking about these mouse-eaten papers in his sleep, because he woke up feeling that he had to look at them, not later in the morning, but immediately. It was no use arguing with the impulse, which seemed like an urgent call, as if Anna Bird herself were impelling him to climb the cold stairs up to the tower room and take out the box that contained the letters.

He had seen them when he came back after Christmas, on the floor where someone—Lazaro, must be—had carelessly knocked them over. At the time, Will scooped them hastily back into the box. He saw they were about Anna Bird, but he put them away unread.

They are all written in the same hand, that of Miss Cordelia Turner, written on very good rag paper, meant to last. Dated at six-week intervals, they chronicle the progress of Miss Anna Bird, a student at the St. Gustav Academy in Hertenstein, Switzerland.

The pupil is learning to read, to do sums, and to sew. The progress of her sewing is especially well-documented, with the different stitches named and commented on. Miss Anna benefits from rough outdoor sports and long walks in the mountains. The letters continue with such predictable regularity that Will begins to get suspicious. Here is a girl growing through puberty into adulthood and the headmistress continues to report on her progress with the hemstitch. Isn't anything else going on in Anna Bird's life?

Will stands and stretches. The moon is gone and there is a pale predawn light in the tower room. The Anna Bird reflected in these letters is faceless, weightless. Vital details are being left out. Why doesn't she go home for vacations? True, it wasn't easy in those days, before airplanes; but still, in ten years—

He could use a cup of coffee, but he doesn't want to risk waking Lavinia. He leans his forehead against the cold windowpane and watches his breath leave a fog print on the glass.

The letters continue, an entire carton of them written by the indefatigable Miss Turner, reporting in the same well-spaced Spencerian hand about the progress of Miss Anna's chain stitch, her hemstitch, her walks in the mountains.

At last, at the bottom of the pile, where the mouse has begun its work, something happens to shake Miss Turner's smooth facade. Her writing constricts, gets taller; the curves tense up into points and angles. Miss Turner was shocked to receive the request that Miss Anna be sent home. Miss Anna has not completed her course of instruction; she is not prepared to leave; she does not wish to leave.

The next letter is terse: there is no one available to accompany

Miss Anna home and she is not capable of making the journey alone.

The final letter, half-eaten by the mouse, acknowledges that Miss Turner is awaiting the arrival of Miss Anna's brother, who will take her home. Miss Turner warns that the girl will need close supervision, a full-time companion.

That's it, the last letter, dated a little over a year before Anna married Will's grandfather. There is nothing more in all the boxes; in all the restless recording of the Bird family, there is not another scrap of information on Anna, only these curiously blank letters, more notable for what they leave out than for what they say.

In all his years of skirt chasing, crazy whoring, this never happened to him, never! Not since the army, and then it couldn't be helped. Then you slept standing up. But after the war, he always, always slept in a bed. It's dangerous for a man of his size to spend the night in a chair. He could have strangled himself, cut off his own air supply. That it should come to this.

The empty bottle on his desk has left a ring on the leather top where it stood all night. He always keeps it in the kitchen so he has to walk out to get it. If he can't walk, he can't have another. That's the rule. It's living alone that's doing it. He has never lived alone.

To have slept the entire night sitting at his desk! He must have been polluted. Slept to seven in the morning at his desk, with his shoes on. Feet swelled up in the night, the pressure of the shoes—but he can't bend down to take them off.

A slow perambulation through the house on painful feet, an uneven-gaited shuffle through the rooms of people he knows (but only at a distance), past pretentious, expensive houseplants that have died because someone neglected to open the drapes one morning a week ago, or two weeks, empty glasses in the sink. There was a woman who used to clean. What was her name? Juanita? Camilla? Where has she gone?

The feet limp into the bathroom, where a grizzled head appears in the mirror above the sink. Staring into these reddened eyes, Nestor feels pity for the lost old man whose wife has left him, gone away with the one who stole his money and his honor. Wasn't money and honor enough? Couldn't Snow have left him his wife?

Nestor knows this is true. Before he knew it, but not fully. He knew it well enough to put a stop on her checks, her credit cards, to draw the money out of the joint account and put it into his private one, but he didn't fully realize it until this morning, when he looked into this old man's empty eyes.

The first thing Lazaro notices, coming out of his house, is that the snow has gone. It melted in the night, even the hard-packed icy parts on the sidewalk. It's all gone except for a long narrow piece of black ice at the curb where the Jaguar was parked.

The second thing he notices is that there is a patrol car parked in Hugo's station. He doesn't look at it, just sees it at the limit of his vision. He begins walking, not fast, but not slow either. As he rounds the corner he senses the bulk of the car creeping soundlessly up behind, but the street is empty.

He takes a long time in the bakery, selecting his breakfast donut, the same kind he always gets, chocolate covered. Instead of running as he usually does, cramming it in as he rushes for school, he takes a slow bite while he's still in the shop, savoring it, considering what makes it so good: the bitterness of the chocolate against the sweetness of the dough; the firm but brittle shell over the yielding, soft interior; the richness of both. The trouble is, when he's chewed it thoroughly, he can't swallow. His throat won't work.

With the gluey mass still in his mouth, he leaves the bakery, hunching one shoulder against the waiting car. But you can't out-walk an automobile, especially if you are trying not to walk too fast or too slow.

"Ortega? Yo! Ortega!"

"You talkin' to me?" The donut goes down in a lump.

"You're Lazaro Ortega, aren't you?"

There's a black cop and a white cop in the car. The white one's driving. The black one is doing the talking.

"No, I mean, maybe. I guess so."

"We'd like you to get in the car, son. We have some questions to ask you."

"I have to go to school. I'm late for school."

The black cop opens the door casually, gets out, and quickly frisks him.

"I think you'd better get in the car."

There's a mesh between the back and the front seats so you can't reach over and strangle the people in the front. Even through the mesh, he can see pimples on the back of the white cop's neck.

The shocks are bad. It rides worse than Appleyard's and nothing near like the Jaguar that rode so smooth it seemed to be floating above these crappy streets.

Lazaro feels something in his hand, the donut, oily, sickeningly sweet. He drops it on the floor of the police car and grinds it with the sole of his sneaker.

Gareth Watts has showered, shaved, dressed, poured his coffee, and read all of section A of the *New York Times* before he thinks of Faye. Maybe he's getting over it. It seemed as if he never would, but he's recovered from countless loves, even forgotten some totally. What happens is, when he loses a lover, even when it's he who does the leaving, there's a terrible hollowness that comes over him. As he said in his latest interview, with *People*, in spite of his work and his success, he is never completed unless he is in love. In that article he was completed by Faye, snuggling up to his side. In the other pictures he was alone: in an empty theatre, wearing his cashmere sweater, slouched down in a seat, a cigarette in his hand; in his aerie, wrapped in a silk dressing gown, with two days' growth on his chin, looking over scripts.

Today he is calm, complete unto himself, surveying the city, feeling the coffee, bitter and hot, opening his throat, watching the patient snakes of traffic winding into the city over the Triboro and the George Washington. He reads about himself in Section C. There's a rumor that he will be directing two different plays on Broadway this spring. He planted the rumor himself. He has worked out a plan where he can do two at once. He's going to put it to both producers that way, subtly, diplomatically, that he will do both or neither. He needs the challenge. Directing hit shows has become too easy, but he'll never say that publicly. Could be misconstrued as arrogant. What he would rather talk about—and might describe, someday, in one of those long, discursive background pieces they like to do on him—is the time he drove his Jaguar to the slums of Wallingford, New Jersey, to have his fortune told and ended up driving a little Puerto Rican kid around town.

The traffic going out of the city on the George Washington Bridge is relatively light. He could be there again in twenty-five minutes. This impulse, so genuine and spontaneous, catches Gareth off guard. It's the kind of thought he would like to imagine himself having, but it has never come like this, direct and unbidden. He almost considers doing it.

The phone rings three times before Delia, buried in sheets and blankets, her clothes in a desperate tangle on the floor, wakes. It rings another two times before she can find her way out of the

wads of bedclothes. The police sergeant has to repeat himself
several times over before she can grasp what is going on.

Her clothes are reluctant to separate. Buttons rebel and fall off.
It is half an hour before, disheveled and numb, she leaves the
house, forgetting to close the door which yawns open like a horri-
fied mouth behind her.

"William? Oh dear. I didn't mean to frighten you."

Will picks up the papers that flew all over when Lavinia came
up the stairs behind him.

"I thought you might want breakfast. You've been working so
hard." She sets a tray on the desk: orange juice, buttered toast, and
two eggs. The eggs are out of the question. They look like yellow
eyes staring up at him. There are two mugs of coffee. Lavinia
takes one and sits on a stack of boxes. "I won't stay if you're
busy—"

Will turns his chair so he won't have to look at the eggs and
picks up his mug. "No, stay. I was getting carried away up here."
He looks at his watch. "Nine already."

"I thought I heard you going up to the tower in the middle of
the night. Is that possible?"

"There were some papers I'd been avoiding—I knew about
them, but I hadn't read them, forgotten about them almost, and
then in the night I woke up knowing I had to look at them. It
pushed me out of bed, the compulsion to act immediately. Has that
ever happened to you?"

"Many times. Then it was always because Nestor hadn't come
home. I'd wake up and I could tell the bed was still level, no big
hulk on the other side weighing it down. And that voice, the one
that only comes in the night when the other voices are asleep, and
when it speaks, it sounds so absolutely right, that voice would say:
'Lavinia, get out. Leave him. He's killing you.' Once I actually

wrote a letter to a lawyer I knew, asking him to start proceedings —sat up until dawn, writing down grievances."

She puts her mug to her lips. On this January day her hand is showing its age, with ropy blue veins, a scattering of liver spots. It's extraordinary that she should speak like this, after the long reticence. Will, of course, never tried to break the facade. He learned early on to respect the wish to not talk.

But now Lavinia is opening up these secrets as if it were the easiest thing in the world. Something in the light, the weak winter light, or maybe a spirit is loose, the same one that sent Will up here in the night to face what he's been avoiding. What spirit? The Spirit of Inquiry, so vital to an historian, but it only comes to him in spurts and then it disappears. Why wouldn't he, in the course of his methodical research through these papers, have come across the note Tuttle wrote to Ferkin about the connection between Anna Bird and Emma Phelps? How could he have skipped over the note? How could he have neglected an entire box of letters? It's as if his need to know is being countered by an equally strong need *not* to know.

"Divorce wasn't so common in those days," Lavinia is saying. "It was a terrible thing to be a divorced woman. I couldn't imagine it in the daylight, so I would cover it all up. It was only at night, when I wasn't in control—"

Will looks away. He hopes she isn't going to cry.

"I guess it would have been better if I had been the one to leave. Then I would have had momentum. The energy of the decision would have propelled me into the world." Lavinia flings her arms toward the window, setting up a whirlwind of dust motes, sunbeams spinning in the winter light. "As it was, I was sort of left behind, like a piece of driftwood on the beach."

"Do you still wake up at night?"

"No. Isn't that odd? I think of Nestor lots during the day. It used to be more, before you came. But not at all at night. He never wakes me up the way he used to. You're not eating your eggs, William."

"I'm not hungry." He drinks his juice as a gesture of goodwill. "This stuff I've been reading, it has to do with me, in an odd way, not a rational way."

"You mean it has to do with the curse on your family—"

"You know about that?"

"Oh, yes. Everyone talks about it, you know, the Appleyard curse. It had something to do with my husband's family, didn't it? There was a broken marriage vow. What was it? . . . When your poor father died, wasn't it, the fall from the horse? There was a rush of talk about it, the old-timers especially. And then you fell off a horse too, didn't you, William? You really should be more careful—"

"Who told you that?"

"Oh, I don't know. Didn't you? Or was it Delia, or Lazaro?"

"I don't remember telling anyone—"

"But you must have, William dear, or I wouldn't know about it."

"It couldn't have been you, because we would have had this conversation then, about the family curse."

"It must have been Delia or Lazaro. Does it disturb you to think that we've been talking about you? You'll forgive us, won't you? We're all so fond of you—"

"It's just strange. I never imagine people talking about me, or thinking about me. I'm used to fading into the background."

"Well, you're definitely foreground in this family. In fact, you were foretold."

"Excuse me?"

"I told you that, didn't I, William?"

"I don't think so."

"It was such a coincidence at the time—the Señora predicting you would come, and then, there you were, at the sally port the next morning. At the moment, it did rattle me." She reaches over to take Will's hand. "I don't go in for this fortunetelling business. It was the Señora's idea. Sometimes she gets these, I don't know what to call them, premonitions. Of course, there was a logical explanation for why you came, because you happened to ask Bubbles and she sent you up here, knowing I was looking for a boarder, but it was odd, wasn't it?"

"Did this woman say anything about the curse on my family? Maybe you heard it from her."

Lavinia rocks back on her seat of boxes, clasping one knee, like a girl. "I believe she said you were coming back, or something like that, because I remember I thought it must be Nestor at first."

"Coming back. That could refer to my family, coming back after generations—"

"And she said you would seek my daughter's hand—" Lavinia is blushing.

"Her hand?"

"I think in marriage, William dear."

14

Will climbs the old stairs to Delia's house, wondering if he's too early. He knows she sleeps late. The door swings open at his approach.

"Delia?"

No one's there.

"Delia?"

No answer. Will looks behind him to see if there is anyone at the gas station across the street, but it seems closed. Now that Will thinks about it, the station was closed the other day as well, for no apparent reason.

"Delia?"

There's a switch in the hall, but the light doesn't work. The plaster saints stand mute in coats of dust. "Delia?" No sign in the dining room. The usual collection of dirty dishes in the kitchen sink. "Delia?" Will stands outside the dresses, calling into the bedroom.

At first he thinks she's in the bed, but it's just the way the blankets are bunched up. She isn't home. Where then? Not far, because she didn't close the door. Lazaro's room is empty too. Maybe she went around the corner, to that bakery, for a cup of coffee and a breakfast roll.

He pulls out a chair. The picture of Emma Phelps is in his pocket. He fingers it, hesitates, then takes it out and lays it on the table.

He has never really looked at it closely. It's like when he was a boy and he came across pictures of snakes in the encyclopedia, he'd close the book quickly, as if they could rise up off the page and come after him. He was a timid child—not like his father, who was always called Billy, even when he was a man. Billy's the right name for a man who rides with the cowboys.

Billy's son, Will, a cautious man, afraid of pictures of snakes, afraid of horses, afraid of going on with life because it might end, sits in the house of Emma Phelps and forces himself to take a long look at her picture.

She is standing in a prison cell. There are iron bars around her. The corner of a neatly made prison cot is visible on the right-hand side. Light comes diagonally from an unseen source, throwing the left side of her face into shadow. She is wearing a dress she made herself out of white dimity, the kind of material a girl would have worn to her first summer ball, trimmed with red ribbons. She made it for her hanging. Did she mean it as a mockery? He can read no spark in those eyes, no humor there. The body stands solid, a little broad in the waist, no longer young. Her patron had found a younger woman, which is why Emma slipped him the arsenic in his rice pudding.

She is displaying her skill with the needle. That's it. Before she dies she wants to show off a bit—all those pleats and ruffles. She's showing off. She chose dimity because she likes to work with it. She sits in her prison cell and works on yards of pure white dimity, taking care not to get it soiled, as if the white cloth can transport her back before the years of degradation. The last thing she will do on earth is sew a pure-white dress.

What a pity she wasn't hung. Of course she wasn't grateful to Tuttle. Why should she be? He robbed her of her glory. She stands in her prison cell having her picture taken in her dress, a disappointed bride. She'll have to wait—how long would a person with a life sentence have to serve before being eligible for parole? Was she paroled?

The telephone in Delia's room. Will pushes past dresses to answer it. A rough voice, British, wants Destiny Ortega, then asks who Will is.

"I'm a friend. I'm sorry. I don't know where she is. I thought she'd be back. She left the door open—" As Will says this he realizes something must be wrong. The caller doesn't want to leave a message. Will hangs up, feeling he should be doing something but he doesn't know what.

The room is dark with the curtains drawn. Will pulls back the drapes, letting in the light, illuminating airborne particles so that they look like magnified dancing photons, reminding Will of his conversation with Lavinia and the elusive Spirit of Inquiry. He might as well. He has a telephone credit card. He might as well make use of his time while he is waiting for Delia.

They're very accommodating in Trenton, very helpful, especially the young man employed by the parole board who says he won't mind at all looking up Emma Phelps. He'll call back.

It's as if he's fallen into one of those late-night science fiction movies where the hero goes away for what he thinks is a day and it turns out that an entire lifetime has been lived in his absence. There are cracks in the driveway with actual small trees pushing up through—silver maples. Damned nuisance. He used to pull them out all the time. Brambles and sumac have grown up around the sally port and young saplings sprout from the gutters. One rusting gutter hangs down from the eaves over the conservatory, and in the window floats the white, pale, frightened face of an old woman.

Nestor stops the car at the end of the drive, giving himself time to reflect, possibly to turn around and leave. It's Lavinia, of course. She's old now, no longer middle-aged. Somehow he had assumed that since Lavinia hadn't changed anything since his departure, nothing would have. But making no changes is not the same thing as preventing change, which takes energy. Keeping things the way they are is an action. Lavinia simply let things run down. She sat helplessly by and let time have its way with her.

He can't take this, not today. He is simply not in the mood for it, not in shape for it. He expected to slip back into time past, into his life as it was before the sad events of the present, but he hadn't anticipated this ghost face at the window. He backs the car around cautiously, trying not to let his eyes stray to the sally port so they won't see her at the door, breathlessly welcoming him back, her dream come true after fifteen years of waiting. He couldn't bear it.

The rearview mirror shows that the sally port is firmly shut, and yet she's had plenty of time to come downstairs. The face in the conservatory is gone. It's taking her longer, that's all. She might have arthritis, although she was always limber, exceptionally so. If he slides the car down the drive now, she will come to the door too late to see him and she can tell herself it was a mistake, a stranger who came up the long drive expecting to find something else. She can tell herself that and save them both embarrassment.

Then again, what if, in her excitement at seeing him, because she did see him, she tripped while rushing downstairs to open the sally port—those stairs always were narrow and treacherous—and she is lying on the cold flagstone floor in agony with a broken leg? Or worse yet, unconscious. Dying on the floor as the big Cadillac, with impassive cruelty, turns its back and inches down the drive.

The car stops, hood pointing down, rear wheels still poised on the edge. Five minutes and the sally port opens not a crack. Even the secret little window at the side, where one can peek out without being observed, remains shut.

The car backs around and pulls up alongside the sally port. He doesn't need this. He really doesn't, in his condition, at his age. The bell, surprisingly, is still operating. He hears it echoing inside, but nothing else, even with his ear to the door, not a moan or a whimper. His worst fears confirmed!

But not. She is not lying unconscious on the floor at the bottom of the stairs. She misled him, conned him, and the sally port door was unlocked. He always cautioned her to lock the door, but she often forgot. Unless she sneaked down here and unlocked it beforehand—"Lavinia!" He means to be stern, commanding, but there's an edge of fear in his voice. It's almost pleading. He would try again, but it might be worse.

He takes the stairs carefully, giving her plenty of time to get used to the idea that he is coming up. They are steeper than they used to be. Blood pounds unpleasantly in his ears; the hangover returns to his stomach. He's sweating everywhere, forehead, armpits, crotch. He leans against the wall, taking in big breaths.

She isn't in the kitchen, but there are two coffee mugs in the sink. Two? Appleyard. He forgot that Appleyard's living here. The floor in the great hall shakes with his footsteps. Dry rot in the beams, or termites possibly.

Mirrors are going gray. The room could use a dusting, but everything is exactly as he remembered or would have remembered if he'd ever permitted himself to think back on it. The high, oversized chairs and sofas by the huge fireplace, the long polished table at the other end. Looks like old blankets wadded up under the doors to keep out the cold. Doors have warped. Have to get new ones.

The conservatory, at the opposite end of the great hall, is open. Nestor steps inside and is greeted with blooming pleiones displayed in a bank along one side, their foliage glowing with health. Underneath the shelves, crouched down on the gravel floor, wearing a dressing gown and Nestor's old workboots, is his ex-wife, Lavinia.

"I was just sponging the leaves of the pleiones for them," she says. "There's some kind of soot on them, maybe from the big fire at Christmas. Do you think it's possible that the soot is still in the air?" She unfolds herself from under the shelves with admirable ease and stands beside him. She's thinner and her hair is gray, but her cheeks are pink as a girl's. She laughs, seeing him looking at her feet.

"I borrow them for working in here. I hope you don't mind."

He backs away, gestures to the orchids.

"You must be spending a fortune. Where did you get all these varieties?"

"I traded them. I took a course at the New York Botanical Society years ago and met some people. Someone's always dividing something and wants to find a good home for a young pleione or paphiopedilum. Your conservatory is the envy of them all. They come out from their apartments in the city and just drool. It's nice to have people who appreciate them. The girls don't, you know. Especially Cass. She thinks they're a waste of time. But I think my happiest moments are spent right here. It's satisfying, isn't it, Nestor?"

"Why were you hiding under the shelf when I came in?"

"Oh, I don't know." She picks up a sponge and carefully goes over one with spectacular bronze-red blooms. "It's awkward, after all this time. I didn't really want, I didn't think I could take, the upset."

"But you wanted it. You told me, wrote to me that you were keeping everything the same for my return."

Her hand stops, poised above the foliage. "What a romantic notion for an old woman. And here I was criticizing Bubbles for mooning over Edgar. I must remember that I wasn't much different."

"It's what you wanted, isn't it, for me to come back?"

"Is that what you are doing here, Nestor, coming back?"

Is he? He doesn't know. "Would you like me to?"

"I'm not sure, now that you are here, in the flesh." She takes off her gardening glove to brush a wisp of hair from her face, revealing a hole in the elbow of her dressing gown. Nestor looks away. "I think I fell into the habit of wanting you back, but I'm not sure I still desire it. Does that make sense?"

"Not a lot."

"I've hurt your feelings."

"No, you haven't, not at all. I just came by to see how you're getting on."

"And how am I?"

"Well. You look well, I mean. And the orchids—it's incredible. But the house is falling apart, Lavinia. The gutters, the doors, the beams under the floor. In ten years the place will be a ruin."

"Is it that bad?" He could never hear it when she cried. She rarely did, considering all his infidelities, but when she did, it moved him deeply. More intimate than sex, to put your arms around a sobbing woman, to hold her while she is in the transport of grief. He tasted the tears the first time she heard of his infidelity. He kissed them off her soft girl-cheeks.

"Why didn't you sell it? You could have reinvested. You were supposed to live off that money. I didn't want this." He touches her bare elbow through the hole in her sleeve, and her face crumbles. In his arms, she's light and bony. He feels a rush of strength and for one delirious moment thinks of carrying her upstairs to their bed. He strokes her hair instead—wiry and dry, where it used to be as fine as silk. He strokes her and rubs her back. Surprisingly, his eyes are wet too. A couple of old people, hugging and weeping, surrounded by banks of orchids.

Maybe she shouldn't be taking this on. Perhaps one of the partners
—but Nestor's secretary called her. They've noticed, in the office,
the special relationship she has with Nestor. They know she's privy
to information. Although he has never talked about his grandson,
Regina has heard about him from others, the illegitimate child, the
mother on welfare. It's common knowledge that Nestor Bird's
daughter lives in the Hispanic slum called Dublin, that she has
taken the Spanish surname of her lover who has been dead for
years.

You'd think someone from the D.A.'s office would have called
—or Marcioni—as a courtesy. It's a bad sign that they haven't. Do
they suspect that Nestor's implicated?

Regina runs up the steep marble steps of the courthouse. It was
the daughter who called, Nestor's daughter. She was looking for
Nestor, but no one knows where he is. They're going to place the
boy in detention until his trial.

Judge Sanders is on the case, which is a good sign. Regina's met
her several times. She has a reputation for being fair, patient, conscientious. She's good-looking but she doesn't use her looks, and
Regina thinks, if she remembers correctly, the judge has a child or
two of her own. That should work in their favor.

The room where Nestor's daughter said they'd be meeting is one
of those that were modernized in the fifties. The paint, public-
washroom green, is peeling off the walls. The stuffing is coming
out of the leatherette armchairs. Under the low fluorescent lights,
even Judge Sanders looks haggard.

There is some confusion when Regina walks in. Judge Sanders
recognizes her, but Nestor's daughter has never met her and Regina is looking for a heavy woman, someone with Nestor's bearing,
not this waif, this wisp, this vacant-eyed, frantic child whose hands
keep flying to her hair, ineffectually trying to push it out of her
face.

It is several minutes until Regina has sorted things out and finally sees the boy. Then she is shocked at how small he is, bent over in his chair, hiding inside an ancient, soiled high school jacket, much too big for him. His eyes are dull, half closed, sunk into their sockets. The only sign of life are the bony hands poking out from ragged sleeves like hermit crabs, tapping out a nervous rhythm on the arms of his chair.

Judge Sanders, peering across oversize glasses which seem especially designed to slip down her pert, unjudicial nose, is trying to get a response from him, trying to find out if he can grasp the enormity of what he's done. The fact that he did it is beyond dispute to all but his mother. The boy seems incapable of understanding. Perhaps he is retarded? The mother, Nestor's daughter, has a strange look to her. The degeneracy of the Bird family. Could Nestor's philandering be responsible—syphilis? No, not in the age of penicillin.

Of course there is no question of the boy being released in the custody of his mother. She looks as if she herself should be put into someone's care. Regina asks to speak to Judge Sanders in private.

Will picks up the photo off the dining table and puts it in his pocket. It's after noon. The sun is now slanting in through the dining room window, revealing sticky smudges on the table. Will finds some paper towels in the kitchen, wets them, and scrubs off the table. Then he does the dishes in the sink. Still no Delia.

He lets the picture lie on the table again and sits in front of it, waiting for what? The dresses to move, or the walls to talk. If Delia were here, maybe, but alone, Will can only see the likeness of a stony-eyed, rather heavy, middle-aged woman standing in a cell, wearing an overelaborate dress.

Beside it, he lays the portrait of a young woman of good family. An unlikely pair, the whore and the sheltered young bride. What did Delia say about the Queen of Swords—a woman thwarted in love or pursuit of power. They were both thwarted, weren't they? Betrayed. Two betrayed women.

My God, listen to him, slipping into this—madness, that's what it is. There's a kind of collective madness going on in this town. Lavinia, Delia, Bubbles, Lazaro's weird grandmother, who, Will now realizes, might be the fortunetelling Señora Lavinia was talking about—all these women with not enough to do, no prospects, no power, have invented him. They've made a gothic hero out of a timid history instructor, given him a curse to overcome and a mission: to marry the down-and-out, possibly brain-damaged descendant of the family his grandfather wronged years ago. Once again he has been the victim of things unspoken, hints and glances. Not intentional. He has no doubt that Lavinia is innocent. But he can't blame her for wanting it. They all want someone to rescue Delia. Like Delia, they've been waiting for her prince to come.

Will pockets the pictures of Emma Phelps and Anna Bird. He needs to get out of here, out of this house, away from this fairy tale that is threatening to become his reality.

The telephone catches him at the door. It's the man at the parole board, with the information Will wants. It seems that when Emma Phelps's name was brought before the board after thirty years, the board turned her down and voted to give her another ten years before considering her case again. Yes, that is unusual. Ordinarily the name would have come up again in eighteen months, or three years at the most.

Will, sitting on Delia's lumpy bed, wipes his palms on his corduroy pants and takes a pencil and pad out of his jacket pocket. There is a record of the names on the parole board at that time. It doesn't take long to get the information. When he hears Socrates Bird, it seems to Will that he already knew that Socrates would be on the board. After ten years, Emma Phelps was again considered by the parole board and again was judged too dangerous (at sixty-three years of age) to be released into society. At that time, Nestor Bird was on the parole board. There is no further record of Emma Phelps in the files. Presumably she died before her name could come up again.

Will hangs up. All right, so Zeus Bird put Emma Phelps in prison and his son and grandson kept her there for some forty-odd years. Emma Phelps had some connection to Anna Bird. All of which is not crucial to Will's dissertation, unless he finds enough about Emma's soothsaying to put her into the chapter on mysticism.

It might have relevance to the curse on the Appleyard family, if Will believed in such a thing, if he were willing to give the curse power over him. This information only feeds it, gives it strength. This is not the Spirit of Inquiry driving him on. It's the demon of self-destruction.

Will escapes through the dresses, past the guardian saints. He gets as far as the street, has his hand on the car door, when he sees Delia coming around the corner, her worn camel hair coat clutched around her, shoulders hunched up. It doesn't take psychic powers to tell that something has happened.

She hasn't seen him. He could get into his car and very quietly pull out of her life, all of their lives, go back to his room at his mother's apartment; he has clothes there. He could finish his research from the New York Public Library. There is no reason why he ever has to see Wallingford again.

Or he could stay, jump into this web of fantasies the women have woven, play his part, the part of the rescuer-prince, the man with the curse on his family. The One.

With a lightness in his chest, the same breathless expansion he felt when he let his horse take him flying down the hill, he turns to her.

But she looks past him unseeing, muttering something. She's distracted, almost looks mad. Will opens the car and slides in behind the wheel. He waits until Delia's gone inside before he drives away.

Two o'clock in the afternoon and he hasn't eaten a thing all day. Sleeping in chairs and missing meals are two things he never does. The morning has been packed with unusual events. Too many at one time isn't good. Puts a strain on the body.

At least he can have lunch. The kid could probably use some food too. He looks even smaller and thinner up close. Can't weigh more than eighty pounds.

"You hungry?"

"I guess so."

"You've missed most of school anyway, might as well take the rest of the day off. Did you ever eat at The Fat Man?"

"Uh-uh."

"It's pretty decent. It's clean at least. Ali, the proprietor, is a friend of mine. I like him because he's the only man in town fatter than I am."

This gets a laugh out of the kid.

Nestor opens the door and lets the kid slip in, quick as a lizard. Ali, wearing an apron the size of a tent, is dishing up soup behind the counter.

"Ali, meet my grandson, Lazaro."

15

What are you taking those for? Do you think you're going to be going to a lot of black-tie occasions with that cowboy?"

"I came to get them because you asked me to. I would have thrown them out, asked you to give them away, but I didn't want to hurt your feelings."

"You have always been very careful about my feelings."

"Look, just give them away, OK? You're right, I'm not going to be wearing these things. I was going to sell them to a place on Madison Avenue that deals with fancy used clothes, if you want to know the truth."

"I figured as much. That's all right. Take them. Take them. You could probably use the money."

"I probably could."

"Remember this one? Kissinger couldn't take his eyes off you when you wore it."

"Kissinger's a dirty old man."

"You met a lot of people through me."

"No one who ever gave me a part."

"We were waiting for the right property. I was waiting too. I didn't work either."

"We would have been better off if you had. Now you're doing two at once. I read it in the *Times* this morning."

"It's only a rumor. I am considering it, but only to keep active, keep my mind off you."

"Is it really hard for you?" There was the slightest softening in her voice, as the last dress, a Givenchy, was folded into the shopping bag.

"You don't believe it, do you?"

"You've always had women—even when I was living here, there were phone calls, letters. I didn't dare leave you for even a day because there were understudies waiting in the wings."

"Which proves what? That I did not, do not, love you deeply—"

Women do come easily to him. It's his gift, and his curse. But it doesn't mean he takes them lightly. He could not get Faye to understand this, even as he watched her packing evening gowns into shopping bags, as he carefully gauged the timbre of her voice, the pacing of her movements, finding the moment when he could coax her to him. He managed it so subtly that she almost believed it was the urging of her own passion. She missed lunch with her cowboy, called him at the last moment, cheeks hot and red, to tell him she couldn't make it. Gareth had already freed up his entire day. While she was packing, he had quietly sent the housekeeper home, used the kitchen phone to cancel appointments, told the doorman he wasn't to be disturbed. It's almost as if he had been planning a murder.

He wrapped her in a blanket and ran with her in his arms out to the terrace. For a moment she really thought he would do it. She screamed and dug her fingers into his shoulders. Then he laughed and set her down, pointed to a jagged line of lightning finer than hair, over New Jersey. They listened for thunder, counting "one chimpanzee, two chimpanzee" to tell how far away it was, but it never came. She wrapped the blanket around him too, and they stood barefoot on the cold cement, their still-sweating bodies sticking to each other in the wool cocoon. He placed his hand on her hip and bent his knees slightly, feeling how easy it would be to pitch her over.

She left at dusk, weighed down like a bag lady who'd struck a mother lode of Paris originals.

He could make her feel the force of his passion, but not the strength of his love. She doesn't believe in it, or she doesn't want to. Even he has trouble believing it. One part remains aloof, even in this moment, watching through a viewfinder how he leans against the rail—waist-level, easy to swing a leg over. Even if he did, that part of him would remain on the roof, observing how the naked body falls, how the blanket billows out and floats behind. The observing self would float down with the blanket and watch as a trickle of deep-red blood escaped from his ear onto the sidewalk. Would he land face down? Do falling bodies land any particular way? They researched all this information for *Traitor Betrayed*, then decided not to show the body, but rather, the horror mirrored on the faces of the onlookers. A much more effective technique. Too many bodies on the screen today, the blood, no art in it.

He's lost it again. He was on the verge of tears, suicide, and the man with the viewfinder took over. Even in sex, at the most painful and exquisite moment, he knows how their bodies are placed, how they are lit, as if he were not in his body at all.

Not Faye. She is totally there. That is what attracted him to her on stage, her abandon, the way she trusted things to come out right. In bed she lets the passion take her, contort her, a beautiful actress without vanity, a rare and precious commodity. What he could have done with her—with the right property, of course.

In the meantime, she's left him alone with no plans for the evening, except for the one to kill himself, which looks like it isn't going to happen.

Gareth closes the door behind him, puts the body which he has decided not to destroy into the shower, where it enjoys, in spite of his misery, the three shower-heads with needle-point spray.

He's hungry. They didn't stop for lunch. He'd been planning a scrambled-egg-and-caviar supper for two, champagne, but now he wants to go out. If he calls a woman, there will be talk and expectations. If he calls a man, business talk and expectations of another kind. He decides instead to go to New Jersey, first because even in his suicidal grief, he noticed that traffic was light on the bridge, and secondly, only the company of a truly off-the-wall uncomprehending eccentric like Destiny Ortega could ease his pain tonight.

"Excuse me. Miss! Young lady! Is there a place to eat around here?"

Carmen knows he is the one with the fancy car who came and gave Lazaro a ride. She saw him on the porch, knocking on the door, but Delia is up with her mother tonight because of the trouble with Lazaro. Mama is working her magic, and all the loose pieces are falling to center.

"Go to Florio's. Take a right and then another right. First right, first right. They've got a lot with a big fence around it where you can lock up your car. You don't want to leave a pretty car like that out on the street at night."

The lightning flashes behind her, and Carmen laughs to see it reflected in his eyes, along with uneasiness, just a suggestion of fear flickering through.

Underneath the distant, muttering thunder she can hear the vibrations of the skin stretched tight on the top of Tio Felipe's drums. In the dark stairway they sound like rain coming down on flat leaves. They call her up the stairs, making room for her in the song.

One of the cousins must have brought him by—he never goes out alone—but no one is here now, just the two old blind people. They are in with the altar Mama had Carmen make for Lazaro's sake, a mound of dirt on a plastic tablecloth in the corner, with candles stuck in, and corn, pumpkin, red beans, and okra scattered around a plaster statue of Santa Barbara, Chango's saint. Felipe holds his drums between his knees, making the little one rattle and chatter while the big one rumbles like thunder. They are singing out to Chango, the god of fire and lightning, god of changes.

Mama doesn't sleep in her bed anymore. When Carmen goes in to make it, it is smooth, unused. Does she sleep at all? Does she doze in a chair when Carmen is at work? Where does she get the strength?

Now she is dancing, her bare feet flashing, moving to Chango's rhythms while lightning licks the walls. She sees Chango in the room. Mama and Tio Felipe see them clustering around, Catholic saints and African spirits coming down to save Lazaro. As if the old gods of Africa, the gods of plowing and harvest, of sunshine and floods, could work inside the windowless rooms of the Anglo court.

"You are praying to corn gods. They can bring you thunderstorms, but they can't get Lazaro out of trouble," Carmen says, but the old woman can be deaf as well as blind when she wants to be. She claps her hands and stamps her feet against the floor, while Tio Felipe, his ugly white eyes rolling in his head, shouts out the ancient words. Sweat pours down his hideous, shining, beautiful face. Why can't they see how ludicrous they are? Why is she forced to see for them, to witness this pathetic show? Why must she get out of bed to see her mother, bent murmuring over candles in the middle of the night, slipping ecstatically away to madness?

"Storms were always worse up here on the mountain," Lavinia remarks to the group in general. She hands Nestor's drink to him—
bourbon on the rocks. They are gathered around the fire in the
great hall after dinner. Nestor, like a king, is sitting in a high-
backed chair, Regina, beside him, a homely prime minister. Lavinia rushes in and out, wanting to serve drinks, after-dinner mints,
coffee, anything to keep from having to sit still. Will is in the
kitchen doing dishes. Delia should help him, but she stays on a
low bench by the fireplace with her arm around Lazaro's shoulders,
monitoring the expansion and contraction of his lungs, feeling the
sharp ridge of his shoulder bone.

Some say the universe began in an explosion of light and that's
how it will end. A piece of the original light of the universe leaps
through the air. Lazaro turns his face toward it. The sound shakes
the floor.

"We used to open both sets of doors, your Aunt Cass and I, and
the lightning would shoot right across the room," she tells him.

"Oh, you didn't," Lavinia admonishes.

Regina is looking down at Delia as if she said something crazy.

"Lavinia," Nestor, imperious, "the floor shook at that last one.
Have you had the timbers checked for dry rot?"

"Oh dear. Dry rot? Regina, won't you have a drink, a little
liqueur? Something?"

"Oh no, Mrs. Bird—"

"Lavinia," she corrects her.

"Lavinia. I should be getting home. You were very kind, to include me in your family dinner—"

"But you are a part of our family, dear. You are the one who
rescued Lazaro. Poor boy would be behind bars tonight. I can't
imagine they would do that to a child, in this day and age."

"I should be going too—"

"Oh Delia, must you?"

"I have clients tonight."

"She's so conscientious," Lavinia tells Regina.

"They send their money in advance," Delia explains, "so I have to be there when they call."

"Are you a counselor of some kind?"

"I'm a clairvoyant."

"Excuse me?"

"A psychic. I have second sight."

Will would have taken Delia home. He was planning to, but she left with Regina. All night he's been trying to talk to her, to tell her that he'll take care of them, to describe the house he'll buy in St. Louis with the basketball hoop for Lazaro. Of course, it's more complicated now. Lazaro will need professional counseling. It's not going to be easy, father to an arsonist, but he's willing to take it on. He wants to.

He's ashamed of the way he left this afternoon, of the passivity that afflicts him when he needs to act. Now he's missed his chance to talk to Delia. Delia left with Regina. Nestor is taking Lazaro home with him.

The long-absent Nestor has stepped in and taken over. Now Will can understand what Cass meant, how his presence can fill the house and you suddenly find yourself doing everything in relation to him. He is too powerful for this family. Will is frightened for Lazaro, for Lavinia, for Delia.

Nestor was looking at Will all through dinner, asking him questions about the history he's writing, about what Will's been finding in the papers up in the tower. He let Will know that he would never have given his permission for Will to go through them, had anyone thought to ask.

"Lavinia, the floor is going to come crashing through to the

dungeon. There's no support here. It's gone rotten, clear through."
The floor in the kitchen shakes at Nestor's approach. Will takes
Lavinia's apron off and tosses it into a drawer.

"Is there any ice in here?"

Will looks in the freezer, although he knows there isn't any.
"I'm afraid it's all gone."

"Doesn't she even keep ice anymore? Don't you people drink?"

"Wine, occasionally."

Nestor sets his empty glass on the counter beside the bottle of
bourbon he brought over, saying he knew Lavinia wouldn't have
any. Lavinia said she did have some she'd been saving, but she'd
used the last of it in the mince pie at Christmas.

"What are you after, Appleyard?"

"Excuse me?"

"Look, Appleyard, I'm an open man; I'm an honest man. It's a
tradition, a family tradition. The Birds are honest men, moral—"

"They did a lot for Wallingford. More than the Appleyards—"

Nestor waves his large, fine hand, generously absolving the
Appleyards. "Past history. Nothing to do with you. Nothing to do
with me."

"History has a way of influencing the present—"

Nestor looks at him from under black, shaggy brows—a wary
look, which surprises Will. "I could have had those papers removed, you know. Those are my family papers. I was thinking of
sending for them. I should have."

"I'm certainly grateful that you didn't. They've been helpful to
me. Your father and grandfather, being public men, so much involved in Wallingford—"

"But there are personal things in there too. I should have gone
through them first, had a chance to take out the personal papers."

"You mean the letters about Anna?"

"Things like that, those personal letters that have nothing to do
with history, with what the public needs to know."

"Perhaps I shouldn't have read them, but I was interested, naturally, because of my family's connection. She was married to my grandfather—"

"Briefly."

"After the marriage, my grandfather, it seems, had a mistress—"

Again, that absolving wave of the hand. Nestor drinks the bourbon down straight.

"The girl wasn't right."

"Anna?"

"I never heard the entire story and I never wanted to. It's gossip, you understand. Of no interest to serious men, a young historian, serious—"

"To tell you the truth, I wasn't thinking professionally, I was thinking of my family. This concerns my family, doesn't it?"

That wary look from under the brows. Is Nestor afraid of him then? The powerful Nestor Bird?

"It did concern your family briefly."

A burst of electricity cracks the sky. The castle shudders. Nestor involuntarily steadies himself against the kitchen counter.

"You can't say you never heard of the curse—"

"Good God, you don't believe in that nonsense, do you? Ouija boards, tables that rap and levitate, all that crap—"

"I'm interested in it as an historian, the way it's cropped up in Wallingford over the years."

"Personal, professional, make up your goddamned mind. Give me your glasses."

Will, too surprised to argue, hands them over. Nestor washes them under the tap, dries them with a paper towel, and hands them back. "That's better. I couldn't see your eyes. Now maybe your ideas will be clearer as well." Nestor pours himself another splash of bourbon. Although he doesn't usually drink it, Will feels he could do with a shot, but Nestor doesn't offer.

"I guess you could say that I'm personally and professionally interested, because of the curse that's supposed to have been laid on my family by Anna Bird before she died."

"Absurd."

"The idea is absurd, I agree, but people have acted as if the curse existed. By so doing, they have given it power, you see. They have made it into a fact—"

"For old women, for the credulous, people who aren't all there—"

"Apparently, and I found this from Lavinia's papers, not yours, there was a connection between Emma Phelps and Anna Bird."

Nestor drains his glass, sets it on the counter, and turns to leave.

Will hears himself saying, "Why did you keep Emma Phelps in prison?"

Nestor stops, blocking the door with his body.

"I found that in the public record, by the way, not in your personal papers."

Nestor lowers his big head and sways, like a bull getting ready to charge. Will stands his ground, although the back of his knees twitch to run. Nestor lumbers toward him, but his goal is the bourbon, not Will. He pours another two inches into his glass and looks up, his face sagging, making Will wonder why he has decided to persecute this old man.

"Bourbon?" He waves the bottle in Will's direction.

"Maybe just an inch." Will sets a glass down on the counter.

"Mind if we sit down for this inquisition? Standing is hard on my joints."

There are real people out here in New Jersey, with real faces. They don't all have plastic surgery and winter tans, upscale hair and capped teeth. The teeth on that black woman! She laughed when the lightning flashed, and he saw them, big curving incisors, like fangs. But she was right, the food is good here. "A black vampire gave me directions to this fantastic restaurant in New

Jersey. . . ." What an extraordinary night it's turning out to be. It helps that they have Barbaresco '77, but it's more than the wine and the food. It's the sense of rightness; he has a feeling that he is exactly where he belongs.

He owes this evening to Destiny Ortega, although she wasn't home. Her spirit alters his perceptions, heightens them. He could be in a foreign country instead of twenty minutes away from Manhattan, more foreign than Europe, where everything turns out to be the same—same people, same food, same service. Europe is a good hotel. This place is something else.

Even the weather is exotic—thunderstorms in January. This is the storm he saw from the terrace with Faye. It seems years ago, but it was this afternoon and the storm has been hovering here all day as if by enchantment. This stinking little has-been city sitting in the rustbelt of America is an island of enchantment.

Three subalterns converge at his side. He's been laughing out loud. The wine. It's a little embarrassing, but what the hell. He's not punching anyone out. He's laughing, that's all. To reassure them he orders the zabaglione. Give them something to do.

Tuning in to other people's anguish; hearing their voices, taut, or quavering; slipping into their lives; feeling out the lines of forces —what sweet relief! It's only in between the calls that the wild grief and panic set in.

She has always had Lazaro here. She locked him in with her carefully every night. She checked his room to make sure he was well, warm enough. She fed him and held him and kept him always in her mind, but somehow he eluded her. And now they've taken him from her.

She never struck him, never abused him, never said an unkind word to him. Other mothers much worse than she are allowed to keep their children.

There is something about her that frightens people. Even when she tries very hard to act in ways that will reassure them, she up-sets them. The woman who drove her home, Regina, kept her big nose pointed away from Delia, her body turned to shield herself from whatever it is that Delia has. Delia can't see it, only its effect on other people. Her gift can open up things far away, in the past and in the future, but it can't see this because it is inside her.

Before it was only an infirmity, making life more difficult but not impossible or unpleasant. But suddenly, now, because of a chance convergence of forces—or was it inevitable?—it has taken away her son.

She must have been reading the signs wrong. The ones that told her the rescuer was near. Or maybe she misinterpreted. Perhaps it was Hugo, or Will.

It isn't Nestor. She had forgotten how enormous he is, how the room shakes when he walks, how small and tight Lavinia is when he's around. He'll take Lazaro away from her. He'll fill up his life so there's no room for Delia.

That was the last call for the night. She wishes there were more, enough to go through the entire night.

No, that's not good either. She must concentrate, think about Lazaro. But her brain isn't good at this kind of thinking. Cass does it, makes one thought build into another, makes a plan, makes up questions, finds the answers. It's just a buzz for Delia, as if there were moths flying around in her head. She can't make it come clear.

Part of the shadow in the hall thickens and steps forward in the shape of a man, standing in the dining room now, indistinct. Jaime, Delia thinks at first, but then remembers the sound of knocking on her door. Someone was knocking and he came in because Delia did not lock the door. She always locks the door after Lazaro is in, and since Lazaro didn't come home tonight—the man comes fur-ther into the room. He doesn't see Delia because she is standing in among her dresses, but she can see him well now, well enough to know that he is the one who gave Lazaro a ride in his car.

She steps out from the dresses. He jumps.

"The door was open. I thought something was wrong—"

"No." Delia wraps her bathrobe around her.

"Were you asleep? I came to see you earlier—"

"No, I wasn't sleeping. I'm glad you came."

Delia turns on the light over the table. "I sense a deep connection between us. I haven't had time to focus on it, but I'd like to. Why don't you take off your coat? It's wet. Hang it over the chair. That's right. Now sit down. I want to look at your palm."

Ordinarily he would be laughing at this, making a story out of it to tell his friends, but he is disarmed, by the wine, the storm, yes, even by the feral teeth of the laughing black woman. And then coming in here like this, with the door open in the middle of the night, and this small person in her threadbare bathrobe ordering him to sit down so she can look at his palm.

Her pale curls fall forward as she bends over his hand. He can feel her breath and her gypsy-child hands tracing hieroglyphics on his skin.

"See, look." She holds his hand up for him to examine. "Here is your heart line, deep and strong, but these feathery little lines all around, can you see them? How they don't quite touch the heart line? Those are your love affairs—many love affairs, many women —but none of them ever quite touch the stream that is the center of your being. Do you understand what I mean?"

"Yes." His throat thickens and his loneliness aches inside him.

"Your heart cries out for its mate, but you are afraid to give in to your heart's desire, isn't that true?"

"They all want something." Gareth is dismayed to hear himself whining.

"Of course they do." The small hands stroke his. "You are rich. You are powerful. They want some of that. But you have plenty. You can give and give and it will only make you stronger."

"I'm afraid."

"You're afraid of the wrong thing. Look, look here at your life line. See how it starts out strong and sure; then look, here in your middle years—"

"What?"

"These lines that come in and deflect the path—"

"Yes?"

"These are your brushes with death."

"What?"

"Think. The fall. The snakebite."

"Accidents."

"Yes, but they can also be considered signs from the heart, the long-starved heart that is pining for its mate, crying, dying for its mate."

"What? Do you see any more? What is this one?"

"Yes. Very good. This one is deeper than the others, isn't it? And it deflects the life line considerably."

"What does it mean?"

"You will leave here, leave my house, and you will drive home in your car thinking over what I have said. It will penetrate very far down. In the morning, all your old life will come crowding in, a busy life, no time to think. You will be quiet for a day or two, and then you will begin to laugh about this. You'll make stories out of it to tell your friends. You'll make it into a little flat story, like a disk you can skim out of your mind. But parts will remain, way down, where you can't see them, can't get at them.

"Now this line right here is your third brush with death."

"What is it? Can you tell? You predicted the others."

"I don't know. It's the heart crying out for its mate, but I can't tell now what it will be. All I can tell you is, if it doesn't end your life, it will change it, drastically."

"My God! Will it come soon?"

She picks up her head, but her face is closed as if she's considering some private matter.

He examines the treacherous line. "Yes, look. It's close to the other two. The other two were—good God! I had my arm in a cast, still in the cast when that sucker bit me! It's coming soon, coming soon. Maybe tonight."

"No, you can't tell. The line isn't like a ruler, calibrated into days and years. Maybe you lived a lot between here and here, in a short space of time, and maybe now your life will be quiet and there will be years before the next—"

"It's tonight! I've had a whole bottle of wine and I was drinking before that. It's tonight. That's why I feel so strange, why I've been doing weird things. I almost threw myself off my terrace earlier. That's it. I can't go out. I can't. Don't let me drive. I'll stay here tonight. Would you let me?" He's holding both her hands in his, clasped, as if in prayer.

"You can have my son's room. The one that used to be his."

The storm is breaking up. Will can see holes where a high altitude wind is biting into the clouds, shredding them and casting them away. The swirling motion overhead makes him giddy. He pushes the sally port shut and leans against it, chilled yet sweating.

With the door closed, the room is darker than night, featureless, without a guiding landmark. But he could find his way back to bed without bumping into anything. He could even take a glass down from the shelf over the bar and fill it with water at the sink. His feet don't need a light to show him the path between the armchair and the television to the bathroom. His body knows the room blind. It's his mind that is making him dizzy, his mind that asks, What is this place? What am I doing here?

All that time spent wanting to know, not wanting to know, finding facts, missing facts. All the time, Nestor knew. He could have told him. All along.

Anna Bird was "queer in the head." That was the expression they used back then, when insane asylums were prisons and people who were mentally ill but not violently so were kept at home. After Zeus Bird's wife died, he couldn't keep a close eye on the child so he sent her to St. Gustav's Academy, a small institution with strong fences and a mixed bag of young people with mental problems.

Zeus left her there until she was nineteen, when he sent for her because he had suffered a mild stroke and was worried that he would die and leave the burden of Anna in the hands of Socrates, who was in law school at the time.

When Anna came home, Zeus was surprised to find she had blossomed, acquired some polish, looked almost normal. She would become overexcited at times; he had to be careful to keep her life calm and ordered, but to the untrained eye, to someone who didn't know, she looked like any other pretty, spirited young woman.

The Birds are honorable men. Zeus wouldn't have gone out of his way to marry Anna off, even though it would be a load off his shoulders, off the shoulders of his son. He wouldn't have tried to pass Anna off. The thing was, William Appleyard, Jr., fell in love. He adored her. The Appleyard parents approved. Could Zeus be blamed for giving his consent, for thinking that perhaps Anna had been cured, that she had only been an excitable young girl?

After the couple came back from their honeymoon and settled in the new mansion the Appleyards had built for them, rumors began sifting through the general gossip of the town. Then one night Appleyard Senior and Appleyard Junior appeared in Zeus Bird's parlor. Socrates was present as well, and it was he who told Nestor the story.

They were all gentlemen about it. No one wanted a divorce. No one wanted scandal. They would try a private nurse at home, and if that didn't work, Anna Bird would be sent away for an indefinite period of time to "convalesce."

What was the connection with Emma Phelps? Nestor didn't

know. Perhaps Anna had visited down there once or twice before the Appleyards caught on to her illness. Later, when Emma Phelps murdered her patron, people recalled that Anna had been seen with her; years later, when William fell from his horse, tongues began to clack.

Nestor told Will this. After living in the man's house for weeks, for months, Will finally met Nestor Bird. After a lifetime of dwelling in murky clouds of rumor, Will finally met the bearer of light, the man who could make it all clear.

The rumor of a curse grew up around a sad, unexplained event. Will's father, Billy, was killed by a rumor. Or maybe not. Perhaps it was only a coincidence and Will is the only one who was finally trapped by the curse.

Now Nestor has lifted it. He has absolved him of guilt, freed him from obligation. Cut him adrift.

Lavinia is crossing the great hall. Will can hear her footsteps overhead, even though she walks lightly in slippers. She can't sleep either. Like him, she is trying to find her balance in a world that has abruptly started pivoting around a different axis.

Will is surprised to see everything dark. Only far down at the end, there's a pale glimmer in the conservatory. Lavinia must be working with her plants. It seems to calm her.

He hears her voice, murmuring low; she talks to the plants. There was a brief fad for that a few years ago. Lavinia seems to think it helps.

The lights aren't on in the conservatory; it's incense candles burning in the back. Moonlight is coming through the glass panes overhead, shining down on Lavinia's hair, which she is wearing loose around her shoulders. She's mumbling something, sounds like a prayer.

"Lavinia?" He stands uncertainly at the door.

"Oh, William!" She giggles. "Oh, William, you scared me half to death."

"I heard you walking around—"

"Oh dear, have you been here long?"

"I just came up and saw the candles, and—"

"You heard me, didn't you. How dreadful and embarrassing. You must think I've gone round the bend."

"It is peculiar, at night—"

"I know, I know, but Señora Ortega made me promise I'd do it, to help Lazaro. She seemed to sense he was in trouble, before it even happened. And there doesn't seem to be much else I can do, so I decided to try this. Actually it makes me feel better. I can consider it a kind of therapy for me, if nothing else."

"I think it's a great idea."

"Are you laughing at me, William? You're humoring me, aren't you?"

He is smiling, grinning even, but only in relief at not having to wait out a long night alone. He'd like to help, sincerely he would.

"We're supposed to recite the Twenty-third Psalm. Do you know it, or should I get the Bible?"

"I think I remember it; if you start, I can sort of trail along."

Will always considered the Twenty-third Psalm a cliché, the Hallmark greeting card of psalms, but in the cloud-scattered moonlight, in the wavering candle shadows, the words lose their Sunday school blandness and take on a primitive immediacy. No longer a churchy petition, the psalm is transformed into an incantation, summoning an ancient war god:

> Thou preparest a table before me
> in the presence of mine enemies;

As they finish, thunder speaks like an answer from the valley. Lavinia looks at him, eyes wide, and takes his hand. "Oh dear, William. Do you think we did that?"

They giggle. Lavinia blows out the candles. Will can still smell the cheap patchouli as he feels his way down to the dungeon.

. . .

It is not unusual for Gareth Watts to wake intimately entwined with a female form and not be able to place exactly who it is. But it is unusual not to be in his own bed. Women usually come to him. This is not his bed. It is not a good bed. He and this female body are sleeping in the middle, as if in a trough, and the mattress is so thin he can feel the springs.

He knows where he is, but he doesn't want to face it. He doesn't want to pick up his head because it will begin to ache. He has a feeling that when he does come to full awareness he will hate what he's done, so he falls back to sleep.

When he wakes again, the fortuneteller Destiny Ortega is standing over him with a glass of orange juice. He takes it from her and the aspirins. She opens the drapes, letting light seep in through unwashed glass, revealing ornate, dusty moldings; an unused fireplace; an ancient silk-covered slipper chair; and the bed, awkwardly placed in the center of this room that was built to be something else. On the table next to the bed where Gareth places his empty glass are a threadbare pack of Tarot cards and a telephone, tools of her trade. What other trade does she ply? What does she want from him?

"It's after noon," she says. "Are you feeling better?"

"My car!"

"It's all right. It's outside."

"Where are my clothes?"

"In my son's room, where you left them."

Gareth fights past her dresses to get through the door. The sleeves cling to him, as if to hold him back. His clothes are scattered around the other bedroom. He throws them on and rushes out. The car is perfectly fine. He owes her an apology, doesn't he? An explanation. But he can't bear to go back inside. He'll call her, write her a letter, send a check.

16

Delia doesn't try to read the signs in weather. There are too many variables: cloud shapes, wind changes, the thickness of dew or frost on the grass in the morning. But weather does have an influence. For instance, in a bright, high-wind day such as this one, people tend to be less thoughtful than they might be on still, overcast days. The light blinds them to subtleties and the wind drives them on to flamboyant conclusions. What bearing all of this will have on Lazaro's hearing, she can't tell.

Her jeans, shirt, sweater, socks, and underpants lie on the braided rug. Delia squats over them, shivering in her nightgown from the wind coming in through the cracks. The tower rooms always were drafty. On cold nights, she and Cass used to camp out on the sofa bed downstairs, the one Will is sleeping in now.

She leaves her everyday clothes in their indecipherable muddle and puts on the dress she brought from home. It must be five or ten years since she wore it last, but it fits fine, a little faded across the top of the shoulders, perhaps. Maybe all the hair flying out at the sides isn't a good idea. She used to know how to put it up in a French twist, but that requires hairpins and she doesn't have any. Lavinia will.

No one's awake in the house, which is odd, considering how keyed up Lavinia was yesterday, her aura trailing off in shreds, every which way.

Each dwelling has its own vibrations. Since childhood Delia has been aware of the castle's, its basic frequency, with alterations according to who's living in it, how the furniture is placed, seasonal changes, leaks in the plumbing. Standing on the second floor outside Lavinia's room, Delia knows that there has been a shift in the night.

Lavinia is still sleeping, young and girlish-looking in the big bed, well over to one side as if she expects someone large to come in and occupy the other half. Delia hates to wake her, but Lavinia would never forgive her if they left for the hearing without her. She lays a hand on her mother's cheek.

Lavinia looks confused for a moment, her mind coming back from a far-off place, and then she smiles.

"Delia. How natural it feels to have you in the house. Isn't that the dress we bought for you at Lord & Taylor? I haven't seen it in a while. It looks lovely on you."

In the kitchen, measuring coffee into Lavinia's old electric percolator, Delia feels the alteration even more, and there's a smell, as if a large humid animal walked through in the night. She plugs the pot in, waiting for the hiss that means it's working.

Where's Will? Still sleeping. From the landing of the stairwell, she can see a long lump in the bed. It's not good to shout a person awake. He must be touched, gently coaxed back into the daylight world. An abrupt awakening could skew his frequencies for the day, or even well into the week.

Will gives her that same initial stunned look that Lavinia did.

Perhaps they were sharing a dream. He sits up, shakes his head. The long piece of hair he keeps to cover his bald spot flops to one side. His eyes are diminished without his glasses. She hands them to him and waits until she comes into focus.

"What an extraordinary outfit."

"I thought I should dress for it, you know."

Will wonders if it is quite the thing for a hearing. He doesn't know much about fashion, but this looks like something left over from another era. As she leaves him, Will notices that she is wearing platform shoes. How long has it been since he's seen a pair of those?

"How about an egg, William?" Lavinia is gotten up in one of her ancient tweed suits, the skirt too big, bunched up around the waist with a belt.

"No thanks, Lavinia. I'll stick to my usual Rice Chex and bran flakes." He can smell incense even here in the kitchen. Delia must have noticed it, but she doesn't mention anything. She is standing at the counter with a can of frozen orange juice, waving a can opener over it, as if she can't quite figure out what sequence of operations results in orange juice. Will takes a pitcher from the cupboard. He takes the can and opener from the small hands, beringed like a gypsy's or a child's. She stands beside him as he stirs the juice with a whisk.

"What a beautiful day," Lavinia exclaims. "The storm cleared up the air. We've been having so many lately. Maybe it's a good sign, that the hearing will go well."

"I don't think you can read it that way." Delia is frowning at the pitcher of orange juice, wondering if she mixed it and forgot. "The weather will have an effect, but I'm not sure whether it will be good or not."

"Well, they can't prove he did it if he's innocent, and we know he's innocent," Lavinia says firmly.

"Of course he is," Delia agrees.

When he's at home with Delia, Lazaro wakes a lot in the night. It scared him when he was little; he'd call for her and she would come and turn on the light, let him hold her hand until he fell back to sleep. But for several years he's been too old for that, so he has to lie awake listening to the whispers and rustlings, the footsteps from the floor above where no one lives.

Here, however, in the Fat Man's house, Lazaro sleeps all night. It's a new house, all one level, with deep, orderly closets for holding clothes and other things. It's peaceful even though it's sad, a good house for sleeping.

The day Lazaro was arrested, the Fat Man drove Lazaro to a mall and bought him clothes: crew neck sweaters, oxford cloth shirts, gray flannel slacks, a navy blue blazer. Lazaro looks like a fruit in them, but the Fat Man told him he has to wear them; it's part of the strategy that Regina and the Fat Man are working out to get him off.

He has to wear the tie today. At first he just knotted it around his neck. That didn't look right. Then he figured that the tie went around under the collar, but the tie is too wide and hangs out underneath. He could turn up the blazer collar in the back. That would look cool and hide the tie sticking out. Yeah, that looks OK, except the knot is too small and the ends dangle down past his waist. He tucks it into his pants.

The Fat Man, in the kitchen, toasting English muffins, is wearing his shirt, one cuff has his monogram in white stitching, *NB*. His silk tie lies completely hidden under the collar in the back. The knot, fat and glossy, fits perfectly into the place where the shirt buttons on top. It ends three-quarters of the way down his grand stomach.

Lazaro pours himself a glass of orange juice and puts plates, knives, napkins, spoons, cups and saucers out. The Fat Man sets a plate of toasted muffins on the table. Lazaro can have jam on only one of them. The other half must have cheese or ham on it. The Fat Man laid this rule down the first day.

The boy is breaking his heart. Nestor passes the milk to him and tries not to look at the way he's done his tie. Twelve years old and no one taught him how to tie a goddamned necktie. Delia, all right—she probably couldn't figure it out herself—but Lavinia, couldn't she have taken it upon herself to teach the kid, for Chrissakes? Couldn't anyone have taken some responsibility for the boy? The total blind incompetency of his family frightens him: Lavinia who can't even see that the castle is falling apart, Delia who willfully keeps herself in the dark about Lazaro's activities, even Cass out in San Francisco, acting out her self-destructive macho fantasy. They're all deluded and helpless.

He blames himself! The self he was twenty, thirty years ago, running his little kingdom, protecting his queen, his princesses, making them into helpless, naive cripples. He knows this now. The irony is that even though he has changed, they persist. They perpetuate the errors he made years ago, and any time he comes in contact with them, his history becomes his present.

Lazaro drinks down his milk. Nestor restrains himself from telling him to wipe his upper lip. Lazaro makes a swipe at his face with his napkin. Good. This is one Nestor hasn't spoiled. He deliberately stayed away. Of course, the kid is a criminal, an arsonist and God knows what else, but at least he is sharp, doesn't trust anyone, and doesn't expect help from anywhere. Nestor likes it that he hasn't asked him to do his tie for him. He hasn't asked him for anything. The kid treats him with the circumspection he would give a boa constrictor.

Nestor never had a son, and a good thing too. He would have destroyed him. But a grandson is another case entirely. There's a distance. What you do doesn't matter as much. The girls had souls like soft wood. Everything he did, good or bad, seared into them, leaving its mark. This boy, this grandson, is protected as if by an electromagnetic field around his heart. He's removed by time, a generation inserted between them, and also by race. By God, the kid speaks a whole other language. He's heard him, on the street, speaking spic—not Spanish, but street spic.

Twenty, thirty years ago, Nestor would have tried to inculcate morals, giving long lectures on the integrity of the Bird family, but now Nestor has broken his own rules and he sees that moral lessons would only annoy this kid. What he needs is practical advice—how to look, what to say. He's been initiated into the two-bit criminal world of the street. Nestor can give him advice on how to handle the more subtle dishonesties of the white professional class.

"Son, why don't you come into the hall with me and stand in front of the mirror. That's right. Now, I think I can give you a few pointers on how to tie a necktie."

Lazaro was expecting something like in the movies, with the judge sitting high in black robes, a jury in the jury box, a railing around the part where the audience sits, flash cameras out on the courthouse steps. There are two reporters here, but they're not allowed to take pictures, or mention his name, because he is underage.

It's that same woman judge, not even in a robe, sitting at a table. Lazaro is at the table, with Delia, the Fat Man, and Regina. Lazaro is proud of his team. His team has class, even though Regina looks a little dykey in her suit, and his mom keeps pulling back her hair, trying to make it neat, which it isn't going to do.

There are seats in the back. Will is there, and Lavinia. Carmen is outside in her guard uniform. She didn't say anything when he passed her, just looked at him. He and Carmen don't need to talk.

Same with the Fat Man, who's a talker, just like he's an eater, but not with Lazaro. With Lazaro he's quiet, only telling him what he needs to know, survival messages. When he showed him how to do the tie, his big neat fingers made the tie look like a piece of string, made Lazaro's neck look skinny, not much thicker than the Fat Man's wrist. The tie obeyed these big calm fingers, neatly twisting into a knot.

"I don't want to say that thing you want me to, about how I was just playing with matches, seeing if that stuff would burn. It makes me sound like a loser. I was getting paid. It was a big job. I dressed up in black and everything," Lazaro said.

The big hands came down around his shoulders, pressing down heavily as if they were deciding whether or not to squash him. "If they think you are just a rather moronic child, they will let you go and you'll have to live here and see a psychiatrist, or a social worker, once a week or something. If they think you were taking money for it, that makes you into a different breed altogether, social vermin, outcast, and they will lock you up in a place where none of us can help you," he said calmly.

"Everyone's going to think I'm just a baby, a dumb jerk baby that plays with matches."

"You think you were so brilliant starting that fire? I went there the day after. It didn't take an expert to tell it was arson. It was a pretty amateurish job. And if you're so smart, how come you are going on trial and the guys who paid you your piddling amount are free? Huh?"

Delia knows by the way Lazaro's vibrations are in sync with Nestor's that Nestor has coached him. Nestor is leaning back in his chair, tapping a pointed yellow pencil on the table, eraser end down, tapping in exact cadence with Lazaro's speech, like a metronome, steadying him, helping him tell his lie. Even the judge seems mesmerized by Nestor's pencil. Her chest, under the silk blouse and gabardine suit, is rising and falling to its measure.

Lavinia squeezes Will's hand, and Will suddenly realizes that he and Lavinia have been holding hands through the entire hearing. Did he take hers or she his? It doesn't matter. It's perfectly comfortable. Their candlelit ceremonies have broken down the separateness between them, like sex is supposed to do but never has for Will.

Lazaro is handling this beautifully. His size was in his favor right away. Will heard a murmur in the room when Lazaro walked in, so small and slight, almost frail, really. It fits that a small, weak boy would be drawn to the power of fire. It fits what people think they know about the way people behave.

The judge wants to believe him. She has no desire to send a little boy to prison. The only one who could wreck it for them, and they anticipated this, is the fire chief, Marcioni, who wants to solve all his fires at one time. Isn't it a coincidence, he asks the judge, that this fire, although by far the biggest, was actually the third unexplained one in an old industrial building, and all of these industrial buildings were held by Grand Land?

Nestor doesn't say anything to this, although everyone knows he's on the board of directors of Grand Land. He waits until someone else, one of the fire chief's own men, recalls that one of those buildings belonged to Grand Land. The other had no connection.

But why so many fires? The fire chief wants to know. His blue eyes, a startling contrast to his olive skin, go to Lazaro, who fidgets under the stare. "I don't want to send a young man to jail, Your Honor, but brave men have been risking their lives. Homes have been lost. We know these fires didn't start from natural causes. Now we have the evidence, the confession, that this young man started that fire. It stands to reason if he could play with matches inside that mill, he could play with matches inside other mills. I think we're letting the small size of this perpetrator blind us to the fact that arson has been committed several times over in our city. This is not a kid who played with matches once. This is a dedicated arsonist, and I would like to bet that he's a professional arsonist at that."

It's time for Nestor to speak. Everyone feels it. He's been keeping quiet, but now it's time to explain what his part is.

"Your Honor, may I have a word?" His voice comes from deep in his chest. He conserves his energy, barely turning his thick neck to make contact with the judge. "Mr. Marcioni, our fire chief, a brave and intelligent man, with whom I have worked closely on many matters over the years, has stated that these fires which have plagued Wallingford over the past eighteen months have not been the result of natural causes. By natural causes, he means lightning, spontaneous combustion. Even bad wiring, if unintentional, can come under the heading of natural causes for a fire inspector. I would like to suggest another natural cause. It is pent-up, frustrated ambition in the young male *Homo sapiens*. Let us think for a moment of all the energy contained in the several thousand young male bodies that live in Wallingford as a natural force, like water power. All of this power, this thrusting, driving urge, has to go somewhere. Traditionally, communities have channeled this energy into athletics. Wallingford, however, long ago lost its middle class to the suburbs. The people who sit on the school board are no longer parents of public school students. They are mainly concerned with how they can keep taxes down within the city. Why spend large amounts of money on athletic uniforms, coaches, fields, so that the kids can steal the equipment and have knife fights in the locker rooms after the games?" Nestor's hand goes up to forestall interruptions, although no one is going to interrupt Nestor Bird. "I'm not blaming anyone. I never raised my voice to say, 'Hold it, we have to have a football team.' I let it go. I agreed. Why cast pearls before swine? I was all for closing the youth center after a gang of kids tore it up five years ago. What's the answer? I don't know. I am simply describing a natural force.

"Now this force, this combined energy of trapped young males, has no legitimate outlet. School is a strange, foreign place. If they succeed there, they will lose their identity. They will become the enemy. So this force, having no escape valve, wreaks its vengeance on our poor forsaken city. The force twists fences out of shape, scars buildings and monuments with graffiti, breaks store windows in the night, and God help us when it gets ahold of a knife, an automobile, or a book of matches."

Where are these words coming from? This is not what he intended to say, but he has them, all of them: Lavinia and Will, holding hands on the sidelines; Regina, her neck going blotchy with excitement; his own dear princess, with round, trusting eyes; Lazaro hardly breathing; Marcioni taking it in; and Judge Sanders intently peering over her glasses.

"I'm not saying," he continues in a calmer tone, "that these youngsters aren't to be held responsible for their crime because of their unfortunate backgrounds. Only that any one of five hundred or a thousand or five thousand young men in our blighted city could have, probably have, and will start similar fires. Just because Marcioni has the boy who started this fire doesn't mean he has the only arsonist in town."

Nestor has not asked his grandson about other fires. He doesn't want to know. It's bad enough, perjuring himself once, although as Lazaro pointed out to him, he is saving his own ass as well. The boy doesn't miss much.

The judge is a good-looking woman, wears earrings with pizzazz, has a beautifully organized mind, but humane. Nestor's counting on the humanity.

She's the mother of boys. She has probably stood with them before a mirror and showed them how to tie a necktie. When you do something for them, even the smallest thing, it unleashes the protective hormones. Judge Sanders has an abundance of those hormones. He can tell because he has the same affliction, just as he can recognize a fellow philanderer (Edgar Snow, the bastard). People who are plagued with an overdose of protective hormones cannot repress the urge to guard the young and the weak.

Can the judge see how the mother and son lean in toward each other, how much the son looks like the mother, just a shade or two darker, the color of milk with a little coffee added to it? What are her views on interracial marriage? Accepting. She's been a family court judge long enough to have seen everything. Does she see how calm the boy is? Too calm? He has everyone here. All his protectors.

Carmen is pacing the hall outside the hearing room, waiting to find out so she can go back and tell Mama. Delia should have given the baby to them when Jaime died. There's something wrong with that girl. She can't raise a child. She can't tell fortunes either. Some girls who went to her told Carmen she's no good. She can hardly speak Spanish.

Carmen isn't going to have babies; that's not for her. She's a security guard now, but she's going to go into the police academy, and after she makes it with the police, she's going to law school nights and become a lawyer. After she becomes a lawyer, she's going to get appointed judge.

That's Delia's sister coming now, running down the hall. Carmen only saw her once, at the funeral, but she remembers.

"Which is the room where they're having the hearing on the Ortega boy? About the fire?" Cass doesn't recognize her, but Carmen didn't expect her to. She points to the door. Cass rushes in without saying thank you.

"I'm sorry," Cass says, her hair swinging back and forth as she cuts into her ham and eggs (Will likes women who eat). "I can't believe he's doing it out of the goodness of his heart. After all these years of never talking to Lazaro, he's suddenly becoming his legal guardian, taking him into his home."

"Maybe he likes him." Lavinia brings the coffee pot to the table. "Another drop to warm it up, Cass dear? Lazaro has a lot of charm, you have to admit it, and he's been living very nicely with Nestor. He looked so handsome in those clothes, didn't he? A little gentleman."

"A little gentleman arsonist." Cass mops up her egg with a piece of toast. "That's another thing. I can't believe Lazaro started the fire just playing around with matches. He's too conscious for that."

"But why would he admit to starting the fire if he didn't do it, and there were witnesses—"

"Oh, I think he started the fire, Mom, but not accidentally—"

"Why would he start a fire on purpose?"

"For money. It's not unheard of, people hiring boys to start fires for them—"

"I can't believe that Lazaro would purposely burn down people's houses—"

"He didn't mean to. He started the fire in the mill. It was the fault of the wind and the clogged water pipes that the fire spread to those houses."

"Who would want to burn the mill?"

"Who would stand to collect the insurance money?"

"Cass! I forbid you. You are going too far. Your father may have his faults, but he would never commit arson, and he would certainly not hire his grandson to do it for him."

"Maybe not, but I bet there's a connection somewhere."

Lavinia takes the empty plate away from Cass.

"Don't wash it, Mom. I'll clean up."

Lavinia sighs and looks at her daughter. For a minute, Will can see how it must have been back before Cass moved out—the rebellious daughter, the hurt, bewildered mother.

Cass studies her coffee. Lavinia's gone to the conservatory. Will can hear the sound of her boots on the gravel.

"Actually," Cass admits to her coffee, "I don't think he'd do it either, but he might have gotten involved in a mess—he's enormously greedy—he may have gotten mixed up in some shady stuff and it's in his interest to keep Lazaro. Poor Delia. She'll never get him back."

"If she were to marry someone—" Will hears himself saying.

"Oh sure, if she found someone reputable with a job, who wanted to adopt her son the arsonist—" Cass looks at him. "You? Are you thinking of applying for the position of rescuer-prince?"

"I thought of it. I thought about it a lot. I get ready to ask and then I chicken out."

"Are you afraid she'll turn you down or are you afraid she'll accept?"

Will smiles. "God, I don't know. It's so crazy here. It is, you know—it's nuts. I think differently here. I spent a lot of time tracking down a curse on my family. I'm not usually like this. Your father seems to be the only one who's sane."

"He's the one who drove them all insane. No, you're right; they're so out of touch, that's what it is, Delia and my mother. I mean, my mother, OK—she's older—but Delia buried herself after Jaime died. I didn't think she'd ever come out of it, but it's a good sign that she's been able to, you know, have a relationship. All those years without sex. I can't imagine it. If I go two weeks—"

"Oh. No, we haven't, we didn't—"

"You haven't even—"

"No, nothing."

"Aren't you attracted to each other? You want to, but—"

"No, not especially. I like her. I think she's pretty, but we haven't ever been attracted that way—"

"Then it won't work."

"If I want to help—I do want to help."

"But you can't, that way, don't you see? It's not love. It won't work. You don't marry someone because you want to help her. That's the worst possible thing."

17

It's a scene that would warm a probation officer's heart (run without sound, of course): the prominent attorney at his desk, and his grandson, former misguided youth from the slums, now in a proper blue blazer and maroon tie (what a difference from the first time she saw him in the judge's chambers, huddled down in that filthy jacket), bringing him a file, going over some information with him. Nestor has put his grandson in a private school. Every afternoon the boy comes here to the office, to help on a special project. When he isn't needed, he does his homework, gets A's and B's, a model student, no trouble. To the outsider, it's a miraculous success story.

"This dude here has a coke habit." Lazaro points to a name on a list.

"What do you mean?"

"He takes coke, you know, man—"

"Sir," Nestor corrects him.

"You know, sir, the drug."

"Guilford? Are you certain?"

"I know where he's buying it. Here." Lazaro pulls a piece of paper torn from his school notebook out of his pocket. "Here's his name and number. He says we can use it to put the squeeze on Guilford."

Nestor takes the paper, smooths it out on the desk, shaking his big head sorrowfully. "I had no idea. That's the entire zoning board. Easier than I thought. Everyone's got something he wants to hide, or someone he has to protect. Everyone has his rotten spot." He pushes the paper away from him, like a loathsome chunk of offal. "Regina, can you handle this one? It will be more discreet, coming from you."

Regina puts the paper in the pocket of her jacket. He knows she won't argue. Regina's not one to fool herself, to comfort herself with lies, to vacillate. Once she agreed to get involved in "Grand Scam," as Nestor calls it, she's never faltered.

Guilford is the last member of the zoning board who hasn't been blackmailed or bribed into voting for the resource recovery center (*i.e.*, the garbage burner). The center will employ many more unskilled workers than the artists' lofts and boutiques would have. Pollution will be kept to a minimum, causing only one extra case of cancer for every one million people. It will cut energy bills, and Nestor is arranging a deal where Ecosource (*i.e.*, the garbage people) will donate a sports center to the youth of Wallingford. Just incidentally, the sale of the property will save Grand Land from bankruptcy, from the publicity of an investigation. It will save Nestor Bird's large, well-cared-for hide.

And, to be fair, the sale will ensure Regina of her place as the youngest and most recent member of the partnership in Bird, Bainbridge & Tulc, brought in over the heads of several older, better-looking male associates, carried in on the broad shoulders of Nestor Bird, who deemed her indispensable, a jewel in the crown, and other hyperboles. There is one advantage to being ugly. No one has accused her of sleeping her way to the top.

Regina takes the piece of paper. Nestor and Lazaro bend their heads over their work in identical gestures. When Regina first saw Lazaro, she never would have taken him for Nestor's grandson, but lately she's begun to see a resemblance. In the lower lip, perhaps? The shape of the head? Or maybe it's the air of assurance, something in the eyes, a concentration of energy.

Regina's neck gets blotchy and red when she takes the paper, like the Fat Man was asking her to pick up a used rubber. Lazaro ducks his head over his homework so she won't see him smile. The Fat Man plays her like a radio. She hates him but she lets him use her because she needs the power and money. The Fat Man tries to charm her, treating her like a woman, and she hates that too because she knows she has a big, bony nose and hips that start where her waist belongs. Besides, she's a dyke. She lives with a girl blacksmith, out of town in a little house Regina just bought. They have a garden and a couple of chickens. The Fat Man is using Regina, but she's using him too. The only difference is that the Fat Man likes Regina and she hates him.

The homework is easy. The Fat Man makes a big deal over the A's and B's even though it doesn't take brains to get A's and B's from the nuns. Getting that piece of paper took intelligence, but the Fat Man doesn't want to think about that. The Fat Man doesn't want to know that he is using Lazaro, so he tells himself he loves him, that he's proud of his grades.

Hugo gave him the piece of paper. Hugo's back in town. Lazaro stopped off at the station on the way home from school. He had to do it carefully, so he wouldn't be seen. He and Hugo had a talk inside the office, away from the eyes. Hugo has his own reasons for wanting the garbage cooker to go through. He's working on it from his side, the underside.

Hugo sat back in his chair. He twirled his leopard medallion on the end of its gold chain and he bragged about the money he was making, mob connections, a house he bought in Puerto Rico. He got up from his chair and strutted around, so Lazaro could see how he'd lost weight. He's jogging, taking vitamins, cutting out fried foods. He wouldn't give Lazaro a cigarette.

"I stopped smoking. You should too, you know. It stunts your growth."

If Lazaro ever gets in trouble again, he said, he should come to him; Lazaro needs a mentor. Lazaro didn't mention that Hugo was the one who got him into trouble in the first place, that Hugo left town while Lazaro took the heat. Hugo, like the Fat Man, wants to think he is helping Lazaro, while he's really out for himself. That's all right. There are things to learn from both of them.

Lazaro jumped down from the edge of Hugo's desk, where he'd been sitting watching his feet in polished loafers moving back and forth while Hugo bragged. "I gotta go. It won't be too cool if someone sees me here."

"You're in good shape. The heat's definitely off." Still, Hugo looked out the window before he opened the door.

"Say, listen," he said, quietly, his hand on the door, blocking Lazaro's way. "There's one person who could potentially do us some harm, you know what I mean? It's that wimp who was writing a history. You know the guy. OK? The thing is, he's been asking some funny questions. I was thinking of sending someone around, to talk him into—just work him over a little—"

"Bad idea. That won't stop him."

"He's just a wimpy guy. He's built like a marshmallow."

"No. You're wrong, man. That's the wrong way to handle him. Let me think about it."

"OK, but don't forget, all right? If you're going to be a criminal, you got to think criminal all the time. That's where your old man went wrong. He was part-time."

Hugo's a businessman, but he's crude. He never had the advantages of a mentor like the Fat Man. Lazaro wonders if Hugo knows how to tie a necktie. Ten-to-one he doesn't.

The Fat Man has taught Lazaro how to tie a necktie, how to polish his shoes. He's taught him that everyone has a soft spot, a way he can be approached. If you know the right place, just a gentle push can change a man's direction.

The Fat Man knows all about Will and what he's doing. Lazaro and the Fat Man have discussed it. The Fat Man gave his furniture away, and he and Lazaro went and picked out four chairs, green leather—"club chairs," is what the Fat Man calls them. At night the Fat Man and Lazaro sit in the living room in the green chairs and go over matters like Will.

Will knows things about the Fat Man. He knows the worst thing the Fat Man ever did, which was to keep a woman in jail— Hot Emma, as it turns out. The Fat Man went to visit her in jail because he felt sorry for her. He was going to let her out, he felt guilty because his own father had kept her in, but when he saw her—ugly, dirty hair, scabs on her face, her arms, and she screamed at him, things about his father, his grandfather, and his aunt—he left her there, left her to die in prison.

The Fat Man had a talk with Will about this. He thought they had straightened things out, but now Will is snooping around, asking questions, and the Fat Man doesn't know why. What has he got against him? The Fat Man says Will is dangerous because he wants something and he doesn't know what it is.

If there's a breeze, it's too much and it blows the papers around, and if there isn't any, it's too hot in the tower to work, so Will has taken what he needs from the archives and set himself up in his room, the old game room, the dungeon, shadowed and cool. It's a more fitting place in which to work out his vision of greed and mysticism intertwining like amorous snakes through the history of Wallingford.

Begin with mysticism, with the falls that the Indians never dared approach alone because the spiritual power was too great for one person; even in groups, they reserved their visits for specific times of the year.

Enter greed in the form of Alexander Hamilton picnicking by the same waterfall, plotting how he will surround it with mills and bleed its life away in a veinwork of canals.

The mighty cascade is hemmed in, diminished, harnessed to the yoke of greed, but the spiritual power lingers over the valley, manifesting itself in the German May Day celebrations, in the rumors of the Appleyard curse, and most recently, in a thriving Afro-Caribbean cult—Santeria. (It has a name and followers, Will has learned; it isn't the particular madness of Lazaro's grandmother, although she may be mad.)

Mysticism is elusive. It forms the underground history of Wallingford. It's the solace, the opiate, of the weak, those who haven't learned to locate the real source of power. Greed, on the other hand, is painfully visible. Wallingford celebrates greed. Mill owners make fortunes from Wallingford and give nothing back. City officials siphon money from public funds and then move to the suburbs, where the schools are good and the streets are clean.

Finally, mysticism and greed come together in a great howling combustion on the banks of the Walling River. On Christmas Eve, a fire-eating, twelve-year-old disciple of Chango, god of fire, burns down the Appleyard mills, thereby destroying evidence of a development swindle.

A halfhearted investigation gets under way. The twelve-year-old is brought in and remanded to the custody of one of Wallingford's leading citizens, who promptly goes into partnership with the boy to subvert any further investigation. The boy has links to the criminal underclass, which has something on nearly all of the legitimate leaders of Wallingford.

The partnership succeeds so brilliantly that—the latest coup—they've managed to push through a zoning change that will permit a monstrous garbage-cooker to go up on the site of the mills. The investors in the original swindle get their money back, and the city of Wallingford pays the price: a round-the-clock rumble of garbage trucks, an increase in air pollution, and a load of dioxin-rich ash.

Wallingford has been sold out again. What was there left to save? the cynic might ask, looking around at the multilevel parking garages which now take on deeper meaning for Will: the mayor at the time they were built had a brother-in-law who put up concrete parking garages, simple as that. One morning's research turned up this little nest of coincidences. Why hasn't anyone ever stepped in and cleaned house, when evidence of corruption lies around like the fossils of scorpions on the red cliffs, just waiting to be picked up? It's too pervasive. There is no one in the whole city who isn't implicated.

Will has told the university he's not going back in the fall, that he needs another semester to write up his research, although he already knows they aren't going to accept it. It's too broad, too literary, and it won't stay in the past but keeps jumping into the present, even leaping into the future. But he can't leave it now, after he's done all his research, and he can't write it any way other than as he sees it. If he finishes he'll have to publish it, privately if necessary. He can't permit himself to worry about what the department heads will think, or what he's doing to Nestor, Lazaro, or even Lavinia.

Will's glasses are fogging over in the dampness. He takes them off and wipes them on his shirt. He's feverish and cold at the same time. His skin feels slimy from being underground too much. He opens the sally port and steps out onto the driveway, startling a snake who, like him, has come out of his hole to dry his skin in the sun. The snake rustles off into the grass and waits quietly for Will to go back inside.

The castle looks less run-down in the summer. The vines help, and Lavinia's pots of geraniums, impatiens, tuberous begonias. She's hoping to sell the place this summer while it's looking its best. Will didn't even know she was thinking about selling until Lavinia came flying down the stairs one day asking him to tidy up his papers because a realtor was showing some people through.

It hurt him more than it should have that she had not consulted him first—shades of his childhood, he supposes. Lavinia is so busy now, showing the house and also working up some business plan with Bubbles, that she's never around. Perhaps it isn't fair, but it seems that after Delia left town and it was obvious she and Will weren't going to marry, Lavinia lost interest in Will.

Looking back, it's actually comical how he had gotten it fixed in his mind that he was the one to save Delia and Lazaro. Even after Cass told him, even after Nestor dissolved the idea of the curse, Will had to see it through to its final absurdity.

He had gone over to Delia's house. She was taking her dresses down, putting them in an old American Tourister suitcase, probably a Christmas present from her parents long ago. She was cramming her dresses into her suitcase with the idea of moving to New York and staying at Will's mother's apartment, working from there until she could find her own place.

Will couldn't help laughing at the image of his mother and Mrs. Jivinsky taking in a homeless fortuneteller. Then his heart leaped, and he heard himself rushing on about the house in St. Louis with the basketball hoop over the garage. As he was saying it, he finally realized how impossible it was.

She drew him into the light, asked to see his palm, examined that one, did the other as well. Then she took both his hands in hers and smiled at him.

"How's my life line?"

"Long. You're going to live a long time."

"Children?"

"Yes. I think so."

"What do you think of my—my idea?"

"You're still doing it. You're still trying to drive your life from the outside. It unfolds, from within. Don't you see?"

She said it didn't matter if she couldn't stay with Will's mother. She had a friend in the city who would take her in.

When Lavinia sells the castle, his connection with the Bird family will be at an end. Lavinia thought he was The One, the savior of the family, or of Delia and Lazaro anyway. Instead, he's turned out to be a viper in the family's bosom.

"What's happenin', man?" Lazaro comes out from behind the rhododendron, grinning like a little monkey, pleased with himself for sneaking up so artfully, for making Will jump.

"You were scared, weren't you?"

"I was startled. You were so quiet, like an Indian—"

Lazaro laughs, like a boy, like any normal twelve-year-old boy. He puts his hand on Will's shoulder, confusing him with his childish affection. A small, slight figure in his T-shirt and jeans, he doesn't fit the image Will has been building from his research. Perhaps Will has missed something, or interpreted wrongly.

Lazaro sits on the steps in front of the sally port. Will squats beside him. The snake slithers a few more feet into the shelter of the hydrangea bush.

"When do you go to camp?"

"Friday."

Will wonders if he'll like it, if he'll find anything in common with those kids from wealthy suburbs, from Park Avenue. Lavinia has been sewing labels into tennis shorts, soccer shirts, bathing trunks—clothes for games Lazaro doesn't know how to play.

"How's your mother?"

"She's OK. She says she's going to have it fixed so I can live with her next fall."

How is she going to manage that? She probably sees it in her cards, or her tea leaves.

"They're tearing down my old house."

"I heard. Are you sorry?"

Lazaro picks up a stone and hefts it in his hand. "Naw. It was full of ghosts, all those dead whores rustlin' around. Maybe that lady will go away now and leave you alone."

"What lady?"

"Hot Emma, the one who put the curse on you."

"Oh. I'd forgotten about that."

"Oh yeah?"

"Uh-huh. See, a curse is really an idea you carry deep in your mind. So deep, that you can't reason with it. Only another unreasonable idea, magical, irrational, has the power to penetrate into the subconscious and cancel it out. That's why that ceremony with the chicken that your abuela put me through could have worked, because it was full of all kinds of powerful symbols that the subconscious could understand. The only trouble was that it was too strong. For my cultural background. If anything, it planted the curse even more firmly in my mind."

"So what do you think got rid of it?"

"History, actually. I found some things out; a lot was up in those papers and I just hadn't read them carefully, and then your grandfather, he told me some more and it turned out my family wasn't as guilty as I thought. And then, I guess, your mother too. She read my palm and said I'd have a long life. Things as silly as that can have an effect with the subconscious. The upshot is I don't feel guilty or responsible or cursed anymore."

Lazaro turns the stone over in his hand. "Yeah, but you still aren't going anywhere."

"What do you mean?"

"You know, you're still hiding out. You're even worse than before. You're skittering around on the edges, like you don't want anyone to see you."

"I've been working on my dissertation."

"Yeah? What's it about?"

"Corruption, greed, mysticism—"

"You're wasting your time." Lazaro gets up slowly, stone in hand.

"I need it to get my doctorate."

Lazaro, stalking something in the grass, seems not to hear, any more than would a cat intent on hunting.

"If I don't get my doctorate—Lazaro, for heaven's sake, don't kill it—"

But the stone has already been thrown.

"I missed him. You broke my concentration."

"Why would you want to kill a snake anyway? They're good for the garden. They're harmless."

"I hate snakes."

"Well, just like you have to kill a snake, although there's no reason for it, I have to do this history, because it attracts me," Will tries lamely.

"You know what I think? I think you got so used to living with the curse that you can't let go of it. You're still lying low. You're still not going anywhere." Lazaro gives one last look at the bush, in case the snake has returned, and runs for the path in the woods.

"Where should I go?" Will calls down the bank.

"San Francisco."

18

The call came in the morning, at that perilous time when the underbrain is most active, when it sends up bizarre Boschian images, sea creatures that turn out to be vaginas with spiny legs, nasty stuff that shouldn't be found in the sleeping head of a man his age with his stature in the community. Other men of his position are not troubled by technicolor nightmares. Their dreams are dim and colorless, ordered, sequential. Who does he inherit this from? Not Zeus or Socrates. Anna. Crazy Anna must have had dreams. Anna, attracted by the underside, and now he, in spite of the best intentions, being sucked down—

When the phone rang, his mind, in its disordered state, flew to the kid at camp, inventing disasters, piling them up one after the other at microsecond intervals. But it wasn't the kid, or some stranger's voice from camp. The voice was one he knew well, intimately, but it was altered by fear and by the necessity of speaking very softly so as not to wake someone sleeping nearby.

She wants to come home. She had no idea what Snow was mixed up in, the hiding, the running. And Snow has changed. He doesn't shave, wears terrible clothes. He even smells bad.

Donna wants to come home to Nestor, or if he won't take her, she'll call her parents. Either way, she's coming back, tainted with knowledge of Snow's crimes, trailed no doubt by a hired killer. She still doesn't comprehend that the fourth-rate city she grudgingly called home has become forbidden to her, more impossible than Lhasa. Lhasa's easy. The Chinese would give her a visa to Tibet, but who can guarantee her safe passage to Wallingford?

He said he'd call her later tonight, but she couldn't give him a number. She's going to call back. Please don't make it early in the morning, he said.

He puts the water up for coffee, still a little shaky. A quick call up to camp would reassure him—no, he promised he'd only telephone once a week. It makes sense. He's got to give the boy room to breathe.

Breathing has become a problem. He thinks he forgets to, because he will suddenly take a breath and it will feel as if he did it just in the nick of time, that he was on the brink of suffocation. The brain stem is supposed to take care of breathing. It's automatic. But if he has a cancer in the brain stem—something the doctor didn't test for when he had his physical—

"You're going to die anyway," the doctor said calmly as he pulled the hypodermic out of his arm. Gareth insisted on the penicillin as a preventive measure, although there were no symptoms of venereal disease. He had meant to get one right after his night with Destiny, but his work prevented it. He's never bothered by concerns for his own health when he's working on a project. It's afterward.

Completion brings on fear of death. And yet, you have to com-

plete. Why? Because we've organized it that way. Because we die.
The urge to finish is a death wish. But fear of completion is a
weakness. You'll never be anything if you give in to it.

"When I read the reviews I figured your name would be appear-
ing on my appointment sheet. I usually see it there a week or so
after reading it in the *Times.*" A tall man, the doctor, English,
with absolutely no bedside manner. He sent Gareth's blood, his
urine, to the laboratory and called yesterday to tell him he was in
no immediate danger of dying, "barring the odd snakebite or tumble downstairs, of course."

Now he has this breathing problem, which he will no doubt die
from because he doesn't want to go back and face his doctor's
sardonic wit.

He's willing to admit that it may be psychological. The problem
did get better as he drove across the bridge. He wasn't even thinking about it until he discovered that the house has disappeared.

He's been around the block several times and he is convinced
this is where it stood, where this vacant lot is now. Weedy, some
old tires scattered around—the lot could have been like this for
years, but the chain-link fence around it is new.

It's reasonable to believe that an old, nearly abandoned house
that was standing—months ago, could have been torn down, that
weeds could have grown over the bulldozed earth. It would be
irrational to think that the house disintegrated or was swallowed
up by the earth after that shameful and disturbing night.

And he does remember a gas station across the street. It was
closed. It's open now, and prospering. A front for something, he
thinks, dope or numbers, a handy drive-in crime center.

A kid comes over to fill the tank, claims to know nothing about
a fortuneteller and her son, can't remember the house across the
street, thinks it was always like that, a vacant lot.

Questions arouse suspicions at the drive-in crime center. The
boss comes over, one of those slick young Hispanic men who know

all the angles, wears a loose Hawaiian-type shirt, gold chains, with a medallion showing a leopard pouncing. Destiny Ortega? Never heard of her. Maybe there was a house across the street, but he doesn't remember.

Gareth sees him in the side mirror, standing with his legs apart, his arms folded across his chest, waiting for him to go, get out. Oh, what the hell. He's got nothing against her. She didn't mean him any harm. "Yo! You! Hey, you!" But he doesn't hear him. With the windows up and the air conditioner on, he could be a hundred miles away. Hugo wonders if he is The One and if he'll find her anyway, if it matters that Hugo did not tell him she went to New York. Does fate have one chance—two? Or does it work itself out no matter what?

Florio's is a perfectly logical place to stop for lunch at one o'clock in the afternoon. But if he's learned one thing in his dealings with Destiny Ortega and her city of enchantment where houses disappear as if they never existed, it's that the laws of logic don't always apply out here. What else besides hunger and the promise of good food draws him in? If this were one of Gareth's cruder, earlier films, there would be a confrontation—Destiny by magical coincidence sitting at a table alone, or her son, big-eyed and skinny, washing dishes in the back. (Gareth would glimpse him through the door, opening and closing like a shutter on a camera when the waiters pass through.) If Gareth were directing the scene at his present level of sophistication, there would be something so subtle going on that it would be unphotographical—a repositioning of the ions in the air that would turn the vector of his life a fraction of a degree, a change so slight that it would not be perceived until days later when he would suddenly see (or perhaps never realize) that the course of his life had been drastically and irrevocably changed.

"Get a chair . . . give him water . . . Jesus-mary-an'-joseph!"

Some commotion here—actors doing a scene Gareth can't remember from the script, and he himself trapped on the wrong end
of the camera. Thick arms thrust themselves under his armpits—
raspy breathing behind him, and from his own chest, nothing,
stillness only, like iron bands around his chest—

He's OK. No problem. Happens often. Asthma. They make him
sit in a straight chair, drink water. They watch him pull air into
his abused lungs. See, he's fine. His Jaguar of course is put away in
the lot by now, not that he could persuade them to let him drive
away after that little show. They're talking ambulances, for Christ-
sake. The captain is still red-faced, wiping his brow and hands with
a big linen napkin, doesn't want to leave Gareth at a table, keeps
looking back, expecting him to keel over.

Gareth smooths back his hair and orders a Barbaresco '77. He
picks up a breadstick, holds it like a cigarette, and longs to put it
to his lips and inhale deeply, a trick he's learned to cut the crav-
ing for nicotine, but he doesn't want to draw attention to himself
again.

He'd feel out of place and exotic here even without the fainting
fit, or whatever it was. The crowd today is all bland-faced and
polyestered, businessmen escaping from the sterile industrial parks
along the highway. None of the remarkable faces he remembers
from the first time, the night of the electrical storm. The whole
place is shabbier in the daylight. The food will no doubt be me-
diocre, not worth the journey from the city.

In fact, aside from that momentary scare about his breathing,
this is turning out to be a flat and pointless journey, one he won't
tell anyone about. Not worth a story, certainly not worth the expense of shooting the scene. No one, not even Eric Rohmer, could
get away with this, allowing the hero's flirtation with witchcraft,
magic, or whatever to flatten out and fade to nothing. But unfortunately, it's the way life often works.

Someone has come in, a local nabob; there's a flurry at the door, a bigger reception than he got, even with his Jaguar and asthma attack. It's a fat man, beautifully dressed in a linen suit, and by his side, a slender gray-haired woman wearing something suitable for a garden party twenty years ago. They can't be husband and wife, or business associates—certainly not relatives. But there's something going on. The old lady slips into her chair as gracefully as a girl.

She caught him staring at her. He switches his focus to the picture of Mt. Vesuvius on the wall behind her. It's as if she could tell him something, but what? The magic is creeping back in, or maybe it's the Barbaresco bringing back the feeling of what it was like that night.

When he woke up that morning in Destiny's lumpy bed, it all seemed incomprehensible. He's been avoiding the memory, walking around it as if it were some putrid carcass, but now these particular circumstances—the wine, Florio's, even that other-worldly old lady over there—are bringing back the feeling of how it was.

Gareth swirls the Barbaresco against his palate, hoping that by analyzing the different layers of taste in the wine he will be able to penetrate through to that feeling. What was it about making love with Destiny Ortega, that quality both familiar and strange? It was like coming home—yes! But at the same time realizing that home is a queer and fantastical place.

Lavinia is not going to tell Nestor that that man has been looking at her since they came in. It would just disturb him. Nestor frequently acts as if she's gone a little soft in the head since he knew her in their previous incarnation as man and wife. But he was looking at her and now he's deliberately not looking at her.

He's wearing soft-looking loafers, moccasins, if moccasins can be that expensive and fine; slacks of interesting silkiness; and a loose shirt Lavinia finds herself wanting to touch. His hair, peaked with silver, is brushed back and grows over his collar. It's his face that is most arresting: deep creases down the sides, hooded eyes, a slightly hooked nose with flared nostrils, full lips, a day's growth to his beard that looks deliberate. He's leaning back, lost in some reverie, sipping red wine. He's not like anyone Lavinia's ever known and yet he looks familiar.

"He must be someone famous," she whispers to Nestor.

Nestor is occupied with the menu although he must know it by heart. "Who?"

"That man. He's a writer, or an artist. Maybe an actor. Do you recognize him?"

She forgot that Nestor cannot just turn his head. Imagine being encased in all that fat! It must be like wearing a big padded suit everywhere. He's not fatter than he ever was, but the flesh is both flimsier—hanging in folds off his jowls, around his neck—and harder to move. His skeleton has stiffened. Poor Nestor. He pushes his chair back and turns his whole body from the hips. "Looks like a hairdresser to me."

Lavinia studies the bas-relief of Mount Vesuvius on the wall. "I think I'll have lasagna."

"Have some meat, for God's sake. You don't eat enough protein. All you had in the cupboard was a package of cookies."

"Lasagna has cheese. That will be enough protein. Shall we have wine?"

"In the middle of the day?"

"Isn't that what you used to do?"

"What do you mean?"

"You know, with your mistresses."

"I don't know what you're talking about."

"Oh, come on, Nestor, sure you do. That's why you would never take me here. You used to come here with them."

"Lavinia, I—"

"Oh, don't sputter, dear. I'm not trying to put you on the spot.

I'm just kind of curious. You don't mind, do you? About that other part of your life I didn't know. There was one I knew, what was her name? Maureen? She worked at the five-and-dime."

"Maureen—"

"She sold nail polish. I went to take a peek at her once."

"Big breasts."

"That's right. She wore pointy bras, and that incredibly silver hair. Her eyebrows were jet black."

That fat man called him a hairdresser. Mistaken for a hairdresser in Wallingford. It's a good story. The feeling of magic, of significance, has passed. Now it's all just funny, this overdecorated, fifties-style, has-been Mafia hangout, with these polyester businessmen and this fat guy who calls him a hairdresser practically to his face. It's a kick. He has to bring some friends down one night, maybe someone who'll take it seriously and someone who won't and wives or dates or something. Look at that couple. They're outrageous. He's growling out some story and she's practically falling off her chair laughing. The whole town is a nut case.

"Here." Nestor empties the wine into their glasses. "We forgot to toast your deal. I still can't believe you got your price."

"I don't think they know anything about houses. They're from the city, you know. They live in an apartment where they don't have to worry about beams and gutters. Or maybe they don't care. They're orchid freaks, did I tell you? They're going to adopt the orchids, so they won't have to leave home." Lavinia swirls down her wine, her eyes still gleaming with tears from laughing over his stories.

"You didn't even ask me about selling the castle, Lavinia."

"I assumed you'd approve. You always wanted me to and you were so critical about the way I'd kept it. It is appalling how much work needs to be done. Lucky these folks are young and rich."

"Yes. Of course. It's a wise move, selling. I agree completely. But it is odd, isn't it, that all these years you've been keeping it until I return, and now that I want to come back, you can't wait to unload it."

"Now that you put it that way, yes, I guess it is odd."

"Will you come live with me, Lavinia? Would you stay with me tonight? I've been lonely since Lazaro left for camp."

"I couldn't!"

"Why not? You can have Lazaro's room if you want."

"How about that girl?"

"What girl?"

"The one, you know, the one you married."

"She isn't coming back."

"Oh?"

"She's very ill."

"Oh dear."

"Yes, she's in a clinic, in the Caribbean. They don't expect her to last long."

"Shouldn't you be there with her?"

"No, she doesn't want me. The disease has affected her brain. She can't stand the sight of me."

"How dreadful." Lavinia has to put a napkin to her mouth to hide the smile curling at the corners. She isn't smiling over Nestor's wife, although she doesn't believe his story about her illness. It's the man Nestor said is a hairdresser, the way he's pretending to smoke a breadstick.

"I just don't think it would be right, do you? Sleeping at your house when your wife is—"

"No, no I suppose not. Do you want zabaglione, Lavinia? They do it very well here."

"No, I want those little cookies, you know, with the sesame seeds on them."

"Have some zabaglione, Lavinia. They make it for two. They make it at your table."

"Order it if you want, as long as I get my cookies."

Look at that fat man, eating two helpings of zabaglione. The calories! The cholesterol! Haven't they heard about heart disease out here? Gareth orders an espresso. Now it seems he knows the fat man as well. He's seen them both before, but where? He feels they could tell him something if he knew what question to ask.

"What on earth?" Bridget sits up in bed, like a little girl, with her straw hair in tangles, her T-shirt falling off one shoulder. There's a yellow sky outside the window and the rain is coming down hard.

"Go back to sleep. It's only five. He called. I have to go over."

"In your lawyer's suit?"

"It's the only way he ever sees me. I have to keep my professional image, even if I'm going over to his place at five in the morning." Otherwise he might try to fuck her, but Regina doesn't tell Bridget that part.

The old man is wearing the same thing he had on yesterday in the office, but it has undergone a metamorphosis. The tie and jacket are off, the shirt wet with perspiration, even though his house, hermetically sealed against the steamy August rain, is air-conditioned. He's been drinking bourbon and offers her some, but she prefers coffee.

He shows her where the pot is and watches as she measures the coffee into the filter.

It isn't until Regina has poured herself a cup and one for him too, although he doesn't drink it, that she begins to make some order out of the information he's been throwing at her.

"Of course she can't come back," Regina says, "to you or her parents. If she does, they'll make her tell where Snow is hiding. They'll kill her."

"If only they could do it before she gets on the plane—oh my God, Regina, help me!" He grabs her arms across the table. "I can't believe I said that. What are they doing to me? I'm an honest man. Look how they've brought me down."

"Besides, it would be just as bad"—Regina casually removes her arms from his grip—"if she were killed down there, wherever she is."

"Yes, yes, but that's not the point. We don't want her dead, do we? It's just that she's so damned inconvenient."

19

———

"You work down here now, I see."

Faye is pacing the living room, brown as a nut, just back from another shooting, in the desert again. She's in tight jeans and a western belt, Rodeo Drive cowboy, a style that brings unwelcome memories.

"I don't use the top room anymore—"

"I don't blame you, after that fall."

"No, I was OK after that. It was, I don't know, after the openings sometime, I was up there late at night working and I had a terrible bout of acrophobia. It took me the longest time to get down again."

"It's the fall," she insists. Why are so many actors amateur shrinks? "It's a delayed reaction, that's all. You're always vulnerable after you finish a project."

As if she's known him all his life, knows him to the bottom of his Welsh soul. But there are things she couldn't even imagine.

The vertigo, for instance, was brought on by an event, a natural phenomenon, not even that unusual, but Gareth colored it with his imagination, gave it power from his subconscious, and he hasn't been able to shake free of it.

The building has been equipped with lightning rods, which serve as conductors between the sky and ground, carrying the electrical charges safely to the outside of the walls, but they do attract electrical energy to themselves. Therefore, to the superstitious mind, it would have looked as if the lightning were coming right down on top of him, a bony three-fingered hand, coming to lift him out of his life into some new destiny. It was well past dawn before he was able to creep down the stairs. He hasn't been up since.

"Shall we start again?" She stands in a new, boyish western pose she must have picked up from the cowboy lighting director, hands in her back pockets, wide stance, pelvis forward. She never used to, he realizes now, stand near the window. She tended to hug the inner wall.

"As what?"

"As lovers."

She'll have some new moves, of course. In the way she has changed since he last slept with her he will feel the methods of the cowboy director. A lot of quick cuts, probably. Do directors fuck like their films?

"What's the matter?" She squats beside him.

"Nothing, it's a breathing problem."

"Can I get you a glass of water—"

"No, no, just get away. I mean, I need room to breathe."

"Of course." She retreats to the sofa, sits down, watches him as he struggles with his own body, raking air down his throat. Must be hideous to look at.

"You should see a doctor," she says, once his breathing is calm and regular.

"I did. He told me to take up skydiving."

She thinks he should go to a chiropractor she knows with healing hands. Most actors are suckers for these kind of things— healers, special diets. "Whatever happened to that psychic?" he asks her in an offhand way.

"What psychic?"

"You know, the one who told you to get your feet on the ground or something like that."

"That girl in the East Village?"

"No, the phone-in fortuneteller who was somewhere out in New Jersey. You left me because of her, because of what she said."

"I left you because of the way you were in Arizona. Trailing me everywhere, looking awkward and out of place, and then you stepped on a rattlesnake—"

"But it was the psychic who predicted all that. Come on, you remember."

"Oh right, the one in New Jersey, the Spanish lady. If it means that much to you, I'll see if I can dig up her number. I must have it somewhere—"

"No, forget it. Come on. I'll take you to dinner."

There are three envelopes on the end of Lazaro's cot when he gets back from lunch. His bed is in the corner under the windows, the best in the bunkhouse.

The Fat Man writes fat, with a fountain pen that makes big shaded swirls on the g's and the y's. He has questions which he numbers. Lazaro takes one of the postcards the Fat Man gave him when he left with his address and a stamp already on it. He dispenses with greeting and writes the number one at the top. Progress in tennis? Not too bad. He's not the worst. He moves faster than most of these kids. Number two. He did learn to swim, the first day. The counselor pulled him out of the water and looked at him kind of strange, but pretty soon he didn't feel sick anymore and he went back in. Number three. He doesn't fight and no one messes with him. Number four. Never curses in Spanish, not even when he's alone out in the sunfish and it tips over. That takes care of the questions. He signs it: *From, Lazaro Ortega.*

The next one is written with three ballpoint pens, all of them running out of ink. From Lavinia. Mostly questions, no information except that she's moving out of the castle. Nothing about his mother. Lazaro's had only one postcard from her, a picture of the Statue of Liberty, when she arrived in New York, but no address. Lazaro answers Lavinia on another postcard. He's warm enough, dry enough, and the weather is OK. Not too many mosquitos.

The last is from Will, pages scrawled with information about San Francisco, mixed in with questions, the kind that take a long time to think up and even longer to answer. That's the way the man's mind works. No wonder he walks around like he's in a dream half the time. There isn't any room in his head for what's happening now. He's full of what came before. What he wants to know from Lazaro is how he's keeping on top of it all, *"moving in a different world"* and all that kind of shit.

Lazaro takes out another postcard, one Lavinia gave him addressed to Cass. He crosses off her name and writes Will's above it. The others come in. Someone turns on a radio. He can't concentrate. He thinks of Will, whose feet go down so deep into the ground that they reach those rocks he told him that San Francisco sits on top of, which is why Will gets stuck. His feet go down too deep. Lazaro stays on top of it. What—he's Hispanic, he's Black, he's White? He's carrying Chango's fire in his belly and he's keeping his eyes open and he's moving, moving like a fireball. Lazaro. He is who he is.

After lights-out, Lazaro will take the postcard under his blanket with a flashlight and write: *Are you making it with Cass or what?*

*Keep your mind on your business, man. You got to learn to look
at what's happening. Everything's cool here. Later. Lazaro.*

"Don't you like it, Lavinia? I thought it would be nice for you,
sitting outdoors." He drove her all the way to Bucks County, to
this restaurant with the waterfalls and ruins. Food's not that good,
bearing out his theory that the quality of the food is inversely
proportional to the setting. Lavinia appreciates surroundings more
than food. He is learning. When they were married he didn't know
these little things about her. Mostly he knew how she would react.
He knew that the tight smile would appear on her face the morning after he'd been out on a bender. That she would speed up,
moving around the kitchen, getting everyone's breakfast—cheerful. So goddamned cheerful all the time. Now, when he is doing
his damnedest to please her, she's pensive, a little sad even, in her
old linen dress tied with a scarf around the waist because she's
thinner than she used to be and the dress has to be anchored some
way.

She lied to him. She promised that nothing was changing, it was
all staying the same waiting for his return, and all the while the
castle was falling into ruin and she was becoming some other
person.

When the waiter comes to take their order, Nestor realizes that
they haven't spoken at all. "Lavinia, you're moving out in a
week—"

"Ten days."

"Which will go very fast, don't think you have plenty of time.
And Lazaro's coming back from camp. Shouldn't we make a decision?"

"About what?"

"About moving in, with me and the boy, making a home for
him."

"I don't think that's a very good example for a young man, Nestor, two old people living in sin—"

"You're mocking me, aren't you, Lavinia. You always used to take me so seriously. We'll get married, if you like."

"Oh Nestor, you didn't tell me. Did she die then?"

"Who?"

"That girl you married. She wasn't expected to survive, you know—"

"Lavinia, I'm delighted that you've come out of your funk, even if it's only to make fun of me. Go ahead, that's fine. Have your little laugh." Nestor hands her the water. "Drink it or you'll have hiccups. If you would sincerely like to know what has happened to Donna, she is living in San Mateo. One of my partner's parents has a beauty salon out there and gave her a position as a manicurist. I hear she's very good. Anyway, she can't—she won't—be coming back here and I'm positive I can get a divorce, and we'll get married, if that's what you want. Then we'll be together, Lavinia, you and me, the boy—a family."

"And what about poor Delia?"

"Delia too. We'll get a big house. She can't live alone. She can't be allowed to—"

"This is the mistake you always make."

"What?"

"The way you always want to take care of everyone. You can't trust anyone to work his life out right."

"I only want to help—"

"You don't want to help. You want to take over. You're greedy, Nestor. One life isn't enough for you."

A terrible indictment. She never used to criticize him. It was a mistake to order prawns here. They're burned and dry. He should have stuck with Florio's. The romantic setting is working to the opposite effect.

Why is it all so disappointing? The waterfalls, the ruins, the impatiens, even the pink napkins and tablecloths annoy her. And Nestor, being so charming, being everything she used to dream he could be, and all she can do is criticize. It's as if she imagined it so long, the reconciliation, that when it finally happens, it seems flat and pale, lacking the dimensions of the dream.

Oh Lavinia, Lavinia, it's you who is the disappointing one. If it wasn't love that kept you locked up in your castle for fifteen years, what was it? Revenge? Were you holding on to Nestor's past so he couldn't move into a future without you? Or was it mere cowardliness that kept you hiding in the remnants of your old life, afraid to start anew?

Lavinia turns to watch the ducks in the waterfall, dabs her eyes with the corner of her pink napkin.

"All those years, you said you loved me," Nestor pouts, making her heart soften. It's his charm, really, this insistent naked greed, no shame, no attempt to disguise it, like a baby at the breast. She grabs his big fat well-tended paws and gives them a squeeze. "I know, you poor old baby. I was calling it love, but I'm not sure that was the right name for it."

Three boys, small, slim, brown, are break-dancing on Columbus Avenue. They wear high-top sneakers, jeans, windbreakers, with hoods pulled down so far it's hard to see their faces. They've gathered a fair-size crowd. One man, standing in the back, is watching them closely, waiting to see their faces in the light from the street lamp. His own features are shadowed by a peaked cap pulled low. Finally, when he has seen enough, he puts a five in the box and walks on.

A tall woman, still young but aging fast, is singing an unfamiliar song with an uncertain melody. A man, older and more weathered, is accompanying on the guitar. Their sign reads: *Family needs sleeping place—basement, garage.* Two small dirty boys are curled on a blanket near the sign. The man in the cloth cap presses a fifty-dollar bill in the woman's hand, then leaves without meeting her eyes.

His plays and films often concern a man or woman with an obsession, driven by an idea beyond the normal limits of sanity. This is not the case with him. He is perfectly sane, but he is, of his own free volition, pursuing an idea to such an extent that it might look like an obsession to an outsider.

Ever since Faye called and told him a friend of hers said Destiny went to New York, to an unknown address, Gareth has been prowling the streets of the Hispanic neighborhoods; he's been calling on psychics and fortunetellers; at night he goes to places like Columbus Avenue where a woman might put out two chairs and a sign that she will read your palm or cards.

It's good for him, an obsession once in a while. It primes the pump, gets him out of his rarefied atmosphere. In his old clothes and workingman's cap, he feels like a prince disguising himself to walk among his people. What he will do when he finds Destiny and her kid is uncertain. He only imagines, vaguely, that he wants to help.

It is not quite as saintly as that, of course, because there is the memory of the baroque and never-before-encountered style of Destiny Ortega's lovemaking.

Later it will seem as if the trailer had been waiting for him, emerging with preternatural clarity from the murky whorls of night strollers on the avenue. A simple sign, no name, on the back window says: *Palms read. Cards. Walk in.* It will seem preordained, that he had no other choice but to obey the sign and walk in.

At first he can't be certain. The light is dim, the windows closed in with red nylon curtains. She sits at a formica table attached by hinges to the wall. Behind her, an accordion-pleated screen closes off the rest of the trailer. She's arranged her hair in a new style, pulled back, escaping in a plume down her back, oddly punk. Her black dress is one of those cheap Indian cotton things girls wore in the sixties. Has she made up her eyes? They're incredibly large and dark.

She doesn't give any sign of surprise that it is he, and yet she knows him. She nods, as if he is a regular, coming at the appointed time. She is shuffling her cards. Perhaps she was already shuffling them when he came in. She puts them on the table before him. He sits in a seat that folds down from the wall and cuts the deck. She pushes one of the stacks toward him; he cuts again. She takes these cards and swiftly places them in a circle: knights and wizards, burning tower, hollow-eyed queens.

"Wait!" He grabs her hands. "Don't tell me. Don't say anything. I don't know what it is, but every time you tell me something it affects my life. It gets mixed up in my head. You tap into the subconscious or something. It's damned dangerous."

She glances quickly, eagerly, over the cards and reluctantly gathers them up. "You keep coming to me, you even interrupt other people's readings with your own messages, and then you don't listen, or you argue with me. You want to hear, and you don't want to."

"Well, look, it's not that—" he takes his hat off and smooths back his hair. "I felt rotten about that night. I don't usually behave that way, and then I got to worrying about you—"

"I understood—"

"You did? I wasn't sure."

"A strong pull like that. It can be upsetting, especially for someone who thinks he's controlling things. '*I am the captain of my ship; I am the master of my fate*—' What's that poem we had to memorize in school? I always thought it was funny—"

"Why funny?"

"Well, because you steer in currents, don't you? With the wind, the weather. So much depends—"

"So you think there's something pulling me toward you, some outside force I can't control—"

"Oh, no no no no. Not that at all. It's an inner force, something inside you, inside me, that vibrates together. You just—" She shakes her head so her earrings jingle and her plume of hair feathers out. "You're just frightened of it. Something inside of you you're frightened of, but it isn't something bad. What scares you so?"

"Look, I'm not frightened, not at all. That's absurd. You know, all of you fortunetellers, you speak in generalities. You never commit to something specific."

She smiles, a childish, impish smile he hasn't seen before. "I could tell you something specific, if that's what you want."

"Like what? Street number, date of birth, how many movies or plays I've directed? You could get almost anything from the articles they've done on me. A day at the library could turn up everything—"

She leans over the table, and his nose, imbecilic organ, rejoices at the smell of her.

"I see things about you, pictures, like, around your head."

It's an easy bluff to call. Whatever picture she turns up will come out of one of those pieces. "Go ahead, give me a picture," he dares her.

Her eyes go off on a nervous, darting dance, as if she actually could see images swarming around his head like gnats.

"I see a lamp, red glass—a red glass shade on a lamp hanging from the ceiling and a woman sitting under it, reading? No, looking at her hands. There's a mug of—tea. The mug is yellow, with a chip—"

"Christ!" Gareth jumps up. His seat snaps back into the wall.

"That's your mother, isn't it?" She's pleased as a child who's just completed a difficult trick. "You're so easy. You're so easy for me to do."

"Whose trailer is this?"

"It belongs to a friend—well, the friend of someone I know. I'm renting it while she's away."

"They let you stay here?"

"Who?"

"The authorities. The police."

"The police! Oh yes. They've been wonderful. They move it for me sometimes, over to the other side of the street. I can't drive. I never learned. There are a lot of things I can't do, which is why I've developed my psychic powers so much. You have psychic powers too, you know, but you have so many things you do well that your gift just gets in your way, or scares you sometimes, I guess."

"How about you? Aren't you afraid, being here alone in this trailer, with the door unlocked? Someone could walk in and—"

"My aura protects me."

"Oh, certainly. That's lovely, to have an aura that protects one, a lovely thought, but if someone were so hard and callous as to not be able to discern your aura—Don't ever point a gun at someone! Christ."

She puts the revolver back on a little shelf by her seat. "It isn't loaded. I wouldn't trust myself with a loaded gun. I can't even have sharp knives around. I'm so clumsy."

His heart is jumping, as if he actually expected her to shoot him. He feels guilty, for the last time he saw her and, aura or not, for the way she is, or the circumstance is, exciting him sexually. It's her fragility and childishness combined with the shabby, almost tawdry, trailer.

"Is there a bed back there?"

"Yes. I live here. I was hoping to move in with my friend, the President of the International Psychics' Society, but it turns out she didn't have room. It's funny, with so many windows, everywhere you look, you'd think there would be a place for me, but all that has come to me is this trailer, so far."

"Do you sometimes take clients into the bed?" Why is he being so cruel?

"You must know I couldn't. You're teasing, aren't you. Or testing."

She disarms him every time. Does she do it on purpose? Is she extremely clever or unbelievably stupid?

"But we could use the bed," she says, "you and I. It had been so long I'd forgotten, but since you visited me that night I've been tormented with forgotten feelings. It even gets in the way of my powers lately."

20

The kid's eating healthy today: toasted English muffins, one side with jam, the other with a slice of Swiss cheese, and earlier from his room came the sound of his weights. He vacillates: body-building and healthy food for a while, then oversleeping, brutal music, and a chocolate-covered donut for breakfast. When he's on these health kicks, Gareth notices, the kid's small body takes on density. He moves as if he weighs three hundred pounds.

No need today to remind him of the time. He's at the door with his schoolbooks. "You ready, Dad?" "Dad" comes with the health kick. At other times, Gareth might be "Boss," or "Man." Whatever mood Lazaro's in, Gareth always drives him to school when he's in town. It's an easy trip on the bus, but Gareth and Lazaro enjoy making it in the Jaguar together.

Lazaro lights a cigarette and hands it to Gareth, then does one for himself. Even on his health kick, Lazaro doesn't give up his morning cigarette with Gareth. Neither of them smokes at home,

just in the car, this cigarette together. Lazaro is solemn and thoughtful this morning.

"Do you have a test today?"

"A speech. I have to give a talk."

"Why didn't you tell me? I would have coached you."

"It's nothing. Just twenty minutes."

"What's it on?"

"Renaissance art."

Renaissance art! Last year he ran with the hoods and this year
he wears a blazer with a school crest and gives talks on Renaissance
art.

As the sun tips away from the northern hemisphere, the boy is
bleaching out. He looks more Mediterranean than African now.
Of course, when the sun comes back, he'll brown up again. Another instance of his remarkable plasticity. Even his skin adjusts to
different climates.

Gareth, on the other hand, retains the fish-belly pallor of his
youth. Not on his forearms or his face, but under his shirt, his
pants, his skin is glaringly white, the white of a Welsh boy who
grew up in cold mists. White skin is a sign of poverty in Wales.
It means you never had the money to buy the sun of Spain.

Gareth is careful to park directly in front of the school so that
the others can see Lazaro carelessly flinging back the door of the
Jaguar. A couple of boys come over. "Yo, 'Zarro, wha'zup?" Tow-
heads, but they talk black to him. Gareth thought they were mocking him at first, but now he sees they are paying him a tribute.
Having some street in him makes Lazaro more powerful. He has a
secret knowledge none of them can ever get.

Gareth eases out of the jam-up of kids, buses, cars and heads
back across the park. Another of his journalist friends, this one a
young woman he's never refused before, called and asked to interview him about his marriage.

He had to explain that he's turning down all interviews. Said
for the first time he has a genuinely private life and he wants to

keep it that way. It's true. He and the journalists created Gareth Watts the director and he almost lost the parts of himself that didn't fit into the image. He was becoming a cartoon. Delia found those parts and she is keeping them safe for him.

There are other reasons why Gareth doesn't want publicity. There's the problem of Lazaro's quasi-criminal background. It wouldn't do him any good to have all of that dug up. And there's the matter of Delia herself. Gareth smiles to imagine his favorite journalist keeping a straight face while Delia tells her that Delia and Gareth were destined for each other, about their "clear psychic channels." And what if Faye were to read about them and put it all together, that the same fortuneteller who advised her to get out of Gareth's life has moved into her spot, even made it official. (She insisted on marriage because otherwise she couldn't have gotten custody of Lazaro.)

Sometimes, strange paranoid imaginings come over Gareth, that Delia planned it all from the beginning, even threw curses on him so that he would have those accidents, that she stage-managed the whole thing. His mind races on. What if he should ever have an affair? Would she give him cancer of the prostate? Cause his plane to crash?

Then he watches her leaving her clothes on the chair at night and decides that anyone who can't fold her clothes properly would never have the concentration to put such a plan into effect.

The story of how they got together does seem loaded with weird coincidences, bizarre twists, but when he talks to other couples (he's always doing this now, asking other couples how they met) their stories too are filled with odd combinations of circumstances ("If he hadn't taken my keys by mistake—").

To Delia it's all perfectly simple. They were meant for each other. The strange coincidences were caused by their urge to come together. She says she knew it the first time she saw him. It took him longer to come to the same realization.

"Don't feel bad. Some people never see it," she told him one recent rainy afternoon when he came home unexpectedly to find that one of her clients had canceled and that she had sent the housekeeper home early so they would be free for some afternoon lovemaking in front of the fire. (Such charming coincidences are so much a part of his life with Delia that he doesn't question them anymore.)

They were watching the city dissolve in a blur of rain, and he was holding her in his arms as she tried, with her usual lack of coherence, to share her vision with him. "Some people never get it. They never see the stream of fate and they keep trying to swim against it, or they miss it completely and they flounder in the desert—" Her voice trailed off as her metaphor became too complicated to follow. "The hardest thing," she began again, "is to know it when you see it. The people who come to me are usually looking right at it, but they need me to point it out to them. It's amazing, the energy people use up, just trying not to see what they see—" She stopped and rested her head back against his shoulder. She doesn't talk about her work much with him for fear he'll tease her, but he respects it, more than she knows.

"He wants a resurrection," Nestor says.

"Who?"

"Snow. He wants to roll the stone away from his tomb and come out all white and clean."

"He wants to come back?"

"He says we're all up here living like free men and he's trapped in the Caribbean, living a nonlife."

"He can't do that, come back after disappearing—"

"Of course he can't. He knows it too. He wants money, darling. It's not enough that he leaves us with this mess, but once we get it cleaned up, he wants money. And you notice who he's asking, not his criminal friends, because they would mow him down in a minute. He's asking us because he thinks our morality makes us helpless. Goddamned snake in the grass." Nestor pours a little more bourbon in his glass and splashes some into hers as well. Regina's acquiring a taste for bourbon.

They are in Nestor's living room, sitting in the green club chairs. Some things are best not discussed in the office.

It was a bad idea. She should have let him wear his gray sweats as he wanted to. She got ahead of herself, became caught up in the vision of what he could be and forgot the reality of what he is. He looks—oh shit, and all these mirrors, the window. It must be like a bad dream to him. A white tank top and black muscle shorts, weightlifter's gloves and a belt. She made him go out and buy the whole number. He looks like a penguin whose feathers shrank at the laundry, waddling splay-footed around the machines. If he could just learn to connect the mind to the body, that's what she's trying to teach him. She points to each muscle as he works it, hoping he'll begin to see.

Charles on the double pull-over is grinning.

"I'm sorry, Will."

"About what?"

"Your outfit. I should have let you wear your sweats."

"Oh no. This is good. You were right. You do better if you're dressed for it. You look great in yours, like a small perfect Amazon, with both breasts, of course."

"Give me a kiss."

"Right here, with all these mirrors and stuff?"

"People do it all the time here."

She makes it long and amorous and doesn't bother to look at Charles to see if he's noticed.

"I'd better go back to sweatpants, if you're going to keep doing that." Will nuzzles her neck. There's a swelling in the muscle shorts, a testimony to the power of love.

This is what it feels like to be inside love, to be the women she used to envy. Now Cass has her man, in her bed, at the movies, by her side doing Saturday morning errands, on the phone with her during the day when she's at work ("How are you feeling? Cold better? I was thinking soup for dinner—").

"He's a professor," she tells people when they ask. He will be when he goes back to St. Louis. His dissertation has been accepted.

He is in love. He says he is, and she knows it's true because he shows it in all the ways Ted does with Laura, and more. In every gesture, look, and word, Will demonstrates his love.

"How many reps is that?"

"Ten, I think."

"OK. That's good. Now, these are for your triceps."

Cass brings the weights over her head and then straightens her arms slowly. Will catches the scent of her perspiration, which is sweet and fresh. Pheromones are secreted by the sweat glands, making a gym a very sexy place to be. Are her ex-lovers present in the room? The guy with the long hair, maybe.

"If I grow my hair long, will you marry me?"

She grins and slips out of reach when he drops his weights. He wants her to go back with him to St. Louis, to be his wedded wife, but she can't decide. "Go anyway," she says. "It will force me to make up my mind."

And what if she doesn't come?

"If you can love me, you can love anyone," Cass said. "It's a question of being ready."

"I'm like Delia," he told her. "I believe there's only one woman for me, and you are the one." It's true. Even when he was engaged to Dagne, it wasn't love. He had no idea. Now he knows and he won't let go.

When Lazaro told him to go to San Francisco, it was like the turning of a kaleidoscope. Suddenly all the pieces fell into a new pattern and the future was brilliantly clear to him. It was as if it had been there all the time but he hadn't known how to look at it.

Lavinia didn't see it that way—in a flash, all at once. She anticipated problems he hadn't even thought about, but then, she had
always known the thorny side of Cass. As they talked about it into
the night, she warmed to the idea and even became excited by the
prospect of "keeping you in the family," as she put it. They ended
up reciting their psalm together in the conservatory, for good luck.

He woke in the morning with a vision of how he would pro-
ceed: steadfast in his love and tolerant of Cass's swings. For an
expert in heat transfer, he's told her, she is curiously lacking in
thermostatic control. She turns hot and cold in a way that could
drive a less confident suitor mad.

"You know why Lazaro sent you here, of course," she said, with
that hard edge to her voice that comes sometimes without warning
after making love.

"Because he could tell that I loved you." He tucked her hair
behind her ears so he could better see her face.

"Because he knew that if you took up with me you would drop
all that stuff about him and Nestor." She shook her hair free again.

It is true. He did drop all the section about Wallingford in the
present but only because the dissertation was stronger without it.
After all, it has been accepted, which is proof enough. "That's
always been my failing," he explained. "I never knew enough to
limit history to the past."

Cass wasn't about to let it go. She said he compromised his work
for personal considerations. But personal considerations were what
gave energy to his work in the first place. Why had he even gone
to Wallingford if not to dig out the curse on his family, to find out
ultimately what was wrong with him?

"And you know, think about it," he said, only thinking about it
himself at that moment. "When did I get on this kick about corruption? After my disappointment. Your mother, her friend—"

"Bubbles."

"Yeah, Bubbles, and that crazy one, the witch, all built me up to be The One. They were making me into a hero, when I had grown up thinking of myself as some doomed victim. I was important to them, to your mother especially."

"She was lonely."

"She opened her house and her family to me. For the first time since my father died, I felt I had a place. And then your father just blasted away the curse and Delia turned down my proposal—"

"So you did offer to marry her—"

"Yeah, but she just smiled, you know—"

"That daft smile."

"But she was right. You were right too. You said it, remember? After Lazaro's trial. It wouldn't work because there wasn't that thing between us, not like you and I have. I was so numb, I didn't even know what that was. But I was hurt because the only home I had was taken away from me. So instead of the prince, I became the viper. Negative or positive, I'm still The One, get it?"

"And now?"

"Now I'm the prince again. I'm your prince."

She leaned across the bed and blew out the candles on the windowsill.

Delia is in the sky cabin—the glass room at the top of the house. When she has clients, they sit at a table an artist painted for her with planets and constellations. But now she is alone, on the lounge chair. She sees the sun plunging down through a layer of smog over New Jersey, scattering its light past particles of airborne debris invisible except for their combined auras of red, yellow, violet. If she turns her head she can see the moon with Venus rising.

Since she's come to live in the glass house high in the air, Delia has been doing more astrology. Before it was too abstract for her, but now she can feel the pull of the planets, observe the approaches and regressions. Someone else draws up the charts. She could never do it, too complicated, but she interprets for her clients.

The charts are beautiful. The clients take them home, along with a recording she makes of the session. She will still do readings over the phone, but clients prefer to come to her. They fly in from Los Angeles, Dallas, Paris, and London. Women mostly: actresses, singers, headhunters, travel agents, gallery owners.

The questions are still about love and money, although why anyone who could afford to pay one hundred dollars would worry about money, Delia doesn't know. She never worries about love or money.

Delia worries about Lazaro, even though she's brought him to a safe place and found him a father, done everything she knows how for him. But still, when she thinks of Lazaro, she sees too many streams of energy, all connecting in one small body. Warnings flash on the perimeters of her mind where she can't see them clearly.

She hears him at the door now, earlier than she expected. He comes up to see her, scattering the ghostly images with his flesh and blood reality. She wants to put her arms around him and feel the bones under his skin, she wants to test the smell and texture of his hair, but he slips by and stands with his hands in his pockets and his back to the window, so all she gets is the outline of him.

"You're home early."

He skipped basketball practice. The Fat Man is coming over, has to see him about something. Nestor and Lavinia come together on Sundays to visit, but sometimes Nestor comes alone at night, carrying questions in his eyes that Lazaro answers privately. Keep the boy out of Wallingford, the judge with the big glasses and the little nose advised Delia, keep him away from bad influences.

Lazaro wheels and crouches at the window, firing an imaginary machine gun at a helicopter patrolling the East River. Delia sees sea gulls rising and falling in the air currents over the water, reflecting the sunset off their bellies, becoming disembodied points of opalescent light. There's something she has to tell him.

"Lazaro!"

"Yeah?"

His eyes turn toward her and catch the sun, not reflecting it but holding it deep inside like an ember, a glimmer of original light being kept alive for another time. It's too late. There's something inside her but she can't call it up. His presence is blocking it. Someone else will tell him, or he'll have to discover it himself. Her time is past.

She moves over on the lounge chair, and he fits himself in beside her. They stay like that until the sky is deep blue-violet with an edge of green over New Jersey.

21

They kept the canal, a nice touch, a run of clear, colorless water in front of the concrete facade. It contributes to the clean look. There was some talk of replacing the old turbines, to use the canal to generate additional electricity, but it proved too costly to be practical. The water is just for show. Its energy is allowed to dissipate into the air. The real business of making energy will go on behind concrete walls, where garbage will be ground and heated, transmuted into bouncing electrons, fine gray ashes, and a gossamer smoke that will steam out of the tall smokestacks. The smoke will be nearly invisible on a warm day.

"Nice touch, leaving the water there," Nestor remarks to Regina, who's walking beside him, bareheaded, her hands in the pockets of her trench coat.

"Smart—the graffiti artists can't get at the walls. It's like a moat, protecting the plant from the hostile public."

"Who's hostile?"

"All those articles—"

"But they're not the people of Wallingford, darling. The city is making a killing on this deal."

"Environmentalists, then. People are worried about the smoke, the ash."

Nestor waves a hand. "There are always those who are going to protest change. They don't see that it has to come. They don't want to see. They want to put their garbage in a can out in front of the house and they want it to go away. That's all. They don't want to have to think about where it's going. Who do you think would have been against the project if we'd given them time to mobilize, if we hadn't rammed it through the committees? The people who live around here?" His arm waves, taking in the burned-out houses and two blocks of brick housing projects. "If they think about it at all, they're in favor, because it's creating jobs and cutting down the electricity bills. The graffiti artists would mark up the building if they could, but only because it presents an unblemished canvas for their work. For them, the plant's just another opportunity for a little ego display, that's all. The people who are protesting are the freeholders up in the hills who are worried about their property values, the same people who will be sending us their trash in state-of-the-art green garbage trucks."

Regina has to smile. Nestor has appointed himself spokesman for the downtrodden ever since he surprised himself with his speech at Lazaro's hearing. Maybe it's a trade-off in his mind: he dirties his hands with the cover-up and washes them clean by championing the cause of the great mute underclass of Wallingford.

He's enjoying this midday walk. Little, self-satisfied puffs of white breath exit from his warm, well-cushioned body. It pleases him that the old brick ruins have been obliterated and replaced by this alabaster behemoth.

Regina allows herself a moment of sentimentality to mourn the passing of those walls which the fire had turned an incredible shade of rose. She finds the resource recovery center chillingly clean behind its moat of clear water. There's something sinister about hiding mountains of foul garbage behind this chaste, elegant facade, behind a technocratic double-speak name, *resource recovery center*. The purpose of this walk, other than keeping Nestor from getting lonely on a Saturday (Can't you tell him that your weekends are for you? Bridget complains), is to examine the construction sites. The burned-out land has been bought up for low-income housing. It's an arrangement that amuses Nestor because it echoes the accommodation for the resource recovery center: surrounding wealthy communities are helping to pay for the construction in order to waive the state requirement that they allow a certain amount of low-income housing in their own neighborhoods. Nestor says Wallingford's main industries are going to be taking in the garbage and the poor for the rest of New Jersey.

He stops to talk to the guard at one of the sites. During the week, when work is in progress, he talks to everyone, from the men driving the cement trucks on up. He jots everything down in a red spiral notebook. Unlike Grand Land, where he turned a blind eye, he is taking charge this time. "The only kind of corruption I'll tolerate is constructive corruption," he told her. The kind of maneuver Snow pulled, where nothing was done, is destructive, but Nestor didn't complete the thought because he never talks about Snow anymore. When Snow's name approaches in conversation, Nestor will veer away. Regina is grateful to him for this, for protecting her. He could have involved her, almost did, but in the end he chose to shoulder that burden himself.

Regina had met Snow several times without ever knowing him. His handsome eyes always slid past hers, as if he sensed that his charms would never touch her, that his regular features and pink, glowing skin would draw no sympathy from her sallow, pocked cheeks, her large and lonely nose.

She must have studied his face more closely than she knew,

however, because it has been coming back to her in dreams. She wakes sometimes with the vision of Snow looking up at her through a mile of clear green glass, his white hair like seaweed around his head.

"Look, darling. The benches are in." This is Nestor's baby, the park by the river, paid for by the wealthy neighbors of Wallingford who are sending them their garbage and their poor.

He invites her to sit down, courtly, waiting for her to seat herself first on the specially designed vandal-proof bench. They admire the future park, a bulldozed piece of flatland with some young trees planted around the perimeter. He shows her where the basketball court will go, the playground equipment. "You can hear the river. That's something. How many years has it been since the people of Wallingford could see and hear the river?"

"There's one thing the fire did that was good. It opened up the riverfront." Regina crosses her legs. Nestor is gratified that she chose to wear a dress even though it's Saturday. She should always wear skirts; she doesn't have that many good features that she can afford to cover them up. Nestor thinks about telling her this but decides against it.

"Inadvertently, you're right. Some good can come from the chaos that was left us, but it takes builders like us to turn things in that direction."

Regina shakes back her hair, which is also good—thick with natural red highlights. She's better-looking these days. She wears power well. It becomes her.

A breeze is blowing off the river. Nestor can hear the water and the future sounds of children playing in the park. The housing units will have space for stores so they won't be those faceless concrete blocks that have been built in the past. It will be a community, messy-looking, sure. There's no way you're going to keep the spray can brigade out. It's not going to be some neat, Disney-esque boutique community like Snow had architects make sketches of to pull in his investors, but it will be alive and people will have roofs over their heads, goddamnit.

Regina lets Nestor look at her legs. It doesn't bother her any-more that he knows she's a woman, not since he's accepted her as a partner. She allows herself to see the children playing in the park—she can be generous enough to share Nestor's vision with him, although she also sees drug dealers doing business under the shade of the growing trees, the strong elbowing the weak away from the basketball hoops, teenagers stealing purses from mothers distracted by babies, and all the while clouds of possibly lethal gas from the resource recovery center sail with the grace of tall schoon-ers over their heads.

"Isn't that Bridget's friend, sitting on the bench with Nestor?"

"I can't look when I'm driving. You know that, Bubbles." La-vinia keeps her eyes straight ahead when she's at the wheel. She just recently took up driving again so she could be of use to Bub-bles in their new business. She loves it, but it takes all her concen-tration to keep on the road. Things can happen so fast, even when you're only going thirty miles an hour. "It probably is. She's a partner in Nestor's firm, and she and Nestor are very close, even though she's a dyke."

"Lavinia, what a terrible word!"

"Oh, that's Lazaro's word. Sorry. He's the one who told me. That girl and Bridget share a bed."

"Lazaro told you?"

"Mmm-hmm."

"Then it must be so. Don't you worry how he knows those things?"

"He had to grow up fast, living where he did. Maybe now that he has a nice home he can learn how to be a child." Lavinia says this, but she feels that Lazaro will be picking up the not-so-nice bits wherever he is. He's acquired an eye. It's remarkable what he still knows about Wallingford even though he's been more or less banned from town.

Lavinia has no illusions about Lazaro, but how she loves him! So much that her heart aches sometimes. Something about that boy draws love to him. Look how Nestor fell for him, finally. He was heartbroken when the judge gave him back to Delia. That girl Regina had to go over to Nestor's a lot when it first happened. Nestor was so lonely.

Lavinia felt guilty for turning Nestor down when he most needed her, but he's better now. He's found a substitute for family in the downtrodden of Wallingford. Nestor was too much for one person, even Lazaro. A personality like his needs to be spread over a large area.

"Left," Bubbles says quietly. Lavinia also can't find her way around when she drives because she's too intent on how she is driving to think of where. They're going up to Bridget's farm, to see her new work and pick up the wrought iron gate. They found a wealthy woman in Clifton who wants it for her garden.

Bubbles has closed down her shop and put her business on the road. They're always going, taking the work of Wallingford artisans to crafts fairs and galleries all over New Jersey, New York, Pennsylvania, even Connecticut. "We live like gypsies," Lavinia loves to tell people.

Lavinia downshifts to climb the hill in back of Wallingford.

"I can't believe it," Bubbles says.

"What?"

"Don't you see it? No, you can't. That big thundercloud over the town. It seems like we're always having thunderstorms, right through the winter."

"I hope Nestor has moved off that bench. He'd make a very big target, in all that open land."

"I thought you didn't see him."

"Maybe I did, out of the corner of my eye."

"It sounds like a dreadful town."

"It's ugly, like any place that's constantly changing. I think of it as a frontier town, because it really is a frontier in human society, the first place all these different immigrant groups come into—"

"And like a frontier town, it's lawless."

"Yes, a good point. Rebellious is a fairer word, maybe. It's in the immigrant's interest to change the law, bend it, circumvent it, because laws basically defend the haves from the have-nots."

"And the part about mysticism is fascinating. I'm surprised they accepted it. Anything that seems faintly literary or interpretive—"

"I was careful to ground it in the agrarian traditions of the immigrants. Originally—"

"Yes?" She encourages him. Tina Reese is genuinely interested. Although Will is the same age as Tina, he always thought Tina Reese was beyond him. She has tenure; she publishes; she has long legs and a quick way of walking with her head thrown forward. Whenever he said hello, crossing her path on campus, she gave him her smile that said, "Sorry, I don't remember your name." Now she is sitting, her long legs crossed, on the edge of his desk.

"And you actually lived right there. What dedication."

"Oh, that was pleasant. I stayed with an older woman, Lavinia Bird."

"Lavinia Bird!" Tina laughs.

"Yes, she lived all alone in a split-level castle that had been built as a movie set in the fifties."

"How funny!"

"I got pretty involved with the family. We keep in touch."

When Tina leaves, Will wonders why he said that, why he didn't say something like, "I'm in love with Lavinia's daughter and I'm hoping she'll marry me." Because he doesn't know. Cass keeps him waiting.

She said he could love another just as easily, that falling in love only required that you be willing to deceive yourself, that once you had picked up the knack of throwing a golden veil over reality, you could do it again. Anyone can be "The One," anyone you choose to invest with your ardor and fantasies.

Cass, the scientist of love. She has studied love closer than most, but she can't bear to jump in because she knows that however much she studies it from the outside, she can never prepare herself for what it's like inside. She's afraid that what happened to Lavinia will happen to her; she'll get locked up in love and won't be able to find her way out.

Will folds his arms and leans his elbows against the windowsill so he can watch Tina Reese striding off diagonally across the green, but in his mind's eye, he sees Cass, her slightly pigeon-toed, athletic walk that bounces at each step.

Cass wakes to the foghorn on the bay and the feeling that she's blown it. At first the calls came once a day. They tapered off after classes began. Now it's been a week. She pushes back the blue and white quilt. The sheets no longer smell of him and of them together.

It used to annoy her that he enjoyed their love-making so much when she knew it only rated a five on the Richter scale of orgasm. She used to envy him for being so in love, for having found his own true mate. She even told him he could fall in love with someone else, now that he had learned how.

She was extremely forthright with him. Frankness, the virtue Nestor always praised. But Nestor would never let honesty get in the way of self-interest.

Cass squats on her haunches, loosening up her hamstrings. She leans over to one leg and stretches the other one out. Should she reject love because it doesn't look the way she imagined? Become a spinster, a nun, who's true to her vision? Should she wait for that cloudy and indistinct shape—The One—to materialize? Or should she try to train her heart to the love that's been offered?

Cass moves slowly over to the other leg. She can see dustballs under her shelves and, folded up, the duffel bag she takes when she travels. She stretches her arms out long until she touches the strap, and then she pulls it toward her.

Not even noon and it's clouding over already. How long before someone notices that every Saturday, nearly, they have a thunderstorm? There was one letter to the editor which blamed it on the big fire, said it changed the climate of Wallingford. But really it's Mama who brings the storms. Saturday she sees clients.

Carmen has to turn sideways to get her grocery bags past the people waiting on the stairs. There are a couple of new ones, young and well-dressed, clutching their tape recorders. She hopes they speak Spanish, or they're in for a disappointment.

She can smell cigars and rum in the stairway. The smell never goes away now, just gets a fresh overlay every Saturday. And the drums are always there, Tio Felipe's tape. Even when it isn't being played the walls retain the beat. They give up the sound when you go by, just like the furniture gives off old cigars and rum. Whatever furniture is left. Mama's cleared it out, made the parlor into a shrine for Chango, tied cloths all around, keeps candles lit, put corn and okra in the corners. That's why he comes to visit all the time, comes around banging his thunder and shooting off his lightning.

The pictures of Jaime are gone. Carmen doesn't know where. Mama hid them somewhere.

Mama is blind but she isn't. Her eyes work fine. It is the part of the brain, the receiver, that isn't there. The nerves burned out when Mama was a baby, but Carmen knows that Mama sees all the same, not with her brain but with her body. She has blind sight.

"What did you do with those pictures?" Carmen asked her. She wanted at least one to remember him by, but Mama said Jaime has been released. His spirit was bound to earth because his family needed protection, but now he isn't needed anymore. Jaime was glad to leave. It won't do him any good to remember him.

Mama has gone too. She's left off worrying about Lazaro, stopped thinking about Jaime. She left Carmen long ago, but that's all right because Carmen takes care of herself.

Mama is holding court on her throne—her favorite armchair, decorated with shawls and afghans of different colors, with streamers coming down from the ceiling like a tent around her. The one in the other chair is about Carmen's age but an Anglo, wearing tight jeans and one of those fancy belts with the silver buckle and tip that they tuck in.

Mama is spewing out words in no kind of order. They stand on their own. The Anglo is drinking them in. Who knows if she even understands Spanish.

Carmen snorts and takes the bags into the kitchen. While she's putting away the groceries, the drums start up again.

Faye has taken off her boots and is following the nimble brown feet of the blind woman across the floor, which is gritty, as the dirt packed into the sides of the room has migrated into the center. Faye was stiff at first, self-consciously following the blind woman's feet, while a flat yellowish light seeped in from under the storm clouds.

But now Faye is moving with the drums—no need to watch the woman, to instruct the parts of her body. They are moving with the spirit. Their hands are raised toward heaven, waving, weaving. Faye thought the scraps of fabric hanging from the ceiling were decorations. Now she understands that they are conduits. They writhe and turn with messages.

Round and round they dance, singing now in a language Faye has never heard, and yet she knows the words.

On the stairway the petitioners sit, hearing the drums, feeling the floor shake with the dance. The ones who've been here before know that the Señora will be giving no more sessions today. Carmen will put her to bed, exhausted. Still, they wait for the word from Carmen, for that dark, angry face at the top of the stair telling them to go home.

The drumming swells, ululations, pounding on the floor. The light bulb in the stairwell trembles, goes black as the air cracks, torn asunder by a fierce, indifferent charge of electricity.

A NOTE ON THE TYPE

The text of this book was set on the Linotype in Garamond No. 3, a modern rendering of the type first cut by Claude Garamond (c. 1480–1561). Garamond was a pupil of Geoffroy Tory and is believed to have based his letters on the Venetian models, although he introduced a number of important differences, and it is to him we owe the letter which we know as "old style." He gave to his letters a certain elegance and a feeling of movement that won for their creator an immediate reputation and the patronage of Francis I of France.

Composed by Maryland Linotype Composition Co.,
Baltimore, Maryland

Printed and bound by R. R. Donnelley & Sons,
Harrisonburg, Virginia

Typography and binding design
by Julie Duquet